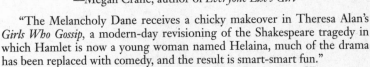

Outstanding Praise for the Nov...

Girls Who Gos...

"Theresa Alan had me up all night! I lov...
moody, funny, and ultimately touching story...
will stay with me for a long, long time."
—Megan Crane, author of *Everyone Else's Girl*

"The Melancholy Dane receives a chicky makeover in Theresa Alan's *Girls Who Gossip*, a modern-day revisioning of the Shakespeare tragedy in which Hamlet is now a young woman named Helaina, much of the drama has been replaced with comedy, and the result is smart-smart fun."
—Lauren Baratz-Logsted, author of *A Little Change of Face*

"A real charmer! *Girls Who Gossip* drew me in at page one and kept me turning well into the night. I couldn't wait to see how it all unfolded. Touching, witty and utterly delightful."
—Jennifer Coburn, author of *Tales From the Crib*

The Girls' Global Guide to Guys

"With *The Girls' Global Guide to Guys*, Theresa Alan delivers a brisk, funny, keenly observed portrait of a woman who wants more out of life than a soul-killing job and a tepid romance—and finds it on exotic shores."
—Kim Green, author of *Paging Aphrodite* and *Is That a Moose in Your Pocket?*

"A wonderful and fun read not to be missed!"
—*Chicklitbooks.com*

Spur of the Moment

"The players come across as real—kudos to Theresa Alan for accomplishing this feat. The sensitivities of Ana and the uniqueness of each member of the troupe as she perceives them make for a solid character study with overtones of a family drama and chick-lit tale."
—*The Midwest Book Review*

"Alan shows that she's capable of handling sensitive issues with an effectively gentle touch."
—*Romantic Times*

Who You Know

"Alan does a masterful job . . . As the three women face the trials and triumphs of life, they assist each other in ways that only best friends can—through unconditional love, unrelenting humor and unwavering support. Reminiscent of *Bridget Jones's Diary* and *Divine Secrets of the Ya-Ya Sisterhood*, Alan's is a novel to be savored like a good box of chocolates."
—*Booklist*

"A delightful chick-lit."
—*The Midwest Book Review*

"A gorgeous book, superbly written with compassion and caring. *Who You Know* should absolutely be number one on everyone's list."
—*Rendezvous*

Books by Theresa Alan

WHO YOU KNOW

SPUR OF THE MOMENT

THE GIRLS' GLOBAL GUIDE TO GUYS

GIRLS WHO GOSSIP

THE DANGERS OF MISTLETOE

GETTING MARRIED

Published by Kensington Publishing Corporation

GETTING MARRIED

THERESA ALAN

KENSINGTON BOOKS
http://www.kensingtonbooks.com

KENSINGTON BOOKS are published by

Kensington Publishing Corp.
850 Third Avenue
New York, NY 10022

ISBN-13: 978-0-7582-0996-2
ISBN-10: 0-7582-0996-7

First Kensington Trade Paperback Printing: May 2007
10   9   8   7   6   5   4   3   2   1

Printed in the United States of America

GETTING MARRIED

Chapter 1

You are not the first, and you are definitely not the last.
*(Graffiti written in block letters with a
permanent black marker in a bathroom
stall at Mickie's Pub in Denver, Colorado.)*

And probably, you are not the best.
(Graffiti written just below in red ink.)

The graffiti makes me groan. I'm trapped in this stall, paralyzed by the words scrawled on the door in front of me.

Here's the deal: My boyfriend, Will, who is sitting downstairs drinking beer and listening to music, blissfully unaware that I'm up here having a conniption fit, is thirty-four and divorced. (I'm thirty-one and never married.) He doesn't have any kids, and his divorce sounds about as amicable as a divorce can get, but I can't help it—I'm wracked with jealousy over his ex. I can't even bring myself to call her by name; I think of her as X. A big, slashing, Zorro-like, blood-dripping-down-like-on-a-poster-for-a-horror-movie X.

It's so painful for me to think that the love of my life once vowed to spend his life with another woman when he should have known to wait for me. I know my feeling is unreasonable, and I'm not even sure why it's so strong. I used to have a long-term boyfriend who had once been married, and I never gave his ex-wife a second thought. Somehow though, with Will, thoughts of X just *kill* me. And the intellectual in me knows that if you're going to wait around until your thirties to get married, your choices are either going to be men who are afraid of commitment or divorcés or the real whammy, men who are divorced and are *now* afraid of commitment. But I still don't like it.

And here's why:

1. Will will always have met X a decade before he met me. He and X were younger, thinner, and he had more hair when they got married. His photos with X will forever be wrinkle free, and I admit it, I'm jealous I didn't get him first.

2. I can't seem to stop myself from asking questions about her. Why I do this to myself is clearly an exercise in masochism. Everyone knows that after a certain point there is no reason to get details about how many sex partners your New Boyfriend or New Girlfriend has had, the wildest/best sex NB/NG has had, who NB's/NG's first love was, etc. You just don't do it.

Except, I do. The answers to my questions inevitably just add salt to my already raw wound. For example, I asked him once what X did for a living. He said that when they were together she worked in human resources, but before he met her, she'd been a stripper. He laughed when he said that. "We were married when I found out," he said. "She waited a good long time to tell me. It bothered me for awhile, but now I think it's funny."

That makes one of us.

A woman who isn't afraid to get up on stage and take off her clothes in front of men is—I'm venturing a wild guess here—going to be a little more free about her body than oh, say for example, *me*. There are women who can pull off high heels, garters, and all manner of ridiculous and impractical undergarments. I am decidedly not one of these women. And while I think my bras and Victoria's Secret underwear are perfectly pretty, sometimes maybe even a little sexy—lace, vibrant colors, lots of black—they are a far cry from see-through merriwidows and crotchless panties. Feelings of merriwidow inadequacy have me in an emotional chokehold.

3. He told me X is outgoing and fun. I fear that I am not. I would never be confused with a party animal, for example, unlike X, whose party exploits are well known among Will's circle of friends.

When I asked Will what made him fall for X in the first place, he told me that he liked how friendly and outgoing she was.

"In what ways was she outgoing?" I, like an idiot, asked.

"Like, say she's at a bar or a party. She introduces herself to everyone in the room and makes friends with everybody. She's always the life of the party. Like this one time we had a get-together, and when everyone was good and liquored up, she went around taking all the women's bras and then threw them on the ceiling fan—"

Let me take this opportunity to assure you right now, if you had any doubts: I would *never* do such a thing. For one thing, this seems a ridiculous activity and it would simply never occur to me. I'm telling you, no amount of drunkenness would ever be enough for me to come up with such a scheme. For another thing, I'm not a go-braless kind of girl. I'm busty as hell, which makes it pretty much a medical necessity that I wear a bra at all times. I mean I need serious architecture to keep things more or less in place. Let's say I was unharnessed and had to move quickly for some reason—a fire, say—the inevitable mammary backlash could wallop me in the face at best, or, at worst, leave me in traction with the kind of concussion where the resulting amnesia is lifelong.

I pull myself together enough to exit the stall. I splash water on my face and look at myself in the mirror. I've met a wonderful man. I have a mostly good job. Why can't I just celebrate how great my life is? Why do I do this to myself:

Indulging in feelings of self-doubt? But every now and then I can't seem to stop dissecting my flaws in painful detail. Like now.

My failings (a sampling):

1. I'm a worrier. An insomniac. A panic-er over things trivial.
2. I can't cook for shit. It doesn't seem like this should be a challenging activity, but I'm hopeless. The other night I tried to make a simple meal of pasta and garlic bread for Will and me. The pasta was just about done, but the garlic bread was still frozen in the middle, so I cranked up the heat in the oven to hasten the heating of the bread, and then I took the pasta off the stove and poured it into the colander. This is where things went terribly wrong. I gave the colander an overly exuberant toss, and spaghetti went everywhere—the counter, the sink, and most distressingly, down the garbage disposal. Will was at the table finishing his salad as I went into panicked pasta-retrieval mode, peeling spaghetti noodles off the counter and salvaging what I could from the sink and then cleaning it all off. Meanwhile, I called from the kitchen, "Everything's fine in here! Dinner's almost ready!" Unfortunately, half of our dinner went down the drain, and as I'd gone on a pasta scavenger hunt, the garlic bread had been solidified to the consistency of a crouton. I served poor Will about four spaghetti noodles and the garlic-flavored crouton and assured him I'd make us some microwaved popcorn right after our "dinner."
3. I have a tendency to focus on the negative, as I believe I've illustrated here.

   It doesn't matter that I know how stupid my destructive thoughts are, I can't seem to stop myself. Logically, I know that Will does not care if I'm the type of woman who gathers women's undergarments and drapes them from the rafters. There are plenty of good things about me. I'm a successful small business owner. I'm fairly smart. I kick ass at Scrabble.

I try to remind myself of the good things about me, but sometimes thoughts of my flaws supersede everything else.

Will and I have only been together for six months, but he's the first guy I thought I might want to spend my life with. After our second date, I emailed all my girlfriends and told them that I might just change my mind about marriage after all. Before Will, I thought I didn't want to get married. I don't mean that I wanted to spend my life alone or anything. I did want to find someone to share my life with. I just didn't think I wanted to do it with all the official trappings that signing a marriage certificate brings. Here's why:

1. My parents are divorced and it was a brutal, fangs-bared type affair. I never want to go through anything like that.
2. Too many of my friends and colleagues have been cheated on and/or gotten divorced. I could blame the failure of my parents' marriage on the fact that they were so young when they got married. Not so with my friends. They all thought they'd be different. They were wrong.
3. I had a friend who was separated from her husband. The guy died in a freak accident, and it turned out he was more than two hundred thousand in debt from gambling and bad investments. Even though they'd been separated for more than a year, she had to pay for it all. Taking on someone else's debt terrifies me. (See point one about my parents' divorce—they bickered endlessly about money. Needless to say, I have issues.)

Then came Will and everything changed. I'm not sure exactly why, but soon after meeting him I could barely stop myself from buying the phone-book-thick bridal magazines adorning the racks at the grocery store. After our first kiss, I could envision the engagement ring on my finger. I actually missed it, almost sensed it on my finger. You know how when you forget to put your watch on, and then all day at work you look at your bare wrist, feeling naked? You can actually feel the ghost of the watch, the palpable absence of it. That's how I felt about my left ring finger except, and this is key, there had never been a ring there to miss. It's lunacy. We haven't been dating long enough to even think about marriage. He hasn't even met any of my family yet since they are spread out all across the country. Dad is still in Chicago where I grew up, my younger sister Sienna is in New York trying to launch a career as a comedian, and my mother is out in California with her second husband. But who cares about them. I want the ring. I've become Gollum from *The Lord of the Rings: Give me the ring. Give me my precious. My precious ring.*

I should defend myself and tell you that it was really more than a couple dates that made me crazy about him. I knew Will pretty well even before we actually met.

I found him online. I'd been searching the online personals for months, and I just could not find a guy I was interested in. The challenge is that I live in Colorado, but I'm not an outdoorsy person, which makes me quite the exception 'round these parts. Coloradoans are a ridiculously outdoorsy people as a rule. I would say about eighty percent of the men around Denver put up personal ads that say something to the effect of: "I love to ski, mountain climb, fish, golf, camp, hang glide, hunt, scuba, snorkel, kayak, snowboard, mountain bike, go four-wheeling, and scale cliff faces. I love watching baseball, football, hockey, tennis, and basketball. I live life to the fullest and would like a woman who I can trek the Himalayas with and train for marathons alongside."

I got tired just reading them. I did not want to be dragged up a mountain on a week-long hike. I did not want to pee in the woods, sleep in nature, or commune with insects. Where was a guy who just wanted to talk, drink, screw, and see a good movie once in awhile?

Of the twenty percent or so who weren't triathletes, most of them had something else about them that was a deal breaker for me like they weren't attractive or couldn't spell for shit. Many of the guys posting ads wrote things that looked like they'd taken a running leap onto their keyboard and then hit SEND. Like this one, repeated here verbatim:

i&*\$%%m lookin for womin who is prety, intelegent (I ask you, to misspell "intelligent"!? The nerve!) *and wers thong underwear. I&*@%%ve a heart of gold*

I'd nearly given up hope. Then came Will. I liked his picture—he has a sexy smile, kind eyes, and cool glasses—so I clicked on his profile to learn more. His ad read: "I think my friends would describe me as funny and smart. I've been told that I tend to wear my heart on my sleeve, and that I am one of the easiest-going people around. I work with computers for a living, which I generally enjoy. For fun, I like live music, movies, restaurants, dancing (though not the ballroom variety—trust me, it's not pretty), travel. I am a guitar player (not bad), a golfer (not good), and willing to try most anything once (anything, that is, that doesn't involve throwing oneself out of a perfectly good aircraft)."

As soon as I read that he had no desire to toss himself out of a plane, I thought, *there's my man*. Also, I needed a guy who was easygoing. I'm high-strung enough for two people. I need a yin to my stressed-out yang. The fact that he played the guitar was also a plus. A guy who plays guitar is somehow intrinsically sexy.

I was out of town on business when I first emailed him, so we wrote each other back and forth for two full weeks before I got back in town. Via three or four long emails a day, we told each other all about our childhoods, our families, our jobs. Before we'd even met, I knew he was hilarious, intelligent, and a damn fine grammarian.

In one of those premeeting emails, I asked him about his divorce. "If I'm being too nosy, just let me know."

"I'm happy to answer any of your questions, Eva, don't worry about it. I'm all about honesty," he wrote back. "Let's see, we were married for four years, and in the beginning, it was really good. The end wasn't about money, nobody had an affair, and no firearms were involved. I think what I learned from the experience is that if there are things that bother you before you get married and you can't even discuss them, can't even talk about how to change or deal with whatever issues are going on, run. It was an exercise in Chinese water torture for me."

I emailed him back. "Interesting. Except what's Chinese water torture?"

"When you get the Chinese water torture treatment, you are strapped to a table or whatever, and a steady drip of water hits your forehead from overhead. The first few drops aren't a big deal—as were the issues my ex and I faced prewedding. Eventually, though, the inescapable, relentless drips are maddening to the point they can simply drive you insane. Drip, drip, drip. You know it's going to come again and again and again, and there is not a damn thing you can do about it."

When Will and I finally met in person at a bar for drinks, it was—I'm sorry to be sappy and dramatic here—magical. When I first saw him, my pulse surged and I couldn't keep a smile off my face. The very first words out of his mouth were, "Wow, you are really pretty. I thought you looked cute in your picture, but now I realize that picture really didn't do you justice."

Our date was completely free of the usual first date awkwardness because we'd already gotten to know each other so well through email. We didn't stop talking or laughing for six hours straight. At the end of the night, he walked me to my car and gave me a kiss that was soft, and warm, and wonderful.

Will had no time for games. The morning after our first date he wrote me that the previous evening had been one of the best dates of his life, and he couldn't wait to see me again. Oh how that put a smile on my face. And I felt the exact same way and told him so.

We went out again the next day, which was a Saturday. It was another whirlwind deal of us talking without pause, laughing so hard it hurt, and having a general blast together. We came home after a romantic dinner and started kissing and then groping and then sort of accidentally had sex for the better part of the night (oops! I didn't mean to sleep with him on our second date!), and, much to my relief, he was great in bed, so he aced the Fun-to-Have-Sex-With test.

My search, at long last, was over.

Now, the only thing standing between me and happily-ever-after is, well, me. I wish I could stop obsessing, but I hate that he loved his first wife and doesn't regret marrying her. He never says anything disparaging about her. It's so annoying. It's really his worst quality.

I inspect my face in the bathroom mirror, decide I look passably decent, and go downstairs where I join Will at the table.

"Is everything okay, babe?" he asks.

"Yeah. I was just writing down some thoughts for my meeting with Woodruff Pharmaceuticals. That's why I took so long."

He smiles and together we watch the band play.

I take a sip of my beer and try to shake my feelings of self-doubt, attempting to enjoy the music. Then a flurry of activity to my right catches my eye and I turn to look at what's going on. The older couple who had been sitting there is leaving, and three young women are snapping up the table. The women are wearing tight, cropped shirts that fall off the shoulders and are loosely draped on, held in place by a couple well-placed knots. I suspect that one overly enthusiastic laugh would cause the blouses to disintegrate. The girls are very pretty: Their hair, their smiles, their laughs, the confident way they move. They are decidedly alluring. I look over at Will. His eyes are resolutely focused on the band, straight ahead.

X. It's X's doing. X trained him not to look at pretty, half-dressed women making a ruckus getting to their table. Men stare shamelessly at women until their girlfriends or wives train them through negative reinforcement that if they stare at other women while in her company, they do so at their peril, setting themselves up for hours-long tirades in the vein of, "What, you think she's prettier than me? You want to fuck her?" Then comes the hours-long protest that no, no, of course he isn't attracted to the twenty-two-year-old brunette with enormous breasts.

A fresh wave of hate for X washes over me. Yes, she'd also trained him to put the toilet seat down and put the cap back on the toothpaste and having him house-trained is undeniably convenient, but the fact that she taught him not to look at other women meant she'd also had jealous feelings about him, and I do not want any more common bonds with this woman than I already have.

Will squeezes my hand, then drapes the arm closest to me across my shoulders. I love how snuggly he is, always holding my hand and giving me hugs.

There's a lot more I like about him, naturally. Sixteen years of dating the wrong guys makes me appreciate all the good things about Will. He's nothing, for example, like my ex, Rick. Rick and I were together nearly three years. Rick was painfully tightfisted with money, so even though at the time we were together he made a great salary and I made no money since I was in school getting my MBA, he made us split everything fifty-fifty. He would gripe endlessly every time he had to spend money on anything—the unfairness of having to spend twelve dollars to get a haircut, the price of gas, the cost of cereal. He was an obsessive bargain-hunter, constantly talking about things like how we could save eleven cents or something ridiculous by switching phone plans. Personally, I'll gladly fork over a few extra bucks if it means not constantly doing research and paperwork on phone plans and rebates and comparing one can of soup to another. My time is more important to me than money.

Will, unlike Rick, is incredibly generous. He tips well, he purchases things based on quality and not whether he can save six cents, and he'll take me out to a nice meal without telling me the entire time how it's wrecking his budget to do so. Early on in our relationship we were at a bar with friends and the waitress brought our check and he reached for his wallet. "But you got dinner and drinks last time," I said.

"Eva, no one's keeping track."

I felt so freed when he said that. A cloud lifting and all that. Instantly I felt I could exhale and relax. After constantly having to pay attention to who had paid for dinner last time and who got the movie tickets last, it was absolutely liberating not to have to keep score.

Also, Will is thoughtful. I'm allergic to nuts, and whenever we go out to eat, he asks if the dish is prepared with any nuts in it. He tells his friends who invite us over for dinner to cook something without nuts and to be careful of the sneaky places nuts can pop up, such as in things like salad dressing and snack foods and even root beer. I love how he looks out for me.

Thinking about how lucky I am to have found Will puts a smile on my face again, temporarily averting my earlier self-esteem crisis. I look into his eyes and we exchange one of those dopey smiling-deliriously sort of gazes that people who are in the first stages of love are wont to do.

We just can't help ourselves.

Chapter 2

The next morning I head over to see my friend Rachel at her shop. Rachel owns her own secondhand clothing store in Highlands, a cute neighborhood in northern Denver. Her shop, Recycled Chic, is in the downtown area, sandwiched in between restaurants, coffee shops, a bakery, a couple of pubs, a bookstore, and some artsy shops selling the work of local artists and jewelry makers.

I really love Rach. We met two years ago at a meeting of the Denver branch of Women Entrepreneurs Incorporated. We were sitting next to each other at a table, waiting for the keynote speaker to go on, and I asked her about how she got started with her business.

Rachel told me that she was the mother of two kids and she launched her store because she had wanted a job where she could be more in control of her hours. She'd worked as a freelance seamstress, but she didn't get enough work to make a decent living.

"My husband works in sales, so some months he makes enough money to get by, but other months are a little rough," she said. "I wanted something steady. I heard about this organization that gives loans to women who want to start their own businesses. I figured a recycled clothing store would be pretty inexpensive to start up since at first I'd just get donations of clothes from friends and stuff, so there would be low overhead. I also sell some original clothes I design myself."

She showed me pictures of some of her designs that she had in the portfolio she'd brought. The clothes were things like funky polka-dot skirts with faux fur trim; dresses whose hems fell at an angle, shorter on the right side and longer on left; denim bustiers with short lace sleeves. I loved her original designs, though they were all a little too risqué for me to feel comfortable pulling off. I tend toward conservative business suits in classic cuts. Rachel always looks cool and hip, though. She is unequivocally pretty. She's thin but with curves in all the right places. She has dark hair, pale blue eyes, and a small diamond nose ring. She doesn't look old enough to be a mom. She reminds me a lot of my own mother, who'd also had kids young and was ridiculously pretty. My mother and Rachel could be described as Hot Moms. They may have children scampering around their ankles, but they are still unequivocal babes.

That day we first met, I asked Rachel about her kids. When she told me how old they were, I nearly fell off my chair.

"You look much too young to have an eight year old."

"That's what happens when you're eighteen and you get wasted and have sex. You have an eight year old when you're twenty-six."

I laughed out loud at how honest and down-to-earth she was. She was such a change of pace from the fake people I'd worked with at the office before I left my corporate job and went out on my own. How could I not love her? And the more I got to know her, the more I grew to respect her. She's both a mother and a successful businesswoman. (She's not rolling in money, but she makes a decent living and has a job she enjoys.) She can cook, and sew, and do all manner of craftsy domestic things that I don't stand a chance at.

Though I love Rachel, I never buy any of the used clothes.

There is something I find disconcerting about the whole idea of putting my ass in a pair of jeans that once housed someone else's ass. And because I'm pretty conservative clothingwise, I never buy any of her original designs either, a fact she thankfully doesn't hold against me.

I hang out with Rachel at her shop whenever I can. She even set up a barstool for me next to hers behind the counter, so that she and I can dish when things are quiet. As with everything she does in her life, Rachel decorated her store in a way that is both funky and classy. Her shop is small but welcoming. She has headless mannequins adorning the place, wearing whatever outfits Rachel wants to highlight that week. Her storefront windows have mannequins modeling the clothes as well, and the window background changes whenever the mood strikes her. This week she has those hula-dancing dolls you suction-cup to your dashboard all over the place—on the ground, taped to the wall, dangling from the ceiling—plus colorful leis draped all around. The headless mannequins are modeling summer clothes, both clothes Rachel designed and sewed herself and preowned items that customers brought in exchange for a few bucks in cash.

Right now, there is only one customer in the place, a teenage girl sitting on the floor with a pile of T-shirts around her. She picks one up, inspects it, then puts it down and picks up another one. She's wearing a consternated expression, as if picking out which five dollar T-shirt she wants to buy is the most important decision she'll make this year.

"Hey, Eva," Rachel says.

"Hey." I slide onto my stool behind the counter. Rachel assumes her usual position beside me.

"So, how are you?" she asks.

"More in love than ever."

"Ugh, shut up, I can't take anymore of your bliss."

"Although, there has been one little dark spot in our relationship."

She looks hopeful. Drama is so much more interesting than happiness.

"I had a little breakdown at this bar last night. There was this graffiti that said, 'You are not the first, and you are definitely not the last. And probably, you are not the best.' I just couldn't stop thinking about Will's ex-wife. I hate that he vowed to love her until the end of time. I hate thinking about him having sex with her. Or with anyone else, for that matter."

"Y-e-a-h," she says in this drawn out, you're-a-fucking-retard way, "you're just going to have to get over that."

"I know. I know. It's just . . . I've dated lots of guys before Will. Chris was even divorced, and I didn't give a shit about his ex-wife. What's going on? Why am I being so psycho about this?"

"You weren't in love with Chris. You love Will. That's why this is eating you up. So you must still be serious about him. Still think he might be the guy who can get you over your fear of marriage?"

"Yeah, I think so. Other times I start freaking myself out, thinking about all the stuff that can go wrong."

The girl who had been looking at T-shirts has finally made her selection and approaches us wide-eyed, like she's frightened of how this whole buying and selling stuff works. There is no question in my mind that she lives in Boulder, a city forty minutes northwest of Denver. She just has the Boulder look—with that messy hair like she just got out of bed or just took off her ski cap. No matter what time of year it is, a staggering number of Boulderites' hair look like it has just been freed from a knit hat. I want to stand out on street corners handing out hairbrushes and explaining as you would to someone who has suffered a head injury, "IT'S CALLED A HAIRRRRBRRRRUSHHHH."

"That'll be five dollars," Rachel says.

The girl hands over a crumpled five, and Rachel rings it

up in her old-fashioned cash register, which spits out a receipt the width and length of a human tongue.

"Thank you so much," Rachel says.

The girl nods hurriedly and makes her escape.

"What were we talking about?" Rachel asks. "Oh yeah, how you were freaking yourself out thinking of what could go wrong. Why does that not surprise me?"

Rachel thinks I have a tendency to overthink things. She's right, of course.

Sometimes I think it would have been so much easier if I'd done what Rachel had done and run off to get married on a deadline—six months to tie the knot before the kid gets here!—and there was no time to think about what it all meant. I should have gotten hitched back when I was still young and hadn't had my heart broken or gone on zillions of disappointing dates that wore my spirit down. When I hadn't yet been hit on by several married men, proving in no uncertain terms that men were scum.

"I don't want to be the second wife. It just seems so seedy. You know, like how in a harem there were like the second, third, and fourth wives, and it was a total step-down from first wife. Being a second wife is less special."

"Look at your mom. She's much happier now with Frank. Same thing with my mom. Some people learn from their mistakes the first time and then they are better able to get it right the second time around."

"It would be different if I'd been married once before, too. Then we'd both be equally sullied. But it's more than that. I feel like there are these shoes I have to fill. I'm the replacement Darren on 'Bewitched'; I'm the new oldest daughter on 'Roseanne'."

"You make no sense at all. What are you talking about?"

"Like I know Will's ex is the kind of woman who can pull off things like garters. He said he likes garters, finds them sexy, and I just can't get the picture out of my head of him having sex with her when she's wearing a garter." I moan at this, the image just makes me ill. A few weary sighs and I recover enough to speak again. "I could never pull off such impractical underwear. I'd look preposterous."

"You would not. Look, at least you don't have to buy your boobs at the Gap—"

Padded bras? I never knew Rachel had faux cleavage! I feel a little like when Mom told me the truth about Santa Claus. . . .

"You'd look great in ridiculous underwear," she continues. "And as fetishes go, his is pretty damn tame. At least he doesn't want to have sex with you and some random other woman or a sheep or something."

"I know all that. I just wish I could get his ex out of my head."

"I get what you are saying. I guess I don't know what to tell you to make you feel better, except that obsessing about this is not going to help."

I love this about Rachel. I think it's the mother in her. She can stay calm while things go nuts all around her—in this case me. Still, I ignore her completely and go right on obsessing. "And then, when I think about things like this, I worry that if we get married, our sex life will get dull because I have all these confused feelings about what is *really* sexy and what our culture says is sexy to sell products like . . . I don't know . . . lingerie, liposuction, fake boobs, whatever. I've never dated a man for more than two or three years. What do you do when you've been together for . . . how long have you been with Jon?"

"Ten years, almost eleven. I'll be honest. It does get boring sometimes. A lot of times we have sex because we think we should, like, well it's been two weeks so we probably should get it on. Sometimes, honestly, it feels like another chore, like cleaning the bathtub or something. It's really hard when you have kids. You only have fifteen minutes to have sex, and even if the kids are over at Grandma's, the screaming and the moaning comes out all weird because you're so out of practice."

I nod, absorbing this information.

"Is sex with Will dull now?" she asks me.

"No, it's great now. I'm just worried it'll get dull someday. Like say, six years from now."

"You're worried about something that may or may not happen six years from now?"

"Right."

"Do you think that's a good use of your emotional energy?"

"No. But on the other hand, it's the whole Boy Scout thing about how you should always be prepared. If you anticipate what things might go wrong, you can take steps to avoid it."

"You have to stop worrying. Worrying gives you the false impression you have control over things. You don't. You don't know what the future brings. Anything could happen."

Worrying gives you the false impression you have control over things. You don't. She's right, but it's not easy to shut off my desire to predict the future. "Seriously, you and Jon have been married for ten years. You must have tips for keeping things interesting?"

"Well, every now and then Jon and I do surprise each other."

"Yeah?"

"For our seventh anniversary he brought home a little . . . toy."

"Really? I want details."

"It was called the Clit Blaster 2000."

"It fucking was not."

"Oh, but it was."

"Verdict?"

"Well, the clit-blasting portion of it was delightful. However, it had certain . . . appendages that seemed bound and determined to venture into places that I would prefer weren't ventured. I think I need a tattoo on my ass that says, 'No entry. Exit only.'"

I burst out laughing. "Aaah!" I say, burying my head in my hands. "I'll never be old enough to hear this stuff." We chuckle for a minute or so. "So tell me honestly, do you think I should buy a garter and see how it goes?"

"It's just a costume. It's not a big deal."

"I know." I think a moment. "I don't mind costumes at Halloween, I mean, then it's kind of fun, but in bed, I don't know, I don't want to feel like I'm putting on a performance. I'm totally comfortable with my body naked in front of Will, I'm not hiding under the covers with the lights out or anything, but I don't want to have to pretend to be somebody I'm not, you know?"

"Then don't wear it. Those kind of things come off in about ten seconds anyway, it's not worth the sixty bucks. Anyway, they encourage guys to come even faster than they already do, so I say, where's our motivation?"

I smile. She's right, where's my motivation?

Feeling better about my lingerie inhibitions, I radically switch conversational gears. "How have things been going with the family?"

"Good. I mean, well, busy. I've got to get the kids in day-care and figure that all out. The house is a mess. I've got to get the dog spayed. Jon has been kind of . . . depressed lately . . . so that's really been a drag. I just want to throttle him."

"What's he depressed about?"

Jingling bells signal that a customer is entering. In this case two customers. Two college-age girls engaged in a loud conversation.

"Hello!" Rachel calls cheerily. "Let me know if I can help you find anything."

"We're just looking," the one girl says, and then continues her conversation in a booming voice sprinkled with a cackling laugh.

"What was I saying?" Rachel says quietly to me. "Oh, Jon.

He's just bummed because he's not doing as well at his job as he'd like to be. He hasn't met his sales goals for the last three months running, and his boss is giving him a hard time about it. Of course when he doesn't meet his goals it means money is tight at home, which leads to all the usual bullshit money stress."

"I'm sorry."

"It's okay. It's the deal with marriage. Sometimes you want to kick your spouse off a cliff. It doesn't mean you don't love him."

"How about the in-laws. Anything new there?" Jon has a very Jerry Springer family. His sister Beth's husband Brent cheated on her when she was just about to give birth to their third kid and then left her for the other woman. His younger sister, Sandy, is currently seeking a restraining order against her ex-boyfriend—now that she's gone through rehab, she doesn't want the thieving, abusive, heroin addict using her as his punching bag anymore. I have to say that listening to tales of Jon's siblings' woes puts my problems in perspective. These people lead such messed up lives that I'm reminded that my life is paradisiacal by comparison.

"Sandy goes to court on Wednesday to get the restraining order. Edward keeps calling and threatening her."

"Threatening her how?"

"You name it. He's going to kill her, break her arms, burn her house down . . ."

"Jesus!"

"Yeah. I know."

"Can't she get a wiretap or something and record this stuff? It seems like he should be in jail for something like that."

"That's a good idea. I wonder how you go about doing that. I hope this restraining order does something. He needs to forget about her already. They've been broken up for four months now. Four months! But when he gets drunk or high, he decides that calling her and threatening her with bodily harm is the best way to win her back. And what makes things worse is that since I haven't gotten around to getting the kids in daycare or summer camp yet, they've been spending all this time hanging out with Sandy and Beth, and it's just not a good environment for them. I mean I'm really grateful that they are willing to help out with watching the kids. It's certainly helping the money situation, but . . . I just don't like the kids spending any more time with them than is absolutely necessary. How about Will's family? Do you get along with them?"

"Well, it's really just his mom. His father died a couple of years ago. He's an only child so he doesn't have any siblings, and he's got aunts and uncles, but they all live far away so we never see them."

"You're so lucky."

"His mom still lives in Colorado, though. They moved here when Will was really young. She lives an hour and a half away so we see her every other month or so. We haven't spent a lot of time together, so we're not really comfortable with each other yet, but we get along all right."

We talk for awhile more and when I can no longer put off getting to work, I sigh, tell her I need to get going, and promise her I'll call her later.

I go home, get myself a supersized water bottle full of water and a soup-bowl-size cup of coffee and go into my office, which is on the second floor of my home. Even though I live alone, I shut the door behind me. I always have the ringer on my phones upstairs turned off so I won't be tempted to flee my study to talk on the phone when I'm supposed to be working. Once I'm in there, I make myself work for at least four hours at a time—I'm only allowed to leave my office to use the bathroom or get more water.

Like I said, I own my own business. I'm an independent management consultant, and I make a good living doing what I do, but I don't trust having money. I'm not used to it. I spent far too many years struggling.

I got my undergraduate degree in history, and, not surprisingly, I had a hard time finding a job after graduation. My father regaled me endlessly with "I told you sos." And it was true, he'd warned me away from getting a degree in history. He'd said I should get a degree in business so I could get a job that paid real money. But I insisted that money didn't matter to me. You have the luxury of thinking like that when your parents are paying your rent.

I had desperately wanted to get away from Illinois after graduating from high school, but we couldn't afford out-of-state tuition, so I earned my degree at the University of Illinois and then moved to Colorado where I managed to get a job as an admin. assistant for the president of the University of Colorado at Boulder. I was quickly promoted to a position in which I did all the mail and email correspondence for the president. My job function was to editorially fellate the donors who gave big money to the school, stroking their egos by endlessly thanking them for their generosity. The job was okay, though it got routine, but the main thing was that it didn't pay very well.

I'd been working there for two years when my father came out to Colorado for a visit. At the time, I lived in a microscopic apartment, and the first words out of Dad's mouth when he saw it were: "I spent twenty thousand dollars on your education so you could live in this hovel? I never should have agreed to let you get a degree in history."

And he was right. I was living in a dump. And did I really want to be broke for my entire life?

I signed up to take my GMAT to apply to business schools the next day.

Some background on Dad: My father has spent his entire life working at a sales job he hates. At night he'd come home and build things down in his workshop. He'd make wooden toys or various kinds of furniture. He'd build shelves or stairs for the house. Dad was always hiding out in that workroom of his. We weren't allowed in it. It was his sanctuary, the place he escaped from his demanding job and needy family. Dad occasionally sold some of the furniture he created, but I don't think he ever considered trying to live full-time off his carpentry. I don't think it ever occurred to him that it was possible to make a living doing something he enjoyed.

Even when he wasn't locked in his workroom, even if he was sitting across from you at the dinner table, he wasn't really there. He was lost in his own world. So for my sister Sienna and me to break him out of that world and get him to pay attention to us involved a lot of jumping through hoops. Mom was always there and her love for us was never in doubt, so therefore we didn't feel the need to impress her with our accomplishments. Dad was a different story. We were endlessly trying to dazzle him with our good grades and successes.

When I was a sophomore in high school I won an essay contest about the history of Illinois. It was a statewide deal, and my name and picture got into the local papers. Never in my life had Dad been more proud of me. The way he smiled at me, the way he bragged to his friends, the way he slapped me on the shoulder with pride—he'd never paid that much attention to me in my life.

Basically, I've spent my entire adulthood trying to get that reaction out of Dad again. I can't help it—I like making Daddy proud.

After I got my MBA I took a job with what was then a Big Six consulting firm. I worked absolutely insane hours and spent more time sleeping in hotel beds than I did sleeping in my own, but I also brought home a very nice paycheck. Even so, right away I knew I didn't want to work there forever. I liked working as a management consultant well enough, but I didn't like the cutthroat corporate culture I was in. And I hated how managers would think nothing of dumping forty-eight hours' worth of work on my desk at three o'clock on a Friday afternoon and tell me it had to be complete by 9 A.M. Monday morning. I started socking away nearly half of my paycheck into a savings account with the idea I'd go solo one day. I wanted to have enough in savings so that if it turned out I was an abject failure at being a business owner, I could still survive for a year or two without bringing in any income. So that's what I did. It wasn't actually that hard because I was used to living simply. I just didn't buy an expensive car or a big house like most of my coworkers fresh out of grad school did. And two years ago, I tendered my resignation and went out on my own. It was rough going for the first several months, but over time I got enough word-of-mouth recommendations that I make more money now than I ever did working for somebody else.

It's a stressful but rewarding job. I take the future of a business—and thus the futures of all the people who work there—in my hands. I'm good at thinking creatively about how to solve problems a business is facing. Somehow at work, I have an absolute confidence in my abilities that doesn't extend to my personal life.

I have a meeting with the executives at Woodruff Pharmaceuticals later this week, and I spent my afternoon researching WP and the company they're considering acquiring, as well as the pharmaceutical market in general. When I look up, six hours have passed and I'm weak with hunger. I go downstairs to make myself a snack. The phone rings and I assume it's Will, since he should be getting off work soon. Then we'll do the whole your-place-or-mine thing. I can't wait until we live together.

"Hello?"

"Hey, you." It's Sienna, my younger sister.

"Hey! How are things?"

"Good. How about you? Is all still paradise with Will?"

"All is still paradise."

"Good for you."

"How're things in New York?"

"Great. I've been working on some new stuff and I performed it for the first time the other night and it went over really well."

"That's great."

Sienna works as a stand-up comedian-slash-administrative assistant. She's been doing stand-up for the last four years, but the money is unsteady, hence the day job.

"Dad called me yesterday and I was telling him about how I performed some new material the other night and it really killed, and he was like, 'how much money did you get?' It was such a buzz kill. I'd been on cloud nine and then it was just like bam! I come crashing to the ground—splat! You can see the little chalk outline of my body. I was just crushed because the truth was, I didn't get paid for the other night."

"Don't let Dad get to you."

"I know . . ."

The unsaid "but" hangs heavy in the air. Sienna and I both constantly struggle with trying to love ourselves as we are, no matter what other people think about us, but secretly we both revel in outside validation.

"How are things with you and Mark?" I ask.

"Good, for the most part. It's hard with both of us working during the day and then performing at night. Sometimes it's hard to find time to spend together."

"I know. I can't wait until you two can both live off your comedy."

"I visualize that every single day. Every single minute, really."

"Do you think you and Mark are going to get married?" Mark is her boyfriend of three years. He's an underpaid comedian too and an absolutely great guy. He's funny, kind, fun—he's just the kind of guy I want my sister to spend her life with.

"We know we want to spend our lives together. I don't know about the whole marriage thing."

See, she's just as confused about marriage as I am. It is so, so nice having another person in this world who was messed up by my parents in just the same way that I was.

"Look, I've got to head down to the bar. I'm opening tonight, so I should get going," Sienna says.

"Well, good luck tonight. I love you, kiddo."

"I love you, too."

I hate that Sienna lives so far away. She and I are a lot alike. We have the same mannerisms and facial expressions. We look alike. We both struggled through low-paying, unrewarding jobs. Sienna is twenty-eight and is still struggling with the low-paying, unrewarding day job bit. She once had the kind of job our parents approved of. She graduated summa cum laude in political science. After graduation she moved to Colorado to be closer to me, and she got a job working for the state of Colorado doing policy research. When the new governor came into office after she'd been working there for two years, he ripped the department up so that he could give jobs to his cronies. All the researchers and people who did the actual work were let go in favor of pencil pushers who could collect fat paychecks.

But Sienna was happy to get laid off. Her job was just too solitary to suit her personality, and it consumed too much of her mental energy, leaving her too drained to pursue her real dream of becoming a comedian. She had occasionally done open mic nights at local comedy clubs in Denver, which is where she met Mark, but it had been hard for her to find the time to write and work on new material. She and Mark had long talked about moving to New York. So after she got her pink slip, they decided to go for it and moved to New York together. They were best friends, and then lovers, and then they finally got around to realizing that they were each other's true loves.

Sienna has held a series of low-paid jobs ever since the move, but she's steadily pursued her goal of being a comedian. My father gives her a hard time about not making more money.

He tells her that he paid for her to have a college education so she could have the kind of opportunities he never had, blah blah blah.

Personally, I think it's great what Sienna is doing. While money is nice, it's not everything. Having a passion—that's worth a whole lot more.

Seconds after I get off the phone with Sienna, I get a call from Will.

"Hi, hon. What's up?" I ask.

"Do we have plans for Sunday?"

"Let me check." I open my Palm Pilot. We're wide open for Sunday. Immediately I wonder what Will has got planned for me. A concert? A party? A romantic dinner and play? "We don't have anything. Why?" I smile with anticipation at the exciting time awaiting me.

"Mom wants us to come down for dinner."

My smile disappears. I exhale silently, my body deflating like a punctured balloon. Like I told Rachel, it's not exactly that Will's mother and I don't get along, but so far we haven't quite managed to connect yet. It's in the little things. She'll tell a joke and I won't get it. I'll try to be funny and she'll look at me like I need to be locked into a mental institution, that sort of thing. Also, since Will is her only child, she has a mother-bear protective attitude toward her cub. She eyes me warily all the time as if trying to figure out if I'm going to hurt her son. She looks at me like I'm after Will just for his money or simply because I like to toy with men's hearts before I rip them out and eat them. I'm not quite sure what I need to do to convince her that I only want her son to be happy, that both of us want the same thing for him.

There are so many millions of things that can put a strain on a relationship. Money, sex, work, a pathological jealousy toward your significant other's ex, what have you. When you add the stress of in-laws on top of that, it's truly a wonder that any relationships manage to survive at all.

"Sounds great!" I swallow hard as my heart sinks into the pit of my stomach.

Chapter 3

The next day, I try to continue doing research for my meeting with the execs from Woodruff Pharmaceuticals, but I just can't focus. Instead, I sit in my study at my big desk and spend my afternoon trying to figure out if I want a wedding. On the one hand, I love weddings. Especially in an era when families are spread out across the country (if not the globe), weddings are a great excuse to get everybody together. On the other hand, I'm a chronic worrier, and I've seen women who are much stronger than me crack under the pressure of planning a wedding. I'm not sure I want to put myself through that. Also, when I was in college I worked at a country club as a waitress and the experience gave me insight into the unsavory dark side of matrimony. The club hosted many a wedding reception and almost without exception, every bride went through the day in a kind of stressed-out trance, constantly snapping at her friends and family. And it's not just strangers who I've known to have a less than paradisiacal wedding day. After Mom married Frank, she and her two sisters didn't talk for two years. Her sisters had been Mom's bridesmaids, and Mom yelled at them over something stupid—because they didn't walk down the aisle just so or something—and boy-oh-boy did they get pissed at her. She was stressed out, and what happened was understandable, but it taught me that a wedding might be the most expensive party you ever throw in your life, but that doesn't mean you'll have any fun at it.

I needed a mother's advice, so I run downstairs, grab the cordless phone off the wall in the kitchen, and give Mom a call.

"Hello?"

"Hi, Mom."

"Eva, darling, how are you?"

"I'm good," I say, pacing around my kitchen. I have an ultramodern kitchen, with a refrigerator with stainless steel doors, a stainless steel cooktop, and a matching washing machine. I have shiny black Corian countertops and white stone tile floors that match the white windowframes and white cabinets. I love this kitchen. It almost makes me wish I could cook so I had an excuse to spend more time in it—almost.

"How are things with Will?"

"Really good. In fact, I think Will and I might get married some day, and I wondered—"

"That's so exciting! When do you think you'll set a date?"

"I don't know. It's not official or anything."

"I'm so happy for you. I have to say I'm still amazed at how quickly everything has been moving with him. Wasn't it after the second date that you started looking at bridesmaid dresses online? That just floored me. After all those years of you thinking you didn't want to get married."

"Well, I still have a lot of fears about it, but it turns out that it wasn't that I didn't want to get married, it was that I didn't want to get married to any of the guys I dated before Will. But Mom, I need to get your advice. I'm thinking I don't want to have a wedding. What do you think?"

"Why not!?"

"You know how stressed out I get about stuff. I think a wedding might just put me over the edge."

"Honey, your father and I eloped and it just never felt right. It felt like something shameful that we sneaked off to do. You can have just a very small wedding with your family in Bermuda or something, but if you don't have some kind of ceremony, I really think you'll regret it."

"I don't know, Mom. I don't want you guys to have to spend a lot of money on a plane ticket to the tropics. Maybe we'll just elope and have a really casual party. A barbeque or something."

"Why don't you let me plan the wedding?"

"What? Mom, don't be ridiculous. You don't have time to plan a wedding that'll take place a thousand miles away from where you live."

"Sure I do. It'll be fun."

"Did you suddenly stop working fourteen-hour days?"

"Well, no . . . but it would be fun. Come on, let me plan it. I'll take care of everything."

Ha-ha, ha-ha. That's a good one. Mom and I have completely different taste in everything. I like ethnic food; she lives off meat and potatoes. I like silver jewelry; she likes gold. I'm a voracious reader; she doesn't have the attention span to read a greeting card. And while her wedding to Frank six years ago was a beautiful one, let me tell you a little story about it that I think illustrates why I don't want to hire her as my wedding planner. After Sienna followed me to Colorado, my mother moved out here from Chicago as well, taking her boyfriend, Frank, with her. They had only been in Colorado a few months when they got hitched, and they wanted a symbolic gesture that brought together their Chicago roots with their new life in the west. So Mom came up with this idea to force her wedding party to dance the first dance to the Blues Brothers' "Rawhide" while galloping on stick ponies. (The Blues Brothers are from Chicago, and "Rawhide" has a western theme, get it?) Mind you, we bridesmaids were wearing floor-length gowns and high heels and were *cavorting on stick ponies in front of all of our friends and family*. Also, you never really realize just how long the song "Rawhide" is until *you have to get up in front of all your friends and family while astride a stick pony while you're wearing a ball gown*. It's four and a half min-

utes long. It was the longest four and a half minutes of my
life, and I was plenty liquored up at the time, so that's saying
something. But she was the bride, so we had to do what she
said. Brides have all the power. You can just imagine their evil
bwah-ha-ha laughs as they contrive ways to humiliate the
people they love.

So did I want my mother planning my wedding? Not so
much. Somehow I imagined that if she planned it, Will and I
would end up in get-ups involving sombreros and tutus.

"Okay, Will and I will have a small wedding. I'll plan it,
though. And it's going to be very nontraditional."

"That's fine." I can hear the smirk in her voice. She's won.
But not really, because like I said, I do love weddings and
there is a part of me that wants to proclaim from the rooftops
that I've found this wonderful man and for whatever reason
he seems to want to spend his life with me. I want to vow to
be with him forever and ever in front of all the people I care
about.

"So . . ." I say. "How are things with you?"

"I'm ready to kill my husband, that's how things are with
me."

"What did Frank do this time?"

My mom married a younger man. Frank is a fun guy, and
after the divorce, Mom was ready for some fun. She felt like
she'd gotten married too young so she never got to do the
fun things young people do. With Frank, she went water-ski-
ing on his boat, riding on the back of his motorcycle, dancing
at clubs late into the night. It's his very sense of boyish play-
fulness that attracted her to him in the first place that drives
her absolutely insane now. She's always complaining about
him not doing his share of the housework, sleeping in on the
weekends, and goofing off when he should be doing whatever
chore Mom feels he should be doing.

"I'm going to have to pay hundreds of dollars to have a
handyman come in and do some housework because my husband is too lazy to do it." Mom launches into a litany of

chores Frank hasn't done: He still hasn't cleaned up the painting supplies from the study. How many times does she have to ask him? And his second car has been taking up half the driveway for weeks with parts strewn everywhere. They look like they belong in a doublewide! What must the neighbors think?!

"I'm sorry, Mom. I know it's tough. How are things with the job going? Weren't you going to meet with that new client? How did that go?" I sit down at my large kitchen table. I spent a bundle to get comfortable kitchen chairs with cushy seats, but I almost never use my table. I either eat at my desk in the study or in front of the TV. I think I had an image of myself being some goddess of entertaining, when in fact I'm more of a solitary TV-dinner sort of girl.

"Oh, I didn't tell you?" She laughs.

"No. What?"

"So I met with these two stodgy men, really high mucky-mucks. I met in the one man's office, and he has those big, big leather chairs for six-foot-tall men that little me just drowns in. I felt like that little girl character Lily Tomlin played. So I went to show them my portfolio," she giggles again. "And they have that kind of plastic mat that goes over the carpet so you can easily wheel around in your chair. Somehow the wheel of my chair got caught under the mat, and I went crashing down with the chair coming right over my head, trapping me. It was a huge chair. I couldn't get it off me. So I say . . . I say . . . ." she's laughing so hard she's having trouble getting the words out. "Excuse me. Can you help me get this chair off my head?"

This strikes me as the most wildly hilarious thing I've heard in months. The image of my petite mother trying to make a good impression on clients, only to go flying upside down, landing with a chair on her head, and then saying in a voice muted by acres of leather chair, "Excuse me. Can you help me get this chair off my head?" It's classic.

Mom and I laugh and laugh. I love that my mother can

laugh at herself. She's unlike my father in that way. Dad always pretends he knows everything and has never made a mistake in his life. Mom is fully willing to admit she's a flawed human being, and it's her genuineness and down-to-earth-y-ness that I love so much about her.

We say our good-byes and instead of getting to work I go back to my study and jot down my guest list. I want to start figuring out how much a wedding is going to cost. I've got money in the bank, but as an independent contractor, I have no economic security whatsoever. When Will and I move in together, that will save me a lot of money on mortgage payments, but until then, I just can't help being stressed out that my savings account is too anemic to fund a wedding. And I don't want Mom and Dad to help out because then they'll want to get involved in planning it, and I'm telling you, that would be disastrous. It doesn't take me long to write out the list. My bridesmaids are obvious: Sienna will be the maid of honor and Rachel and my girlfriend Gabrielle will be the bridesmaids. My list has fifty people on it. I'm guessing that's about what Will would put on his, but it's really inconvenient that I can't ask him to write his list out so I could know for sure. It's really going to hinder my ability to plan this thing if the groom doesn't know that we're going to have a wedding. I look at the clock. It's nearly six o'clock. I've managed to squander my entire day with dreams of wedding bliss rather than doing my job. That's one of the really hard things about owning your own business. When you slack off, you're the only one who pays for it. It's not like you're sticking it to the man, you're just sticking it to yourself. Alas.

Will and I see each other just about every night, unless we have a girls only or boys only kind of event with friends. He usually gets home from work around six, so I drive to his house in downtown Denver and wait for him there; he gave me keys to his place after we'd just been dating about a couple of weeks. With any other guy, I would have thought it was too fast, but everything just felt so right with Will.

Will's condo is a small, nicely decorated place. He's got the same taste in furniture and decorations that I do. Light wood floors, classy paintings, and a modern pale green couch. His hallway is lined with pictures of him and his friends. I hate, hate, hate the pictures where I can see his gold wedding ring. I hate having photographic evidence that he was married to somebody else. If we get married, he'll have to get a platinum ring so we'll have color-coded evidence to be able to figure out who he was married to at the time the picture was taken. Of course, the fact that he's lost a good portion of the hair on his head would also be a clue, but the wedding ring color will be the ultimate test.

As I stand in the hallway, looking at him wearing a wedding ring representing a marriage to another woman, my mood just sinks. Suddenly I don't know if I can marry a man who was married to someone else, even if I do have a guest list all written out back home. I want a guy without a past, without entanglements. Everything seems too hard and too messy and I want to break up with him and run away from the pain I feel when I think about him and X together.

Will opens the door, and I feel a flush of guilt for speculating on the possible demise of our relationship. I wish I could just believe in happily-ever-after without having bursts of doubt and insecurity.

We kiss and hug. I love the first after-work kiss and hug of the day. All the fears I battle all day rush out for that moment and I feel happy and safe and secure.

"I'm starving," I report.

"Good. I was thinking I'd take you to this little hole-in-the-wall Greek restaurant."

"Okay. Sounds great."

"I can't believe I haven't taken you to it before. You're going to love it."

He's right about the restaurant. It's great. We have saganaki and Greek salad to start and then share a nice meal. We discuss how we spent our day, except I have to lie about how I spent mine since I can't exactly tell him I've been plotting our wedding plans all day. Then, just as we're about done with our meal, he says, "So, I wanted to ask you something."

Immediately, visions of an engagement ring and Will on his knee and declarations of "Oopa!" filling the restaurant flood my imagination. Will I react in a suitably teary-eyed, delirious-with-happiness way? These are the things I worry about.

"We spend nearly every night together, and I love waking up to you more than anything. I was thinking maybe we could move in together."

I smile. It's not a wedding proposal, but it's not bad. "I would love that. I would love that a lot. Which one of us should sell our place do you think?"

"Well, your place is bigger, so I think it would make sense for me to sell mine and move in with you. What do you think?"

"I think that would be great. When do you think you'd want to move in?"

"Well, as soon as you want me to, I guess. And then I'll work on selling my place."

"You can start moving in tonight!"

He chuckles. "Well, I do have to pack."

"Details, details." I smile moonily at him. We stare at each other in silence for a moment as the conversation ebbs. Then I think of something else we can talk about—my phone conversation with Mom. I tell him the story about the chair and he laughs.

"I can't wait to meet her. I can't wait to meet all of your family," he says.

"I know. I can't wait for them to meet you."

"Who should I meet first?"

"It doesn't matter."

"Why don't we fly out to New York sometime in the next month and visit Sienna?"

"This weekend is the barbeque for Jon, but any other weekend after that would work for me. I'll call Sienna and see what would be good for her."

As Will drives us back to his place, I call Sienna on my cell phone and ask her if there would be a weekend when Will and I could come out sometime in the near future.

"I perform every Saturday night for the next month," she says.

"Perfect. We want to see you perform. I want to show off how talented you are to Will."

"Let me talk to Mark. Hang on." She puts the phone down for a minute and then gets back on. We decide we'll come out three weekends from now.

"Just call when you get your flight information," she says.

"Will do. Later, kiddo."

I click my cell phone off and smile. I'm excited about not having to live in two places from now on. I'm excited about being able to wake up to Will next to me every morning. I suppose that maybe I should be more nervous about this. After all, it's a major life change, but it's one I've been anticipating almost since we met. It seems silly to have to pay two mortgages and have to commute from one place to the other every day.

I reach my hand out to hold Will's and give it a warm squeeze.

Chapter 4

One thing about working from home is that you get addicted to lounging around in sweats. However, I suspect that I'd appear somewhat unprofessional if I showed up to my meeting with the executives from WP in PJs and bunny slippers, so I wrestle my way into nylons, heels, and a sedate slate gray skirt and jacket.

I've done some work for them before, primarily helping with new product launches. I worked for the company when Warren Woodruff was still running things. Warren had launched the business as a small-scale manufacturer of drugs like headache medicine and cough syrup. He built it into a major cutting-edge biopharmaceutical firm that was one of the top producers of prescription and over-the-counter drugs in the country. He'd done it by being a marketing powerhouse and by heavily investing in research and development, which enabled the scientists who worked for the company to make major discoveries and breakthroughs. Warren stepped down a year ago and handed over the reigns to his eldest son, Kyle, who had almost no management experience. Kyle's appointment caused a major buzz among the in-the-know businesspeople in the Denver area.

The receptionist guides me to the boardroom where I wait for twenty minutes for the four men I'm meeting with finally to show up.

"Eva Lockhart? So good to meet you! I'm Kyle Woodruff."

Kyle is my age but he seems much younger. He's thin and he apparently skipped over the part of puberty that was supposed to add bulk to his chest and shoulders. Doogie Howser comes to mind. He smiles at me and it takes me a second to figure out what is jarring about his smile. Then I realize that it's a caricature of a smile. Everything about it is big. Big teeth, thin lips that stretch wide as rubber bands, large gaping open-mouthed *big*. I shake hands with him and he crushes my fingers with his grip. He doesn't look like he's capable of crushing my hand, but I guess that's the point, he needs to prove he's not the lightweight he looks like.

"Glad to meet you! Glad you could stop by!" Kyle says.

"It's nice to meet you, too," I say, shaking Kyle's hand.

He points to the three men flanking him around the business table. "Eva Lockhart, this is Michael Evans, the senior vice president and my right hand man. Michael, this is Eva Lockhart."

"It's good to see you again, Michael," I say.

"You two know each other?"

"We do. I've done some work for WP in the past," I say.

"So, do you also know our chief scientific officer Doctor Edward Lyons and Anthony Victorino—"

"Your chief financial officer. Yes and yes," I say, nodding to both men, who nod back.

I take a seat at the table with the others. Kyle remains standing.

"Well, as you know, we called you in because WP is at a crossroads," he says. "We have the opportunity to make bold strides into the future or to let opportunity pass us by."

"I would phrase it more like, 'we have the opportunity to ravage our reserves on a risky and untested product, or we have the chance to ride the rocky economy out by staying true to our core competencies,'" Michael says.

"But Michael, our cash flows are strong—"

"Our cash flows are strong, but if we don't have the reserves to weather a downturn in the market, we risk becoming another WorldCom, growing too far too fast."

"It is a gamble, but I believe as you research this acquisition, Ms. Lockhart, you'll find that this new product of Ridan's will revolutionize how diseases are diagnosed, using a noninvasive methodology in which a tube is inserted down a patient's throat—"

"Ridan is not the first to patent such a product," Michael says. Dr. Lyons nods in agreement.

Kyle ignores Michael and continues touting the strengths of Ridan's new diagnostic equipment, only to be contradicted at every point by Michael. You don't have to be a psych major to figure out what's going on here. Michael has twenty years with the company while Kyle has eight. Michael is well into middle age while Kyle is in his fresh-faced early thirties. Michael was responsible for the acquisition of one of the leading drugs on the market for fighting osteoporosis and a major moneymaker for WP. Kyle has not yet accomplished anything of that scale. My guess is that Michael thought he should have been named chief executive officer and he will do anything to prove that Kyle was the wrong choice. Kyle knows that his appointment has upset a lot of people since he has so little experience, but if he can make a successful acquisition, it will earn him authority and respect he doesn't currently command.

The meeting lasts three long, heated hours, and when I leave, I feel like I've put in a ten-hour day.

Chapter 5

It's Rachel's husband Jon's birthday today, and Rachel is throwing a barbeque to celebrate. The barbeque starts at four on Saturday afternoon, and the sun is roasting the dry air of Colorado when Will and I pull up to Jon and Rachel's house. As Will parks, I recognize the car in front of us as Gabrielle's.

I met Gabrielle when I was working on getting my MBA. Gabrielle was working on her PhD in sociology at the same time I was getting my master's. I was waiting in line to get coffee from the stand at the student union and I went to pay for my latte, handing the kid behind the counter my twenty because that was all I had. He pointed to the handmade sign that had a twenty dollar bill sketched on it with a red bar in a circle over it, like you have on no-smoking signs.

"I know you'd prefer not to take twenties, but it's all I've got," I said.

"I'm sorry, I can't take it. I'll run out of change."

"But you don't understand. I'm in graduate school and I'm having a caffeine emergency. My entire future could be destroyed if I fall asleep at my final presentation tonight."

"No can do, lady."

"Here. I'll buy you a cup of coffee."

I turned to see a petite woman with dark hair and glasses

forking over the three bucks I needed to obtain the precious beverage.

"Thank you, so, so much. You are a life-saver. You're earning like a million karma points."

"Don't worry about it. I'm a grad student too." She ordered a latte for herself. "We have to look out for each other. I'm getting my PhD in sociology. How about you?"

"MBA."

The kid behind the counter set the two lattes down. I took one and handed the girl the other.

"I'm Gabrielle Leveska."

"I'm Eva Lockhart. It's nice to meet you. I don't have to be in class for another hour. Do you want to share a table with me?"

"Sure."

We sat at a nearby table and I asked her what she was doing research on. She told me she was looking at the representation of self and social interaction in online gaming communities. Which meant nothing to me, and I said so.

"Well, there are these games you can play online against thousands of other people from all over the world," she explained. "You get to choose the character or persona you play these games with, and you can be male or female. The vast majority of people who play these games are men, yet many of the men choose female personas. Sometimes they'll be given a hard time about that, but these guys will explain that they choose a female personality as a strategy because other male characters will give the female character gifts, like extra ammunition and supplies."

"Really? But don't the people playing male characters know that the females are in all likelihood played by other men?"

"Yeah, but it happens anyway. Characters even fall in love and get married online."

"I don't get it. How do you get married online?"

Gabrielle explained about online weddings where communities of characters met in cyberspace to have a ceremony and celebration. I'd had no idea such things happened, and I was fascinated to learn about this strange new world.

We spent the next hour talking about gender and identity and how people socialize and don't socialize with each other in an era of the Internet. It was so refreshing to talk about things other than business plans, economic forecasts, and the bottom line. I learned that Gabrielle was married. I told her that I was single and I was beginning to think I always would be.

"What are you looking for in a guy?" she asked.

"Someone who's kind and funny. Someone who's thoughtful and interesting."

"It's interesting that you didn't say anything about his looks."

That's the tricky thing about befriending a sociologist. They're always noticing that kind of thing.

"Well, I don't want him to look like an ogre, but attraction is such a tricky thing. I've dated some really good-looking guys who were boring as hell and I just didn't care how chiseled their cheekbones were or how ripped their abs, I just can't be attracted to someone who's nothing more than a pretty face."

"Well, I know a guy I think you might like, and he's pretty cute, too."

She invited me to join her and her husband, Dan, for a dinner where I'd meet Steve. It turned out Steve just didn't do it for me, but Gabrielle and I kept calling and seeing each other. I didn't get a boyfriend, but I did get a girlfriend.

Her relationship with Dan was the first marriage I saw that I thought, *wow, I want what they have.* Most married couples I knew seemed bored and irritated with each other most of the time, like the spark had died a long time ago. I'd take years of bad dates before settling for something like that.

But not Gabrielle and Dan. They'd been married for three years at that point and had been together two years before that, but they still were passionate about each other and they still really knew how to joke around and have fun together. They were both good about expressing their feelings. Several times I witnessed Gabrielle saying to Dan or Dan saying to Gabrielle something like, "When you said (or did) —————, it made me feel—————." Then apologies and "you're rights" and "I didn't mean that at all. What I was trying to say was . . ." would flow. It was so much different from my parents' marriage, where the argument style was for Mom to yell and scream and cry and bring up every possible way my father had wronged her over the fifteen-year course of their relationship and my father wouldn't say a word and wouldn't listen, either. (Truly, it's a wonder my parents stayed married the fifteen years that they did.)

Gabrielle and Dan had a true partnership. They laughed together, played together, and exchanged passionate kisses with applause-worthy regularity. Through the years I spent with Rick the money-grubbing skinflint, I compared our relationship to Gabrielle's and Dan's and found it wanting. I despaired of ever having what they had.

Then, about six months after I'd broken up with Rick, when I was in one of those I'm-going-to-be-single-forever-and-never-get-laid-again moods, I went to a party with Dan and Gabrielle. Gabrielle went out to get more beer, and I volunteered to get more ice from the freezer in the basement. Dan followed me downstairs. He asked how my love life was going.

"It's not."

"Relationships are hard. Gabrielle and I have become more like brother and sister these days."

I knew for a fact they had an active and interesting sex life—Gabrielle gave me juicy details regularly—but before I could even make a confused expression, Dan plunged his tongue so far down my throat he could have used it to clean out my small intestine.

I pushed him off me, demanded to know what the fuck he

thought he was doing, and raced up the stairs, leaving the bag of ice behind me. I didn't know what to do, whether I should tell Gabrielle or not. I tried to convince myself that he'd just been drunk and it didn't mean anything, though he hadn't seemed drunk.

In my usual way, I did my best to avoid the problem by leaving the party immediately and avoiding Gabrielle and Dan for the next two weeks. Then one day Gabrielle called me crying. She'd come home to find Dan watching television with a woman in bed. They were both naked.

She'd extracted the following information from Dan: The affair had been going on for nine months. It wasn't his first affair, just the first one she'd known about.

Needless to say, he was booted out on his ass posthaste.

I knew my sorrow couldn't compare to Gabrielle's, but I truly was devastated. If the one relationship I knew of that I actually admired and coveted was nothing more than a trick of smoke and mirrors, how the hell could I expect to find and nurture the real thing?

That was two years ago. The divorce was a relatively quick affair since they had no kids and no money and thus no assets to divide. Gabrielle had been a basketcase for the first year, as could be expected. She'd finished her coursework for her doctorate, but she left school without completing her dissertation, making it impossible for her to land a job doing what she really wanted to be doing—being a professor of sociology. Instead, she got a job as an executive assistant. It's unbelievable, really, that someone as bright as Gabrielle should have a job she dislikes so much, but academia gave her no skills other than teaching and research, and she can't teach unless she gets a teaching certificate to work in a high school or finishes her dissertation so she can teach at the college level. It's a brutal catch-22.

"Gabrielle, my love!" I say as Will and I get out of our cars at the same time she does.

"Hey, Eva. Hey, Will."

Gabrielle is looking good. Much better than she did in the days immediately following her divorce when she went around looking like a zombie, a haunted expression in her eyes. Gabrielle is cute, with a button nose and a sweet smile and gentle brown eyes that sparkle with humor. She wears glasses, but even so you wouldn't suspect her of being the genius that she is. She can pass for a completely ordinary person who likes reality TV shows and can watch hour after hour of "The Simpsons" reruns, but if you get her started on politics or current events, she can spout complicated theoretical concepts using vocabulary words that mere mortals like myself can only wonder at.

We walk to the backyard together and say our hellos. Following right behind us are a mom and a dad with their little girl.

"Well, hello. And who are you?" I ask, bending down so I'm eye level with the little girl.

She buries her face in her hands, smiling shyly.

"This is Deidre," the dad says. I'm sure I've met him before at another of Jon and Rachel's parties, but I can't remember for the life of me what his name is.

Deidre peeks out from behind her hands and smiles at me. When I smile back she squeals and runs over to her father.

Just then Rachel's three year old, Julia, plucks a dandelion from the ground and hands it to Deidre. Deidre takes it in one hand, then takes Julia's hand in the other, and the two run off squealing and laughing together. The entire exchange is done wordlessly.

"That was the cutest, most precious thing I've ever seen in my entire life," I say.

"Wouldn't it be nice if it were that easy to make friends as an adult?" Gabrielle says.

The two little girls are over in the corner of the lawn by the plastic kiddie pool, tossing the dandelion in the water. Then they run off to gather more dandelions in the bobbly way of three year olds, then run back to the pool, dandelions in hand, and toss those in the water, too. I watch Rachel's ten-year-old son across the lawn. Isaac is sweet and ridiculously brainy, excelling not just at math and science but at English and spelling as well. He is always writing horror stories. Cannibalism tends to feature heavily in his short stories. I find it a little creepy that a ten year old could be so addicted to the work of Stephen King and Dean Koontz, but Rachel thinks his fiction is a good outlet for his active imagination. Both of Rachel's children have the dark hair and blue eyes of their parents. Isaac is a cute kid, but Julia is truly precious beyond words, with long ringlets of curls, big eyes, and a smile that could charm the Devil himself.

I turn my attention to Jon and Rachel.

"Happy birthday, Jon," I say, giving him a hug.

"Thank you."

"You're looking surprisingly chipper for an old man of thirty."

"I do try."

And it's true. He looks younger than he is. He has an enthusiasm toward life and a perpetual brightness in his blue eyes. It's hard for me to think of him as a father because growing up, I associated fatherhood as being something that involved constant worrying, endless stress, a propensity for brow-furrowing, and writing lots of checks. It's hard for me to grasp the concept of a father who is cheerful and happy.

My exchange with him is cut off when someone else arrives and wishes Jon a happy birthday and starts telling him about the new truck he bought.

"I'm going to grab a beer. You want one?" Will asks me.

"Yeah, sure."

"Gabrielle?" he asks.

"Please."

Now that we're alone, Gabrielle and I look at each other and exchange dumb hmm-what-should-we-talk-about smiles. It has been tricky for me to talk to Gabrielle since the divorce. I don't like to ask about her job because I know she hates it; I don't want to ask her about her love life since I don't want to rub it in that she doesn't have one; and I don't want to ask her if she's working on her dissertation again since I'm pretty damn sure the answer is no, and I don't want to make her feel bad about putting off her life dream indefinitely. One thing Gabrielle and I can usually talk about is current events and politics, but I have to be in the mood to hear about how the environment is being destroyed by evil corporations or how innocent victims are dying of AIDS in Africa or how trees are being clear-cut all across Canada (and the world) even though paper could easily be made out of hemp if the U.S. government weren't so terrified of allowing it to be planted, and as it happens, I'm not in the mood to get depressed and angry about the injustices of the world just now.

"Did I tell you I've been trying the online dating thing?" Gabrielle says, rescuing me from my deliberations over how to start a conversation.

"No! That's great!"

"I figured if it worked for you, it might work for me. And guess what? I have a date for tomorrow night."

"Really? Cool. Tell me about him."

"He's a doctor, an MD, internal medicine."

"So he's smart, that's a start."

"He's cute. He's divorced, two kids."

"Ooh, another divorced guy. How old is he?"

"Thirty-five."

"How long has he been divorced?"

"Separated for three, officially divorced for two."

"Has he dated since then?"

"One woman."

"Good, so he's got the transitional woman out of the way."

"My thoughts precisely."

"How long have you guys been emailing each other?"

"About a week."

"I'm so excited for you. Why didn't you tell me you were trying the online thing?"

"I just did! Honestly, I'd looked at a few sites every now and then over the past few months, but usually it just depressed me to see what's out there. So many guys brag about how they are just typical guys. I don't want a typical guy. I want more than that. It's as if there is a large contingent of people who are afraid to be different and think for themselves. Then I saw Jeremy's picture, and when I read his ad, I thought, what the hell?"

"Good for you. I want a full report as soon as you get home."

"But of course."

A woman carrying a paper plate filled with food smiles and joins Gabrielle and me in our little circle.

"Hi, I'm Lisa. I'm a friend of Rachel's. I live just down the block."

"Hi, I'm Eva. This is Gabrielle."

"You two looked like you were discussing something interesting." She bites into a carrot, crunching loudly.

"We're just talking about the joys of dating when you're in your thirties," I say.

"I bet it's not easy."

I take this opportunity to notice the colossal rock she's wearing on the ring finger of her left hand.

"Well, it's fun when you meet a good guy. I met Will a few months ago and I'm in heaven. He's over there." I point to where he's talking to Jon over an open beer cooler. "It's been great. He's great. It's just been a little hard for me to deal with the fact that he's divorced. I just have to get over it, but still, you know, it's a little painful."

"That must be so hard," she shakes her head as if I've just told her I have terminal cancer. "I guess I'm lucky. My husband and I got married when we were both twenty-five."

I nod and smile. What does she want me to say? Yes, you

did the marriage thing right. I'm sorry I didn't hop to it in my twenties; I will never forgive myself.

Through my defensive feelings, I get this sudden flash of emotion, this sinking feeling *I'm getting used goods.* Nobody ever won a gold medal for coming in second. Second is just not as good. Everyone knows that.

"It's actually kind of good that he was married," I say. "He was with her for six years, so that cuts down on the number of sex partners he could have racked up."

Apparently Lisa doesn't see the humor or truth in my comment, and she just gives me this fake smile like she just smelled something awful.

"I'm doing the online dating thing, too," Gabrielle says. "But it's exactly like you say, Eva. I want a guy around my age, so I'm looking at all these guys in their thirties, and if they're single I think, 'why are you still single?' and if they're divorced I think, 'why did you get a divorce?'"

"It's tricky isn't it?" I say.

"I'm so glad I never had to go through that," Lisa says. "I guess that's what you get when you put a career before family."

I know Lisa is the one being the bitch here, but I feel judged by her. And even though I know that when people judge other people it's just because they're not happy with themselves, I start feeling anxious and uncomfortable.

"Can you excuse me for just a moment?" I say.

I make a hasty retreat into Jon and Rachel's house to their bathroom. I lock the door and sit on the closed toilet seat and try to steady my breathing. Why do I let people get to me like this? I lock myself in the bathroom because some judgmental stranger looks at me funny?

Retreating is how I've "dealt"—which is to say not dealt—with every unpleasant thing that's happened in my life. When my parents got divorced, I didn't cry, or talk about how I felt, I just became withdrawn and sullen and lived my life in an emotional fog. When my senior math class suddenly got hard, I just gave up. I didn't need the class for college, so I failed every test the rest of the semester, squeaking by with a D, thanks to some initial strong test scores at the beginning of the term. Is that how I'll deal with things if Will and I get married and things start to get a little tough? I'll just give up, retreat into a silent trance?

I stay in the bathroom for several minutes, just trying to get my breathing and heartbeat back to normal. Every fiber in my body just wants to run out the front door, drive home, and dive into bed, pulling the covers tight over my head. I finally force myself to go back outside when I realize I've spent far too long away from the party.

Will has returned with the beers, and happily Evil Bitch Woman Lisa has moved on. Will, Gabrielle, and I start talking about this movie we heard was good and haven't seen yet, and I look over and see Jon talking to a male friend of his. Rachel is talking to another male friend of theirs across the lawn. The thing about how she's talking to him is that it's a definitely flirty kind of chitchat. Extra enthusiastic laughter, eyes lowered and then raised with lashes aflutter, the occasional touch of her hand on his arm. I excuse myself from Will and Gabrielle, and sidle up next to Rachel.

"Hey, Rach, how's it going?"

"Eva! Eva, you remember Shane, don't you?"

"You look familiar, yeah."

"I think we met at the house-painting party," Shane says.

"I think he means the hours-of-back-breaking-labor-in-exchange-for-some-beer-and-chips party," Rachel says, and the two of them howl with laughter. What the hell is going on here? Doesn't Rachel know she's the one married role model I have in this world? Rachel has never given me any delusions that marriage is easy, but she and Jon have gone through a lot of hard times and managed to stick it out, and I really admire that about them, so I strongly feel that she shouldn't be flirting with another man, for my sake if nothing else. I need role models, for heaven's sake!

I stand and talk with them for a few more minutes, but I'm so uncomfortable with their unrestrained flirting I can't take it anymore and I return to Will and Gabrielle. Will, Gabrielle, and I make our move on the buffet table and help ourselves to the fattening barbeque and potato salad type foods. As I eat, I watch Rachel's interaction with Jon and her interaction with Shane. Whenever she's around Jon, she becomes stilted and tight, and whenever she's around Shane, she's flirty and loud and full of laughter.

After awhile, I notice that Rachel is by herself, filling her plate at the buffet table. I put my paper plate down and approach her.

"Hey, Rach, is everything okay?"

"What do you mean?"

"I mean did you have a fight with Jon or something?"

She nods.

"What happened?"

"It's stupid . . . but he said he'd help me get ready for the party today, and instead he spent the entire day at Home Depot buying stuff to build shelves in the garage. And yes, we do need shelves in the garage, but we've needed shelves in the garage for the last two years, so I'm thinking we probably could have lived another weekend without them. Why did he have to pick *today* to go shopping for them? I was running around all day, trying to cook and clean, and you know what it's like with kids, as soon as you have one room clean, you turn your back for ten seconds and the place is destroyed again . . . I just really could have used Jon's help today, even if all he did was entertain the kids and keep them from wrecking the house . . . ." She exhales a tired breath.

"I'm sorry, Rach. I just . . . it sort of seems like you're flirting with Shane."

"Yeah? Well, I don't know, I guess maybe I am."

A stricken look overtakes my face.

"Nothing's going to happen. It's just . . . sometimes it's nice to know someone finds you attractive. Sometimes when you're married, you feel like you're no longer this sexual being. Every now and then you need to be reminded that you are."

Rachel takes a decisive bite out of a celery stalk and, with a parting smile at me, returns to the guests out on the lawn.

For the rest of the night, even as I talk to Will and Gabrielle, my eyes drift back over to Rachel and Jon. I watch them as they orbit each other as if the other person were nothing more than a piece of furniture, something you get used to having in the background.

Chapter 6

I'm at home, working in my sweats. I go downstairs to get more coffee, and when the phone rings, I answer it, even though I'm not supposed to answer the phone during working hours since it might distract me. As it turns out, it does.

"Hello?"

"Hi."

"Gabrielle! How did your date with the doctor go?"

"It went really well, I think." Gabrielle goes on into detail about her four-hour long dinner and after-dinner drinks. I'm interested enough in her story that I only cast a few guilty glances at the clock, noticing twenty minutes, thirty minutes, forty minutes tick by as she gushes about every syllable uttered, every glance exchanged. "We're going out again tonight."

"Good for you."

"It was the best date I've had . . . maybe ever. I just haven't been able to talk with someone like that since Dan left."

"Did you guys smooch?"

"We did."

"Okay, if you get some tonight, call me in the morning with all the salacious details. Even if you don't get some, I want to know everything. Good luck."

*   *   *

Will and I drive down to Colorado Springs to have dinner with his mother, Doris. She makes lasagna for us. She knows I don't like red meat so she makes a vegetable lasagna just for me. She gives me a slice the size of a brick. It's about twice as much food as I can comfortably eat, but I eat every last bite of it until my stomach is about to explode.

"Can I get you some more?" she asks.

"Oh, no, thank you. I'm stuffed," I say.

"Don't you like it?" she asks, a hurt expression on her face.

"What? No, no. I mean yes! I do like it. I meant 'no,' like, 'no, you don't understand' . . ." My tongue is coiled in knots.

"I'm going to have so much extra food," she says with a hurt look on her face. Does she think I can eat an entire pan of lasagna by myself? I finish my glass of wine and quickly pour myself another.

"So, Mom," Will says, "I'm getting ready to put my house on the market. I'm going to move in with Eva."

"Really?" She smiles. "That's nice. Why did you decide to move into her place rather than have her move into yours?"

"Her place is bigger."

"Hmm. How big is your place?"

"We have two bedrooms and my study," I say.

"So you'll want a bigger place someday when you have kids." She nods, considering this thoughtfully.

"Oh, we don't want kids."

Her eyes bulge.

Uh-oh. It occurs to me that was not what she wanted to hear. But it's not my fault! It just slipped out. I wasn't thinking.

"But why not?"

"Well, for a lot of reasons. For one thing, I feel very strongly about having no desire whatsoever to have a bread box with limbs come popping out of that area of my anatomy." I hope that my attempt at humor will defuse the tension.

"Oh, giving birth is agony. Will nearly killed me. His

birth was awful. Just awful. I was in labor for twenty-eight hours. I wanted to die."

"Well, see, you understand then," I say.

"But they have much better drugs today," she says, as if you could squirt a baby out as easily as you could pop a zit.

"Even so, they can't give you nearly enough drugs to make it easy. It's still agonizing. Anyway, even if giving birth were easy, there are other reasons I don't want kids. I personally don't want to try to be a superwoman trying to balance work and kids. I like my job, so I don't want to give that up."

Will's mother spends the next hour trying to persuade me to agree to have kids. I've never wanted kids. I like them, don't get me wrong, but being a good parent is a huge job, and I'd rather leave it to people who have more patience and less anxiety than I do.

I get the uncomfortable feeling that if I don't come around on the kid issue, she is going to do whatever she can to break Will and me apart.

Which, of course, means war.

Any doubts I had about marriage have just flown out the window. I'm going to get Will to marry me no matter what it takes! I will become a Bridal Dominatrix like the world has never seen. I will have my way! All will submit to my bidding!

Bwah-ha-ha-ha-ha!

Chapter 7

Every night after work I go to Will's place and help him pack to move. He brings a few boxes with him to my place each night. Will is still at work and I'm unpacking a box of books he brought over the night before when Gabrielle calls me on my cell.

"Hey, babe, how's the doctor?" I ask.

"Awesome. We've gotten together every night this week."

"For conversation or for sex?"

"A nice mix of the two. Very nice. In fact, I know this is soon, but I think I'm in love with him. I'm crazy about him."

"Love! Wow! Congratulations."

"Can you and Will meet us for dinner tonight? I want to show him off."

"I'm sure we can."

I get the details about when and where, and then I hang up the phone. I have to say that instead of feeling happy for Gabrielle, I'm a little worried about her. I hope like hell she's not jumping the gun. Of course, you'll notice that I told all my friends Will was the man I wanted to marry after our second date, but because that was completely out of character for me, my friends took my comments seriously. Usually my MO is to discuss everything I think might bother me about the guy a few months down the road. Usually I can just look at a guy and foresee the demise of our relationship. I imagine him getting bored with me and cheating on me and breaking my heart; I imagine him being a lazy slob and not doing his share of housework and me ultimately getting so sick of nagging him all the time that it's easier just to break up, whatever. For me to feel hopeful, for me to feel like things really have a chance to work out, means something. I'm not one of those cry-wolf, fall in love with every guy who comes my way kind of girls. And the thing of it is, I never pegged Gabrielle for one of those girls, either, but I've only known her married and then picking up the pieces of her broken marriage. I've never seen her do the whole dating thing before. I just hope she doesn't get hurt.

New love is like a pregnancy—you should wait three months before telling anybody about your exciting news. When you are just falling for somebody, you can tell people you are dating, but you want to keep quiet about just how excited you are until you've passed the critical three-month mark; things are just too fragile and unsure before that. Not that things can't go wrong after that point, but there's a better chance that things are healthy and will stick.

Chapter 8

At the last minute, it turns out that Will has to work late because the new software release his company just launched has bugs in it that need to be fixed pronto, so it turns out I'm on my own to meet Gabrielle and the doctor.

We meet at a noisy pub and order some nachos and beer. Right away I can see Gabrielle's attraction to him. He's gorgeous. He wears glasses and all I can think of is a model wearing glasses ironically—in a sort of "look, I'm gorgeous yet smart" way.

"Eva met her boyfriend online, too," Gabrielle says. "How long has it been now, seven months or so?"

"Yeah, that's about right. I'm sorry you couldn't meet him. He had to work." I shovel in an enormous bite of nachos—I'm determined to get the perfect mix of bean, cheese, salsa, and sour cream on the chip, which requires a heaping, quivering mass of food. I wash it down with a swig of beer. I am in heaven.

"It's been this whirlwind affair," Gabrielle adds. "I've never heard her talk about marriage before, and after her second date with him she was telling everybody that she could see herself spending her life with him."

"He's changing your mind about taking the plunge, huh?" Jeremy says. There's something I don't like about his tone of voice. An edge of warning or sarcasm or something.

I decide I don't want to be talking to two divorced people about getting married. I don't want them to tell me that love dies and marriage is a one-way ticket to monotony and resentment. Note to self: Befriend people who subscribe to more of "love conquers all" attitude toward life.

"Yeah. I still have fears, of course, but the majority of the time I just look at him and feel so lucky and absolutely delirious with happiness. Of course, every now and then I get these panic attacks over the thought of actually saying 'I do.'"

"I think being terrified from time to time is normal," Gabrielle says.

"Do you mean you're literally having panic attacks?" Jeremy asks. "Describe the symptoms."

"I just have these meltdowns. I just want to shut the world out and hide until it passes."

"Does your heart start beating rapidly? Do you feel faint or nauseated?"

"My heart pounds. I feel light-headed, I guess."

"Do you sweat or tremble?"

"I don't think so."

"Do you have trouble sleeping?"

"Always."

"Do you worry about things a lot?"

"Constantly."

"You might have G.A.D.—Generalized Anxiety Disorder."

Ridiculously, I'm actually thrilled by the prospect that I have a real disease and may not just be your run-of-the-mill basketcase. Having a disease means there is some medicine out there that can treat it. Yeah for drugs!

"Really? What can I do about it?"

"You could take a serotonin inhibitor like Paxil."

"Oh. But don't those kind of meds make it hard to ah, you know, enjoy sex?" I say.

"It can be more challenging to achieve orgasm, but it's not impossible," Jeremy says.

"Well, I tried just about all of them in the year after Dan and I separated," Gabrielle says. "I was still on them when I started dating Ken, and I had no sex drive whatsoever. I'd think, am I supposed to want sex? Because I didn't, not at all."

"Is that why Ken only lasted a month?" I ask.

"That was part of it. Part of it was also that I still just wasn't ready to date."

I'm no longer excited about the possibility of having something technically wrong with me. G.A.D. just seems like a medical term for basketcase. I don't want to go on anti-anxiety meds unless it's a life or death issue.

"Well, thanks for the free advice, doc."

"What do you do for a living?" he asks. I know Gabrielle said he works in internal medicine (What the hell is internal medicine, anyway? Except for skin treatment for rashes, isn't all medicine pretty much internal?), but the way he asks me this makes me think of a psychiatrist trying to determine whether I'm fit for society.

"I'm an independent management consultant."

"Do you like your job?"

"Most of the time."

"What do you do for fun?"

"Well, this isn't going to make me sound very exciting, but the way I like to relax is to read."

"What do you read?"

"I read a lot of nonfiction. Mostly history. I got my undergraduate degree in history."

"I loved my history classes."

"Yeah? I was lucky because in high school, every history teacher I had was really good. They got me excited about the subject. And so I studied it in college, along with some anthropology and sociology classes, and it just opened up the whole world to me. I think sometimes we think the world we live in now is 'just the way things are' naturally. But then when you look at various cultures over the eras of time, you realize that the culture we live in now is very different than the culture we lived in a very short time ago or even other modern cultures. Like the differences between the Europe of today and the America of today are pretty staggering. Even the gap between America and Canada in terms of things like how news is covered is really different. In America, the news is all murder and mayhem all the time. The nightly news isn't like that in Canada at all. Anyway, I'm babbling. What about you, what do you do for fun?"

"I'm a bit of a film buff," he says.

"Ahh, just like Gabrielle."

Gabrielle's undergraduate degree is in film. She likes to go to movies that are utterly dark and depressing. After she dragged me to enough movies in which I left the theater longing to slit my wrists, I realized that whenever she recommended a film, I should never agree to accompany her, and instead I should run as fast as I could in the opposite direction. Gabrielle notices things in movies like what the camera angle "signifies" and how who was in the foreground versus the background of a shot has some kind of metaphoric importance. When she tells me this stuff, I nod as if I know what the hell she is talking about, but secretly I haven't a clue.

She and Jeremy are talking about some movie they saw together (in which all the characters are either dead or in jail at the end, very uplifting stuff), discussing metaphor and meaning and what the director's *intent* was with such and such a cutaway shot (whatever that is), and I smile as I listen to them talk. When you're as smart as Gabrielle, you clearly need a guy who is your intellectual equal, and Gabrielle has had a hell of a time finding guys who challenged her intellectually. It looks to me like, with Jeremy, she has found a match.

The waitress comes by to take our dinner orders. I'm already full from the nachos and beers, but since Gabrielle and Jeremy are ordering meals, I order a chicken breast sandwich, swapping the fries for a salad. We all order another round of beer.

We spend the evening talking and laughing, and after getting to know Jeremy, I'm feeling better about Gabrielle going crazy over him. I can see why she would. He is handsome, and smart, and successful.

It's not until we stand to leave that I feel how uncomfortably full I am from all the beers, the nachos, and a full dinner. I feel grotesquely fat and bloated and I'm mad at myself for not showing even the slightest bit of self-control. When I was a kid we had a dog named Happy who would gorge himself and then be forced to puke because he'd made himself so sick from overeating. You'd think I'd have a little more self-control and self-awareness than a schnauzer, but no, apparently I don't.

I'm officially in a crappy mood when I get to Will's place. It's about 9:30, too early for bed, so after we kiss and hug for a minute or two, we park our asses on the couch and Will pops in a DVD. We've hardly watched any of it when Will starts kissing me.

A little voice inside my head says, "Just tell him you're not in the mood." Then another voice says, "You've only been dating a few months. What'll he think if you are already squirming out of sex? You have to be a perfect girlfriend, always voraciously ready for sex." Voice number one then retorts, "Don't be a fucking idiot. You've got to learn to speak up. How are you going to have a successful marriage if you can't communicate how you feel over such a minor thing? What are you going to do when a real problem rears up?"

By now we've been kissing for several minutes. I let my hand skim lightly over his penis to see what's going on down there. He's fully hard, and now I feel I really can't say no. I should have pulled away a few minutes ago, I'm a tease. Voice number one, the voice that took Gender and Society classes in college and is good friends with Gabrielle Leveska knows that his hard-on is not my responsibility, but somehow logically knowing that doesn't lessen the guilt I feel.

Why can't he just realize I'm not really into this? I'm showing none of the enthusiasm I normally have over such activities.

Will pulls off my shirt, unbuttons my shorts, and I help him take them off. He takes off his own clothes and then moves to go down on me. I grab him by the shoulder. He looks up at me.

"Just come inside me," I say. Because I want to get this over with. Really, I don't want it at all. Why don't you know that?

He's kneeling on the floor and I'm awkwardly splayed on the couch. He uses his fingers to lubricate me.

It's not terrible, even though I'm not into it, but out of nowhere, I decide I want to break up with Will. I don't want to do the whole relationship thing. Will will do like so many husbands I've known: Once they get the ring on their finger, they know there's nothing to work for, so they let the women cook, clean, and do the bulk of the work in child-rearing, even though they, too, work hard at jobs outside the home. I imagine that Will will never go down on me again after we get married. He'll belch rudely and publicly. The romance will die, the sex will all be like this, and nothing good can possibly come of us actually getting married. We can live together. That will be much better and far less terrifying. We won't have to get divorced.

There is the knowledge somewhere in the back of my mind that my thoughts are ludicrous. I would love to blame this torrent of emotions that has walloped me out of nowhere on PMS, but my mood swings can plummet by the minute and can come at any time of the month, any part of the day. Something bigger is going on. I feel like some God is playing with my emotions like He's trying to get the shower temperature just right, but every now and then it goes from scalding hot to bitingly cold for no apparent reason.

Will finishes and we go upstairs to bed.

The next morning I wake up feeling completely fine, utterly happy. I wrap my arms around Will's sleeping form, smiling, feeling like the luckiest woman in the world. This is my reality: Mood swings of seismic proportions one second that calm just as abruptly for no particular reason.

Chapter 9

With Will moving in, the house is a mess. Boxes are strewn everywhere. I silently mourn the loss of my closet space.

Will comes over every night after work with a load of stuff, and then he works on unpacking it. He's so easygoing, letting me dictate exactly where I want him to put things.

My house has three rooms. They aren't huge, but we have a master bedroom, the guestroom that will double as Will's study, and my office. Still, with all of Will's stuff being added to the fray, the house seems smaller by the second.

The weekend after we get back from Mark and Sienna's, Will's friends will help him move the last of his furniture in, and then it will be official: Will and I will be roomies at last.

Will is at his place tonight and I'm at my place packing for my trip to New York, when I call Gabrielle and ask her how things are going with Jeremy.

"It's good, but it's hard, you know, because of the kids," she says. "It's hard on me that he sees his ex-wife every other week. I'd really rather that she lived in Alaska and they didn't have kids together. I was supposed to meet his kids for the first time this weekend, and Jeremy and his ex got into a fight while he was over there, and it turned out that he was over there for more than an hour. The whole time this was going on I was sitting at my house, wearing nice clothes and trying not to rub my lipstick off, waiting expectantly. By the time he got the kids, he was so wound up that he called and said he didn't think it was such a good idea if I met them that day after all and that he'd call and tell me the details later. He didn't call me all weekend, so then I felt like an idiot and called him on Monday and he gave me this abbreviated story, you know the way men do. I'm sure so much more happened, but I couldn't get any details from him. It's so hard that I don't get to see him every other weekend, and his work schedule is already really crazy. Relationships are hard enough without an ex-wife and two kids and child support payments and eighty-hour work weeks. But I don't know, I really love the guy."

We talk a little more and I tell her about how Will and I are leaving for New York in the morning. When we hang up, I'm instantly restless. I realize that I've gotten used to spending every night with Will and I'm not used to being by myself anymore. I had lived alone for more than two years before Will came along and I was happy enough with that arrangement at the time, but now being alone feels strange. It's amazing how quickly new patterns can be established.

I can't stand the silence, so I call Rachel. "Hey, Rach, what's up?"

"Nothing." She expels a long and weary sigh, so I know that there is, in fact, something up. "What's going on with you?"

"I'm just packing. Will and I are going to New York for the weekend to visit Sienna. I've never seen her new place. And Will will be meeting her for the first time."

"I'm so jealous. I wish Jon and I could get away for the weekend."

"Is something wrong, Rach?"

"It's Jon's mother. She can't meet her medical expenses, but she doesn't qualify for Medicaid. Jon wants us to make up the difference. It'll be about eight hundred dollars a month. We've got seven hundred dollars worth of student loans per month that we should be paying off, but we're deferring those loans as it is. We can't afford the bills we already have, let alone new ones."

"Can't one of his siblings help out?"

"Beth and Sandy make even less than we do, if you can believe it. We're still trying to pay off the money we borrowed to help Sandy get through rehab."

"What are you going to do?"

"I don't know. I don't have a clue."

"Can I help?"

"Yes. If you win the lottery, give me some of the money."

"I will. Absolutely. You can count on it. But if I don't win the lottery, what then?"

"The only way you can help is to listen to me bitch. You're doing a commendable job. What's up with you?"

I tell her about the dinner with Will's mother, making Doris out to be this evil villain and me to be a put-upon heroine boldly facing the injustice and adversity flung my way. I'm the one telling the story, so I'll be heroic and valiant in my version of the tale if I want to.

"She's acting like I'm denying Will fatherhood for my own selfishness or something," I say.

"I don't understand how she can be upset with you. Obviously, Will didn't want to have kids or he would have had them the first time he was married."

"Well, that's not true. His first wife wasn't able to have kids, so it simply was never an issue. Who knows? Maybe I can't have kids either. Maybe all these years of birth control pills and condoms have been a giant waste of time."

"Maybe," she laughs. "I better let you go. I'm meeting with Shane."

"Shane? Really? Why?"

"Oh, you know, just for lunch."

"Just the two of you?"

"Yes, just the two of us. It's lunch, Eva. That's all."

I squirm. I get the distinct feeling that that's not all. "Well, have fun. I'll talk to you later."

After Rachel and I get off the phone with each other, I wonder what would happen if Will and I did get married and he lost his job and suddenly his mother got sick and we needed to pay for her to have hospice care or go into a nursing home. Or maybe she'd come to live with us, and since I work from home, what then? Would she finally begrudgingly show me affection, or would the remainder of our lives be an endless stream of conflict? These aren't the typical things you worry about before you agree to spend your life with someone, but maybe they should be.

How would Rachel's life have been different if she hadn't gotten pregnant at eighteen? Would she have married Jon? Would she and he have broken up, dated other people, and ultimately end up with each other because that's the way it was supposed to be? Or maybe Rachel would have fallen for an eccentric millionaire who didn't want children. Or maybe she would have become a career-oriented lawyer and ended up on the Supreme Court. Would another path in life have been a happier one for her? Less happy? Or just different?

How would Gabrielle's life have been different if she hadn't been married to Dan? Were those years she spent with him a mistake? Of course, wondering about these things can't change anything. We each have our personal histories that shape who we are.

I think about Evil Bitch Woman Lisa from Jon's birthday party who bragged about getting married right on time at the age of twenty-five. When I was twenty-five, I was going back to school to change my career and my future completely. I've always been a mature person, but I needed several more years before I was at a place in my life where I could even begin to consider marriage. Will and I needed a little more time to rack up life experiences, sex partners, and mistakes before we were ready for each other. Our histories are messy, but they're ours. But now we are in the places we need to be to make things work for us. That's the important thing.

Chapter 10

Sienna and Mark live in a cute but microscopic studio apartment in Brooklyn. Will and I have made reservations at a hotel close by since their place is too small to entertain visitors.

After dropping off our stuff at the hotel, Will and I walk the few blocks to Sienna and Mark's place so we can get a tour of their apartment before we head downtown.

Sienna screams and squeezes me in a tight hug when she opens the door and sees us. When we finally stop crushing each other, she backs away and says, "Will, it is so good to finally meet you." And she gives him a hug, too, though not of the internal-organ squishing variety that she gave me.

Mark is standing behind her, and when she's done having her way with us, he embraces me and shakes Will's hand.

"I'll give you the tour," Sienna says. She stands in the middle of the room and spreads her arms out. "This is the living room, bedroom, home office, study, and, if occasion calls for it, the guest bedroom. Through that door you'll find the bathroom, and this," she walks into the kitchen, which is only demarcated from the living room by a counter with stools on one side, "is the kitchen. It's small, but we just need it to store our beer and leftover Chinese takeout, so it works out fine."

"Please tell me you don't work at this desk," I say. Sienna works from home as an administrative assistant to a best-selling author, answering her fan mail and scheduling her speaking tours and trips to writing conferences. Sienna's desk is clearly made for an extremely tall man and not for five-foot, four-inch Sienna. Her desk chair is a five-dollar wood hunk of junk, and I'm certain that any amount of sitting at it would cause severe neck and back pain, not to mention a supremely sore ass. And because the chair and desk are completely not at the right levels for her height, she's created an elaborate set up using cardboard boxes and phone books to adjust the heights to something resembling an ergonomic working environment.

"I know. I'm an ergonomic mess. You ready to head out?"

Sienna is modest about her place, but it really is cute. She has a way with decorating the exposed brick wall and wood floors with bright colored touches that add up to a decidedly cute little space.

"Ready," I say. I take Will's hand and follow Sienna and Mark out.

We have to walk several blocks to catch the bus that takes us to the subway and then catch another bus, then we get out and walk several more blocks.

"Ah, so where is this place exactly, Canada?" I wouldn't mind except I stupidly wore my new shoes that aren't broken in yet, and I can feel the blisters forming with every pinching step.

"When you're going from between boroughs or from the west side to the east side, it can take awhile," Mark says.

"That's one thing I love about when I visit you in Denver," Sienna says. "It's so amazing to just get in your car and drive exactly to where it is you want to go. Point A to point B, just like that."

"There are advantages to living in cities that are like hick towns in comparison to New York," I say. I always try to play up the good things about Denver when I'm around Sienna. I want Sienna to succeed at her goal of being a comedian, but I also want her to come back to Denver. I'm hoping that she gets so famous she can be based anywhere she wants, and she chooses Denver. The important thing, to me, is that she gets this New York crap out of her system and comes back to me. I want to live near my sister, but there is no way I'm going to move to New York, unless I become a multibillionaire. Even if I were wealthy, I'm not sure I could ever bring myself to spend four hundred thousand dollars on a condo the size of an Easy Bake Oven, which seems to be about all you can find in the city.

"Yeah. But there are a lot of great things about New York," Mark says. "Is this your first time here, Eva?"

"No. I came here several years ago for a visit," I say. "And you're right. There are a lot of wonderful things about New York. I remember walking around Central Park and there was one outdoor concert after the other and all these plays and performances. I was staggered by how much there was to do all the time everywhere. And then the next day, my friend and I were just walking around checking out the city and we started seeing all these gay pride flags. We realized there was going to be a parade, and it turned out it was the Gay Pride Parade recognizing the thirtieth anniversary of Stonewall. We look up and we just happen to be standing in front of the Stonewall on Christopher Street, the freaking epicenter of where it all went down. We were witnessing history. It was so cool. There's always something to do or see in New York. That's definitely not the case in Denver."

"Sometimes that's a bad thing," Sienna says. "Some nights I just want to stay home watching TV or reading a book, and in New York I always feel guilty if I don't go out every night to enjoy all that the city has to offer."

The place they take us to is a little Thai restaurant full of funky lighting, brushed stainless steel tables, and black lacquer plates.

When we go to order, Will asks if the green curry has any nuts in it.

"Oh, are you allergic to nuts, too?" Sienna asks him.

"Nope, he's just looking out for me," I say.

Sienna nods and smiles approvingly at me. Score points for Will!

We gorge ourselves on green curry, kung pao tofu, and plum wine.

"So, Mark, are you doing the comedy thing full-time?" Will asks.

"I've got a day job working at an art supply store."

"Are you an artist as well as comedian?"

"No, but I am capable of ringing up art supplies for people who are artists."

"How long have you been doing the comedy thing?"

"About five years total, but it has just been this last year that I really started getting serious about it."

"I think that's so cool that you're brave enough to get out on stage," Will says.

"What about you, Will? Eva tells me you're a guitar player. Were you ever in a band?" Sienna asks.

"No," he says, "These three buddies of mine also play instruments, so every now and then we'll get some songs together for a party, but that's about it. Like, for this Halloween party, we decided we'd play three or four songs, but change the lyrics. Like we took the Stray Cats' 'Stray Cat Strut' and turned it into 'Costume Rut', about someone with no good costume ideas, that sort of thing."

"Oh god, don't bring up Halloween, I'm still feeling queasy from last Halloween," Sienna says.

"The trouble began with spiked punch . . ." Mark says.

"As so much trouble does," Will says.

"I seriously don't know if I've ever been that ill in my life before," Sienna says. "I don't know what they put in that punch, but it tasted like Kool-Aid."

"Sienna made an absolute spectacle of herself," Mark says, affecting a lisp.

"Excuse me, was I a giant purple orc attacking Darren's tree with a battle-ax?" she says.

"Ha, yeah, I guess I did do that," Mark says. "I wanted to see how sharp my little sword thing was, so I started attacking the tree, and after a couple of minutes I turned around to see my friends Darren and Carlos. They'd been sitting behind me in lawn chairs, and they were just covered with wood chips."

"And Darren's poor tree had this huge bald spot on it; it looked so sad and pathetic. I don't understand men's attraction to weaponry. Will, do you have any experience with guns or knives or anything?"

I know this is another test for Sienna, and it is for me, too. Neither of us believe in having guns around the house.

Will thinks a moment. "The only thing I can think of is when I was in college, and I was living in the dorms. I had this bow and arrow and I wanted to see if an arrow would stick in the wall of my dorm room, so I let it rip. It went straight through the wall. A second later we hear this shrill scream, then footsteps thundering over to my room. Turns out it had gone through the neighbor's wall and got stuck about six inches away from where my neighbor's head had been."

"Boys are so weird," I say. "Sienna, would you ever think, hmm, I wonder what would happen if I just launched this weapon of mass destruction in my dorm room?"

"That would be a negative. A big N-O."

"It's in our blood since we were wee lads," Mark says, this time adopting a Scottish accent. "To fight the good fight. To defend our bonnie lasses on pain of death!"

"Yeah, you two are total warriors. Just need a little war paint," I say. Mark is scrawny and Will has the athletic prowess of a KitKat bar. I'm not convinced they could protect us from an enraged butterfly.

"Well, my gracious, I do believe our manhoods have been insulted," Mark says to Will.

"You know I think you're a manly man," I say to Will,

sidling up to him, fluttering my eyelashes coquettishly. He gives me a long, deep kiss.

"Get a room!" Mark and Sienna start heckling.

"All right, all right," I say, pulling away from him. "Let's go find someplace where there's music."

They take us to a jazz club several blocks away. We dance for maybe half an hour, though really Will and I just kind of make out in a swaying sort of way to the music. Sienna and Mark start teasing us again. We smile sheepishly. Really, we can't seem to resist each other. Although in truth, we don't try very hard.

"Come on, Sienna, let's go get the next round," I say.

Sienna follows me up to the bar where we order four more beers.

"So, what do you think?" I ask.

"I approve. He's cute and funny and kind."

"I told you."

"I'm so happy for you. You two seem really happy together. I'm jealous of how you can't keep your hands off each other."

"Well, we've only been dating for seven months. Give us time." Really though, I think Will and I are both just snuggly, hand-holding type people.

It's late when we finally decide to head home. Will springs for a taxi so we don't have to walk eighty-six blocks, switch buses fourteen times, and take the subway to get home. It's nice that you don't need a car in Manhattan, but if you don't live in Manhattan yourself, getting around is a complicated public-transportation relay race.

We sleep in late the next morning, and the four of us meet up over bagels and coffee for breakfast before heading to MoMA for the day. Naturally, Mark and Will make smart-alecky remarks about the art work they don't approve of. And they're right, there are some paintings that I just don't get why they are considered "art" and not "dreck." Is it the-

emperor-is-wearing-no-clothes situation or am I just an ig-
noramus? I don't know. But other paintings make me want to
get down on my knees and bow down in supplication to the
artist, they are that good.

When our feet are museumed out and pleading for mercy
we grab some dinner and then head over to the club where
Sienna is going to perform that night.

The club is tiny and tables are packed so tightly together
that I can tell what brand of hair products and skin cream the
woman sitting next to me uses because my nostrils are essentially squashed against her lightly scented flesh. I tell Sienna
to break a leg and she leaves us in the audience and heads
backstage. Mark, Will, and I order drinks. The opening act is
blessedly hilarious—there is nothing more painful than a bad
opening act, whether it's comedy, music, or whatever—so I'm
relieved.

Just before Sienna is supposed to come on, Will says, "I'll
be right back."

"But Sienna is about to come on."

"I just need to use the bathroom real quick. I'll be right
back, I promise."

When Sienna is introduced moments later and comes out
on stage, I'm thoroughly annoyed with him for not using the
bathroom earlier. Half the reason we came to New York was
to see her perform!

When the applause dies down, Sienna begins, "So, my sister is in town with her boyfriend. Now, usually I don't like to
travel down the blue road of comedy . . ." Sienna sighs deeply
and hangs her head in mock shame. "But my sister reminded
me of a trip we took together, and it's going to require me to
talk about the important issue of male crotch-thrusting."
Naturally, the crowds whoops and hollers at the word
"crotch." And by the way, I have no idea what Sienna is talking about regarding me reminding her of a trip we took. Comedians make stuff up, but sound like they are telling a true

story. Comedians never let the truth get in the way of a funny story. "Since I'm doing stand-up comedy, well, I don't know if you know this, but I'm actually required to use the word 'penis.' If I don't say 'penis' twice within the first two minutes of my routine, I get kicked out of the union. There, I've met my quota! Phew! Anyway, my sister and I went to Cancun during spring-break vacation one year. Cancun connotes a tropical getaway, but really you're just visiting a frat house near a beach. The bars in Cancun are just a sea of drunk, horny Americans. My sister and I were trying to dance in our own little space, but the boys were attaching themselves to us like barnacles. We'd be dancing to techno music," Sienna starts making techno music noises with her mouth pressed up close to the microphone. "Because it's all bad early eighties American techno music down there. Apparently, they don't have any music in Cancun since CDs were invented. So these guys would just attach themselves to your leg, thrusting their pelvis into you like some horny dog that just found a spare pillow on the living room floor." Sienna begins thrusting her crotch and makes a funny face as she does it. The audience loves it. I love seeing her make people laugh.

"So, we came up with a move to defend ourselves." She does a little side shuffle and then does a karate chop with her hands across her leg. "It's called 'the Erection Dodge.' Use it. It works. But now . . ." Sienna takes a dramatic inhale, smiling solemnly and looking heavenward. "My sister doesn't need the Erection Dodge to defend herself from drunk men in bars anymore because she has her own, nonscary man at her side. If you don't mind, I'd like to take just a couple minutes out of my regularly scheduled routine . . ." My heart stops as I see Will walking out onto the stage, guitar in hand. "And give the mic to my sister's boyfriend, Will Cummings."

Will clears his throat and gives a little wave to the audience. "Hi, everybody."

"Hi!" the audience calls back.

"Leave it to a guy in love to make an ass of himself in a public place," he says. The audience laughs. "I'll try to make it quick."

He begins strumming his guitar and sings into the microphone:

I met a girl who has captured my heart.
She's kind, and funny, and smart.
When I'm with her, I always have a great time.
I met a girl, and I want to make her mine.
She means everything to me . . .

At this point, Will stops singing, gets down on one knee, pulls a ring box from his pants pocket, opens it, and says, "Eva Lockhart, will you marry me?"

I needn't have worried about getting teary-eyed when the marriage proposal came. Tears are running down my face and I can barely breathe.

I can't move or think or do a thing until Mark nudges me. I begin nodding and don't stop. Finally, a distant part of me remembers how to speak and the words form on my lips, "Yes. Yes, I'll marry you." As I walk toward the stage, the audience erupts in thunderous applause. Will helps me climb the couple of feet to the stage and slides the ring onto my trembling finger.

Chapter 11

Naturally, as soon as we get home, I have to run around telling everyone I know that it's official, we're getting hitched.

I call Mom and after she congratulates me, she orders me to take a digital picture of the ring and email it to her. I call Gabrielle and ask her if she can meet me for lunch. She seems kind of distant and out of it, but she says she'll meet me at noon. I'm bursting to tell her my news, but I force myself to wait until I can tell her in person. Then I run over to Rachel's shop. Well, not literally run, of course. The last time I ran was when they forced me to in gym class when I was in grade school. But I do amble over at a speedier-than-normal pace.

She's sitting on her barstool behind the counter reading a newspaper when I get there. There aren't any customers in the store. I sit beside her, say "Hi," and try to act natural, but she gives me this odd look.

"What is wrong with you?" she says. "You've got the stupid smile of a baby who's just farted."

"Will asked me to marry him this weekend."

She drops her newspaper and snatches my left hand so hard I nearly fall off my stool. "It's beautiful!"

"It's antique platinum. Sienna helped him pick it out. She insisted that he buy antique so he wouldn't be raping the

earth for precious metals and contributing to the whole diamond trade business . . ."

"With the African children losing their limbs in the
mines . . ."

"Yep, all the cheery things you normally associate with
marital bliss. But I think she made a good consultant. Apparently, they've been emailing each other for the last month,
plotting the whole thing."

I tell her exactly how he proposed, about how he got up
on stage and sang me a song, and she clutches her heart and
deems it all "so romantic."

"Why do you think he asked you up on stage?"

"Well, early in our relationship I'd told him this story of
one of Sienna's comedy friends being proposed to by another
comedian at the end of one of their shows and how romantic
I thought that was, so maybe that's what gave him the idea.
He definitely surprised me anyway, that's for sure."

"What date are you thinking of?"

"I was thinking May. May is usually a pretty nice month
weatherwise in Colorado. But Will and I haven't really talked
about details yet."

I go on and on about my blissful, happy, perfect life, and
every detail of how my weekend went, then I finally get
around to asking Rachel how things are going in her life.

"Well, Jon and I are fighting . . ."

"Is this still the garage shelves' fight or is this a new one?"

"It's a new one. Apparently, he gave Sandy the keys to our
place—"

"No way!" When Jon's sister Sandy had been in the deep-
est depths of her heroin addiction, she'd stolen a bunch of
Jon and Rachel's stuff (their TV, stereo, and computer to
name a few) to sell for money for drugs. Personally, that
would have been enough for me to cut off ties with her forever, but Jon and Rachel are better people than I am, and
they forgave her. However, to forgive her and to give her the
keys to their place are two different things entirely.

"Yes, way. He is just so gullible when it comes to his sisters. He thinks that because she's been clean for six months, she'll be clean forever."

"How did you find out about it?"

"I'll tell you how I found out about it. First, on Monday I came home and the half gallon of milk I had in the fridge was gone, and there were all these dishes in the sink, as if someone had cooked lunch there. When Jon got home I asked him if he'd come home for lunch, which is not something he usually does, and he just kind of looked sheepish and changed the subject. I *wished* I'd pressed him then, but I didn't. Then yesterday I was at home with the kids making dinner, and I saw her in the window at our backdoor, so I was going to walk over to the door to let her in, but my hands were wet from rinsing the lettuce, and in the few seconds it took me to dry my hands, I just watched her unlock the door, open it, and march right in."

"No way!"

"I know. I was like, 'where did you get a key?', thinking maybe Jon had lent her his as a one-off or something, but she said he had made her a set. I was so pissed at Jon. We had this big fight. He said she could be trusted now. I said even if she could be trusted, that didn't mean she needed a key to our house. Then he said that sometimes she watches the kids, which is true, but they always go over to her and Jon's mother's place, specifically because I don't want her in my house. I mean, I'm not even worried about her stealing our stuff . . . well, maybe I am. But I think what I'm really mad about is her audacity to come over whenever she feels like it and clean us out of milk and eat whatever she wants," she sighs. "Although, I mean she has been helping us out with the kids, so maybe I was too hard on Jon. But even if I was, he should have *told* me he gave her the key, he shouldn't have just *given* it to her."

"I think you have a right to be pissed."

"You do? Thank you for saying that. I'm always worried that I'm being a crazy bitch."

A female customer enters the store, and then moments later two teenage girls come in. The three of them orbit the store, running their fingers over the clothes, and then taking the folded sweaters, unfolding them, and then doing a half-assed job of refolding them and putting them back all lopsided, a particular pet peeve of Rachel's.

Rachel and I talk a little more and then I tell her I have to go because I have a lunch date with Gabrielle.

When I get to the restaurant where Gabrielle and I always go for lunch, Gabrielle is already there and sitting at the table with a beer in front of her. It's not like Gabrielle to drink before five, so as soon I sit across from her I ask her what's wrong.

"I'm that transparent, am I?"

"Kind of."

"Jeremy went back to his ex."

"What do you mean? He and his ex-wife are back together?"

"Not his ex-wife. His ex-girlfriend."

"Transition woman?"

"Transition woman."

"I'm so sorry."

She nods glumly.

"What happened?"

"I don't think he ever really stopped seeing her."

"Why do you think that? What did he say?"

"Last night he called me and said he wanted to give it another chance with Susan and that he didn't think things were working out between us. I wish he could have figured this out before we slept together. God! I feel so stupid!"

"But . . . how . . . did he say when he decided to get back together with her? Did you have any idea when they'd broken up?"

The waitress comes to take our orders. We each get the soup and the sandwich deal.

"When we were emailing each other, I asked him when he'd gotten divorced and if he'd dated anyone since then. He said it had been three years since they'd separated and that he'd dated one person seriously in that time. I didn't ask for any more specifics than that."

I think about how I grilled Will endlessly about his ex at the beginning of our relationship, and while I didn't always like to hear his answers, I got a good sense that he was telling the truth. I've always made it a habit to do what journalists do—ask the same questions worded differently over and over again to see if I get the same answers. Guys who change their stories are lying about something. Maybe asking lots of questions at the beginning of a relationship isn't such a bad thing after all.

"So, what did he say last night? Do you know how long they'd been broken up?"

"He didn't say this outright, but from reading between the lines, I think what happened was that she was getting serious more quickly than he was ready for, so they fought and sort of broke up and about ten minutes later he was looking for somebody new to date, and that somebody new turned out to be me. But then they made up and got back together. I don't think they'd really been apart at all. He didn't say that, but that's what I gather. And I know we only dated a few weeks, but . . ."

"A lot can happen in a short time," I finish for her. "I was insane over Will after just two dates. If he'd abruptly dumped me to go back to his ex, I would have been crushed."

"I was actually proud of letting myself really fall for Jeremy. With the two guys I dated after Dan and I split up, I worked really hard not to let them get too close because I was still in so much pain over the divorce. I don't know how to strike a balance between being too cautious and opening up too much."

"I know. It's so hard."

"I hate dating. I hate it. I hate Dan for making me go back out into the world and date."

I keep mumbling useless "I'm sorries," until the waitress brings our lunches. We eat several bites in silence and then Gabrielle says, "God, I'm so wrapped up in myself, I didn't even ask you about your weekend in New York. Did you guys have fun?"

"We did, as a matter-of-fact." This really doesn't seem like the time to tell her about how Will asked me to marry him, but I feel like if I don't tell her, I'll be lying.

"Did you guys do anything interesting?"

"Ah, well, yeah, some interesting things happened. Will asked me to marry him and I said yes."

She chokes on her bite of sandwich and then forces a smile. "Oh. Congratulations."

"You don't seem very excited."

"No. I'm happy for you."

I stare at her for a long moment until she continues.

"It's just, you know, men tend to get more out of marriage then women do. All the surveys show that married men are happier than married women."

This is really not the reaction I was hoping for. "Why is that? Because women tend to shoulder more of the domestic responsibilities?"

She nods ominously.

"You don't believe in marriage anymore?" I ask.

"I believe in two people mutually supporting each other, but I don't think I believe in marriage, no."

Instead of trying to get her to feel my happiness, I immediately find the doubter in myself, as if I feel the need for the two of us to be in agreement on all that could go wrong.

"Part of me wants to elope secretly just so his friends won't be able to throw him a bachelor party," I admit.

"Have you talked to him about it?"

"Oh, he knows my feelings on strippers."

"Do you really think that if his friends wanted to take him to a strip club, he would say, 'No, Eva doesn't want me to'? He'd never hear the end of it. You know how guys are. They act all tough, but secretly they're gutless. The homosexual taboo is just too strong. Heterosexual men constantly have to prove to their friends just what manly men they are."

I lose my appetite, mostly because I know Gabrielle is right. Will loves me, but I'm genuinely not sure he's strong enough to stand up to his friends on this issue, particularly since he doesn't share my feelings about how the stripping industry is manipulative and degrading to everyone involved. (Plus, it makes me hate men a little bit that they'd squander their money in such a ludicrous way. Hello, they can't touch you, you can't touch them or yourself, why would you put yourself into such a situation á là Tantalus—the guy who was condemned to an eternity of hunger and thirst with satisfaction always just out of reach—seems the height of stupidity.)

"Ah, well, I was hoping you'd stand up for me in the wedding," I say to veer the conversation in a less depressing direction.

"Of course I will," she says.

"I wasn't sure what color dresses you guys should wear. It'll be you and Rachel and Sienna."

"Whatever color is fine."

We talk a little more about how Will proposed and what my thoughts for the wedding are, and I leave the majority of my lunch uneaten.

When I come home, I feel incredibly depressed. Why can't I just believe that now that the man of my dreams has asked me to marry him, my major goal in life has been accomplished and I can now get started on the happily-ever-after portion of my life? I wanted to marry Will, I wanted to get engaged, so what the hell is my problem? Why am I so scared?

In bed that night, just after I turn the lights off, I ask Will about the end of his marriage. "When did things start going wrong?"

"The first few years were pretty good, but then the last year . . . we fought a lot. About everything. And we couldn't talk about it. When I tried to talk about things, she just exploded, like I was accusing her, like I was trying to blame things on her. I offered to go to counseling, but she'd had a bad experience with counseling in high school and didn't trust it."

"Did you leave her or did she leave you?"

"She came home one day and said she'd rented an apartment and was moving out."

"How . . . what was that like for you?"

"It felt like a personal failure. Nobody thinks *their* marriage is going to end in divorce."

Nobody thinks their *marriage is going to end in divorce*. I turn these words over in my mind again and again. He was willing to go to counseling. That seems to me a very positive sign for us. But I have to say, I'm extremely curious to hear X's side of the story about how things ended.

Then I think about my conversation with Gabrielle and I turn on the light beside the bed.

"Ouch," Will says, shielding his eyes.

"Sorry. I just need to tell you, I feel really strongly that I don't want strippers at your bachelor party."

"Who even said there is going to be a bachelor party?"

"I know your friends. There will be a bachelor party, and I don't want there to be any strippers there."

"Okay."

His tone is casual when what I really want is a zealous response along the lines of, "I'd sooner have my scrotum pummeled by a sledgehammer than be subjected to the sight of a naked woman other than you!"

"No, Will, I mean it. This is a big deal for me."

"Okay. I get it."

But I can tell that he's just trying to agree with me so I'll turn off the light and let him sleep. "I don't think you do get it. It's not okay with me that you go off and pay a woman to take her clothes off."

He lets out an exasperated sigh, which infuriates me.

"I'm sure your *ex-wife* wouldn't have a problem with it." I hiss. "God, I hate that you were married to a stripper."

He sighs again. "I'm sorry. There is nothing I can do about my past."

And, even though I know he's right, I'm irrationally angry with him anyway. I grab my pillow and stomp downstairs to the living room, where I take an afghan out of the closet and make a bed on the couch. I'm crying and my breath is jagged and I hate all men right now and I vow to become a lesbian.

Except, God, can you imagine how much time it would take to get *two* women off? You'd be there for days.

I *would* absolutely become a lesbian, though, if it weren't for the time-constraint issue.

There is a distant part of my brain that knows it was completely illogical of me to get enraged at Will for crimes he hasn't even committed yet, but I'm still angry: Angry at Will for being a typical guy when I want more than that; angry at culture in general for treating women like background decoration; and angry at Gabrielle for taking her bad mood out on my good news.

It takes awhile, but eventually I cry myself to sleep.

Chapter 12

In the morning, I wake up when Will walks through the living room as he's getting his things to go to work. I quickly shut my eyes and pretend to be asleep because I don't feel like talking to him right now—that's just how mature I am. I hear him leave, and the next thing I hear is the phone ringing. Apparently, I'd fallen back to sleep, because the ringing phone wakes me up.

"Hello?"

"Hi." It's Gabrielle. "I'm sorry about yesterday. I'm sorry I was such a bitch. I was just upset about Jeremy. And Dan. And life. But I shouldn't have taken it out on you. I'm happy for you, I really am. Will is a great guy. I think you two will be really happy together."

"Thanks. Thank you. That means a lot to me."

"Are you busy today?"

"Yeah. Why?"

"No reason. I just called in sick because I couldn't face the office and I was wondering if you wanted to play hooky. Maybe we could look at wedding dresses or something."

My bad mood vanishes entirely. I'm thrilled by the prospect. "Really? That sounds like so much more fun than crunching numbers all day. I really should work though. Although the work will all still be here tomorrow, and I can put in a few hours on the weekend if I have to, right?"

"Right."

"Okay. I'm convinced. Let me shower. I'll pick you up in an hour."

I pick Gabrielle up and drive us to Cherry Creek, an up-scale neighborhood with several bridal stores. I tell the sales consultant that I don't want anything puffy, and she keeps bringing me dresses that look like they have hoop skirts built into them.

"No, I don't want a puffy skirt," I tell her for the tenth time. "That's puffy. I don't puff. No puff. Puff-free please."

Finally, she brings me a couple dresses that don't look awful, and Gabrielle and I go into the large dressing room with a plush velvet curtain. I take off my clothes, and before I can get the dress on, I catch sight of my nearly naked body and wish I hadn't. My hair looks limp, my skin looks yellow, and I have more than my fair share of belly pooch and upper arm fat.

"Ick," I declare. "Look at me. I need to get highlights. And maybe dermabrasion. I've heard that makes your pores look smaller. And I may even have to get really drastic: I may actually have to start working out."

"The lighting in here is bad, don't let it get to you."

"I don't think we can blame the lighting on me being overweight and out of shape."

"You're not overweight. You're not out of shape. Your hair is beautiful. Your skin is nearly flawless. You are just believing the crap that advertisers tell you. Advertisers want you to think you're imperfect because then they can get you to think that buying their product will make you thinner and prettier and *then* you'll be happy. If people loved themselves, they wouldn't go out and spend money on clothes and jewelry and makeup they didn't need in a useless exercise in trying to feel better about themselves. Loving yourself is the most radical political statement you can make against a consumer culture that tries its damnedest to convince you that you're not good enough as you are."

When she says that, I'm reminded of why I love her so much. *Loving yourself is the most radical political statement you can make.* She's absolutely right. I have to work on loving myself, on focusing on my good qualities. Then I try on the first dress and I look like a wiener dog in taffeta, and I decide that whatever might be good about me is clearly all on the inside. I try on the other two dresses and my suspicions are confirmed. I'm hideous.

"Let's get lunch," I say.

We grab burritos at a fast food restaurant nearby and I take a too big bite and half the burrito pours into my lap and cheese and sour cream drips onto my hands and down my face and all I can think is, *What kind of bride am I? Is this bride-like behavior? I think not.*

"You seem pretty calm for a bride," Gabrielle says, and I laugh.

"No. I'm not. I guess in some ways it hasn't all hit me. But . . . I don't know, I'm happy, but I'm also just terrified, too. There are so many things I'm scared of."

"Like what?"

"Well, like last night Will and I got into a fight. No, that's not true. I screamed at Will over nothing and then stomped off to sleep on the couch. I mean, with communication 'skills' like that, there's no way our marriage stands a chance."

"But you're aware of it, which means you can change, which means your marriage does stand a chance. What did you get mad about?"

"I told him I didn't want him to have strippers at his bachelor party, and he said that was fine, but he wasn't taking it as seriously as I wanted him to take it. I couldn't communicate that this is a really big deal to me. The whole thing reminds me so much of the way my parents fought. Dad would say nothing while Mom screamed about everything. I sort of feel like my communication style is a cross between theirs. Mom's accusatory and confrontational approach coupled with Dad's retreat and ignore tactics."

"That's pretty common to adopt your parents' argument style. It becomes very ingrained after years of living with it."

"Well, how am I supposed to change?"

"Practice. Communication is a skill you have to learn like any other. Next time you want to stomp off in a huff, you have to force yourself to take a deep breath and try to communicate the emotions you are feeling."

"That *sounds* easy, but in practice . . . well, I'll try."

"What else are you scared about?"

"What?"

"You said there were so many things you were scared of. What else?"

"I guess I just have residual fears from my parents' divorce. After they divorced, Mom couldn't get credit cards in her name for seven years because when Mom and Dad were in the really ugly bitter throes of divorce, Dad hid his money and he didn't make the mortgage payments or pay off their credit cards for a few months in a row and it just ravaged their credit rating. But Dad already had credit, so he could keep his credit cards, but Mom couldn't get any new ones on her own because she'd only ever had a joint account. And I'm just so terrified of becoming dependent like that."

"Eva, you've got an MBA. You own your own home. That's not going to happen to you."

"I know, I know. I'm not making sense. It's just . . . I have a real fear of being vulnerable, and so the whole thing is really scary. I just worry . . . I don't know, I don't really think Will would ever cheat on me, but you never know. I'm trying to think of all the bad things that could happen to us and whether I'm strong enough to be able to get through the hard times. Like what if Will suddenly becomes a gambling addict or if he quits his job as soon as we get married? I had a girlfriend in college who that happened to. Her husband almost never worked the entire decade they were married."

"Man, Eva, your anxiety disorder is out of control. Calm down. Of course, a lot of bad things could happen, but you'll be gaining a partner, somebody who can look after you when you get sick. Someone whose shoulder you can cry on when you have a crappy day."

"I don't want to get sick. I don't want to be vulnerable."

"I hate to break it to you, but you are going to get sick. There are going to be times when you need help whether you like it or not. That's what brings people together. By opening yourself up, you make yourself vulnerable, but you also get the opportunity to connect with someone on a deep, authentic level, and that's really something."

"I guess. Let's not talk about love and commitment. Let's talk about something fun. Like weddings. Any ideas where I should have mine? Where did you and Dan get married?"

"We just said vows by ourselves at a botanic garden, and then we spent the weekend at this cabin in the mountains making love."

"Oh. That's nice. But it doesn't help me any."

She shrugs. "Sorry. Maybe you can ask Rachel."

"I already did. She had her mother throw something together in just a couple months. She and Jon just showed up and got married and five months later it was Mom and Dad and baby Isaac makes three. Why do I have to have such nontraditional friends?"

"Maybe because you're a nontraditional girl?"

Chapter 13

The night passes and Will and I don't say anything about the tiff we had the night before. Will and I don't argue often, and it's because both of us aren't fans of confrontation. He does-n't mention a word about our squabble, and I sure as heck am not going to bring it up, in part because I don't even know what to say or how I feel. How am I supposed to communicate my feelings when I don't know what it is I'm feeling?

The next morning, I wake up early and work hard on the Woodruff Pharmaceutical project for several hours. The sense of accomplishment makes me feel good, and I allow myself to take a break in the afternoon. Foolishly, I begin searching for information on weddings online. At first, I look up practical stuff about what Will and I will need to do to get hitched in the eyes of the law in Colorado, but then I'm quickly off looking at wedding dresses and bridesmaids' dresses and sites that offer wedding tips. At some point, I admit to myself that I'm not going to be getting any more work done today, and I head off to the bookstore, where I do my best to give away all of my money buying every book that I can find on planning a low-budget wedding. I spend so much on books there is no way the adjective "low-budget" can be applied to my wedding any longer. I buy every bridal mag-azine I can get my hands on and books on wedding traditions and how to write your own vows. I'm embarrassed about the vow book because the whole idea of writing your own vows is to be original and not worry about what other people have done, but when I see the book, I snap it up instantly, because I have no idea how to even begin writing vows. I feel like it has been decades since the last time I went to a wedding.

There were summers in my midtwenties when it felt as if I went to weddings every weekend, but eventually, after everyone I knew was married, the pace of the weddings I was invited to slowed considerably. The last wedding I attended was last summer and I can't remember anything about it. I wish I'd taken notes.

I flip through the planning books, and instead of feeling like I'm beginning to get a handle on what it will take to plan a wedding, I'm starting to get alarmed because there are so many things I never realized I should be worrying about. The book admonishes me about the importance of a centerpiece for the tables, and I'm suddenly thrown into a panic. What makes for a good centerpiece? I can't even begin to imagine, and even though I shelled out hundreds of bucks at the bookstore, apparently none of the books I bought have suggestions for this particular topic. Where is help when you need it?

Then I read about how some reception halls won't let you have a family member cut your wedding cake for you, yet they insist on charging $1.50 for every slice *they* cut. $1.50 a slice! The more I read, the more I learn about how everyone who comes in contact with the bride and groom are going to try to screw them out of money at every possible opportunity. Like the photographers who insist on holding on to the negatives so if you want extra copies of a particular shot, you have to pay them exorbitant prices for it. I read how you can't bring your own bottles of wine to a reception hall so you have to buy the wine from them, which naturally costs twice what it would to buy it wholesale. Bastards one and all.

When Will gets home from work, I get started on making

us dinner. Tonight, I'm going with a Middle Eastern theme—falafel and hummus and couscous and pita.

When dinner's ready, I call up the stairs to him, "Will! Dinner's ready!" Right after the words come out of my mouth, I'm struck by this weird feeling, like I'm playing house, and somebody is going to catch me pretending to be a grown-up.

We sit down to eat and the odd feeling passes. The dinner turns out to be highly edible, which is a pleasantly surprising and unexpected development.

"Do you care if we have a wedding?" I ask Will as I stuff a pita full of falafel and onion and tomato.

"I'd be happy just to elope."

I nod. "I figured you'd say that. Mom sort of talked me into a wedding, and at first I thought I agreed with her, but then today I went and bought a ton of books on planning a wedding, and now I'm not so sure anymore."

"Whatever you want, hon."

I tell him about all the dastardly evil-doers out in the world who wanted to cheat brides and grooms out of their money, but then I go on and on about how much fun it would be to get all of the family together.

"Except for Mom and Dad, of course. There is some serious potential for ugliness between those two, especially if they get some alcohol in them. The last time they were together was for Sienna's graduation, and they fought like caged animals. I hope they've grown up since then, but I wouldn't count on it."

I ask him to make up a list of people he wants to invite, and how many family members he thinks he'll ask to come. Will's father died two years earlier of a heart attack, and so his mother is the only close family he has. It makes me sad that Will had to mourn the loss of his father without me in his life. There are all these huge life events that Will has experienced that I wasn't a part of, and I hate it. I hate that I wasn't there for him.

After dinner, I go to put on one of Will's T-shirts to lounge around in. I'm wearing just my bra and underwear when Will comes into the room. "Can I wear this one?" I ask, pulling a T-shirt off its hanger in the closet.

"Sure. Anything you want."

I snap off my bra and before I can put the T-shirt on, Will is kissing me, and his instant erection is pressing into my thigh. I abandon thoughts of putting the shirt on and instead shimmy out of my underwear and pull Will on to the bed with me.

Will drives me wild with kisses along my inner thigh and his fingers do magical things to my clitoris. (I did mention that Will is a guitar player, right? The boy knows how to use his fingers, that's all I'm saying.) Finally he enters me, and it feels so exquisite that I can't suppress a moan. As I hear myself, I think, *I bet she screamed louder, bucked more wildly, moaned with more enthusiasm.* And once X is in my mind, I can't get her out. I've seen pictures of her (I asked to see them, because as I mentioned earlier, I'm a masochist.) and she was pretty. Not gorgeous, thank God, but definitely pretty. I keep thinking of Will going down on her, and the image is grotesque to me, but I can't shake it. With X being foremost in my thoughts, an orgasm is out of the question, so I just moan encouragingly (I don't want him to think his effort is for naught), and the sound works as I'd hoped, putting him over the edge. He comes with an explosive groan that I find sexy as hell, and then he collapses on top of me.

We lie in each other's arms for a long time. I hear my cell phone ring, but I let voicemail take it.

When Will and I finally muster the energy to get out of bed, I check my messages.

"Oh shit! Oh shit!" I cry.

"What?" Will asks when I hang up.

"My dad. He's coming for a visit. The weekend after this weekend. That is so like him. He just buys the tickets and *then* tells me he's coming. He knows I travel all the time for work. And the worst thing is, I'll be in town next weekend, so I'll have no excuse not to see him."

"You don't like your dad?"

"No, I love him, I just . . . my dad kind of makes me nervous. When I'm around him I feel like I can't do anything right. Anyway, it's the principle of the thing. Once he planned a trip and had to spend nearly twice what he paid for the ticket to change it around once he bothered to find out that I wasn't going to be here when he'd planned to come."

"Why does he do that?"

"He gets these whims and he'll go online and goes right ahead and buys the tickets if he finds a good deal and *then* remembers he needs to tell me he's coming. Not that he'd call to check if it was a convenient time for him to come, just to let me know he'll be here. Shit."

"Well, I'm looking forward to meeting him."

"I guess it will be good for the two of you to meet. We'll meet his new girlfriend, too."

"It sounds like fun."

Will, my love, you couldn't be more wrong.

When darkness comes, Will falls asleep in moments. I, however, lie in bed, fretting. Fretting about something new for a change, but fretting all the same: Dad. I'm not looking forward to him visiting.

Dad's parenting skills wax and wane. Sometimes he's superdad, being thoughtful, calling just to chat, sending presents just because. Other times it's like he forgets he has children. Mom waited several years before remarrying. Dad waited about four minutes once the divorce was official. Granted, that was a full three years after he and Mom separated. He dated a lot of cool women in those three years. But he married Deanne.

I didn't like Deanne from the beginning, and not just because she had three kids from three different marriages, or because she wasn't smart, wasn't interesting, and decorated her house with things I would give away as white elephant gifts. I stood up at his wedding, though, as if I approved of the whole thing.

Dad and Deanne wrote their own vows. They gushed about how meaningful this would be, but with four failed marriages between them, it would be more honest if they said something like: "I'll be beside you whenever you need me, as long as you don't get fat/go bald, your kids don't drive me up a wall, and we don't argue about money too often."

It's not that I didn't want Dad to get married again. I wanted him to be happy. Which was why he should not have married Deanne. Basically, she told him she was thirty-eight years old and did not have time to waste in a relationship that wasn't going anywhere (i.e., to an altar, and quick), so he had to propose or get lost. My dad doesn't do well with loneliness; I understand that. But marrying someone like Deanne to combat loneliness is like drinking too much at a party because you feel a little uncomfortable making small talk, and then you end up puking into the centerpiece before passing out and wetting your pants. The short-term solution makes things much, much worse in the end.

At Dad and Deanne's wedding, they had the poem on their invitation about how some people come into your life, leave footprints on your heart, and you are never, ever the same. What they should have written was that some people come into your life, poison your heart and mind with their toxic bullshit, and you are never, ever the same.

Deanne seemed relatively benign at first. She did little things that, by themselves, seemed harmless enough.

Like how she started to infiltrate Dad's wardrobe. I was home from college for Christmas when I first discovered Dad's newly errant fashion ways. Dad and Deanne weren't married yet—the threat of impending nuptials hadn't even been mentioned, but already Deanne was imposing her will.

At the time, Dad was taking me and Sienna to the mall to

finish our Christmas shopping. Sienna was fifteen then, and still skinny as ever. She'd developed some curves while I was gone, though she did her best to hide them, shrouding her figure in enormous sweatshirts and baggy jeans.

It was cold out, and we were all wearing coats, which is why I didn't see the shirt at first. Dad was talking about how he and Randy tried to get an armoire Dad had built into this old lady's palatial-size house. Randy is Dad's wildly unambitious younger brother, who spent his days getting high and his nights bartending and getting drunk. Dad sometimes tried to give him work that he had to do sober, so when Dad needed a hand with the furniture he built, he'd give Randy a call. Sienna leaned forward from the backseat to hear what we were saying.

"Randy was, as usual, not paying attention. We had to get this enormous armoire up dozens and dozens of stairs that curved around up to second floor. That wasn't even the hardest part. The hardest part was trying to get it through the narrow door into the bedroom. Randy kept knocking into the side of the door. Each time he was surprised that it kept crashing into the doorframe and didn't go through." Dad affected Randy's perpetually confused expression. Maybe there's something just intrinsically funny about your father pretending to be high, maybe it was just our dad's ability to make comical facial expressions, but Sienna and I cracked up. "Googe, googe," Dad continued, imitating the sound of the armoire slamming into the side of the door. "Fortunately, the old lady was deaf, and didn't hear that we were smashing her extremely expensive new furniture into her door." Dad would never let a piece of his crash into anything even once, but he always exaggerated to make his stories funnier.

As he talked, I finally noticed the top of his shirt peeking out from where the zipper on his jacket stopped.

"What the hell is that?" I asked when he was done telling his story.

"What?"

"That shirt."

Dad laughed. "Deanne. She thinks I need more color in my wardrobe."

Dad had always had decent taste in clothes. He wore subdued, high-quality shirts in greens and blues that looked good with his hazel eyes and brown-blond hair. Except that day he was wearing an atrocious shirt with vertical stripes in red, orange, white, and brown. It's not that I would have ever accused Deanne of having good taste. She had from-a-box blond hair that she hairsprayed until it was crispy and encircled her head in an ironic nimbus and she wore bright blue eyeshadow with her blue eyes. Still, this shirt of Dad's was unconscionable.

Sienna peered at the shirt in question. "Jesus, Dad," she said, shaking her head. "What was she thinking?"

Dad chuckled. "You should have seen the pants she got me. Light blue corduroys with inch-thick ribbing. I told her I'd wear this shirt if she returned those pants to the store, and I never had to lay my eyes on them again."

We had a fun day with Dad, joking around and catching up on things.

All the fun faded as soon as we got home to Deanne and her brood. I didn't like any of them. I didn't even like their dog, and usually I love dogs. He just seemed dumb and contrary and without a shred of personality, just like the family who'd raised him.

Deb was Deanne's oldest at thirteen. She was probably about twenty-five or thirty pounds overweight for her height and already wore a C-cup. Like her mother, she had faux blond hair that was white in places and yellow in others. She wore skintight jeans and cropped sweaters that hugged her prodigious chest and revealed the ring of fat that hung over her jeans.

Trevor, eight, and Dillon, four, were strange-looking, with dark, sunken eyes, sullen expressions, and too-large heads.

They looked dim-witted, as if they'd been dropped on their heads as babies.

Dad had dated some cool women since the separation, and Deanne wasn't smart enough, witty enough, or classy enough for him. I just couldn't take her seriously. I thought Dad would surely come to his senses soon.

My friends thought that I wouldn't like Dad to fall for anyone who wasn't my mom, but that wasn't true. I'd spent too many years listening to my parents endlessly bicker about money and mortgage payments and credit card bills to think they could possibly be any good for each other anymore. I wanted him to find somebody. Somebody who wasn't Deanne.

I did my best to be polite when I was around Deanne and her kids, but it was a relief to go back to school so I could stop the charade.

The next time I came for a visit was late in March, over spring break. I stayed with Mom and Sienna again—the house Dad was renting was small and every available inch of space was taken up with power tools and carpentry supplies. On my second night home, Dad took me to a fancy restaurant. He joked around over appetizers and salads, but as the entrees were being served, his expression became serious.

"I have something to tell you," he said.

"Yeah?"

"I proposed to Deanne a few days ago and she accepted."

"What? I had no idea you were even thinking about marriage."

"Deanne's very eager to get married. She pointed out that at her age, she can't afford to waste her time in a relationship that's not going anywhere."

"So basically, she bullied you into proposing."

"I've just come to see that this is the best thing."

The best thing, like having a hysterectomy was better than having cancer or saving one cojoined twin was better than letting them both die. Like he wasn't happy about it, but he didn't see what else he could do.

I sat there for a moment in stunned silence. "But you're still married," was all I could manage.

"Your mom and I met yesterday, and we got the last details agreed on. It's been three years. Three bitter years. We're ready to be done with it. The divorce should be final by the end of the month."

"So when is the wedding?"

"August. We'd like you and Sienna to be bridesmaids."

I agreed, but after I returned to school, an uneasiness settled into my stomach that wouldn't go away.

I stayed in town at school that summer, waitressing at a Mexican restaurant known as *the* place in town for margaritas. I told Mom and Dad that I was staying in town because I didn't want to lose my job, but that was only partly true. I didn't come home because I didn't think I could handle it. Sienna made it sound like she was living on a set of a soap opera. Every day was filled with overblown theatrics and hysteria. Mom was crying daily over the fact that Dad was moving on so quickly while she was still reeling from the demise of her marriage. Dad was going through life mechanically, doing what Deanne told him to do.

Sienna and I talked often that summer. Whenever our conversation came around to Deanne, our words began flooding out, tumbling over each other's. We didn't care that we interrupted each other and essentially had the same conversation a thousand times. We just wanted to talk, to get all the tangled emotions out.

"Dad dated so many cool, intelligent women since the separation," I said, for the twentieth time that summer. "Women who were funny and had a shred of personality. I thought he'd get bored of Deanne, find someone worthy of him. Instead, she's the one he's marrying."

"I was staying over at their new house last weekend—can you believe they got a new house already?" Sienna said. "A month after the divorced is finalized they're moving into this enormous place. It's got five bedrooms and a swimming pool. She works as an assistant to a tax attorney. She's like an administrative assistant or something, so I'm sure she can't help out that much financially. I don't know how the hell they could afford the place. Anyway, I woke up and came downstairs and nobody was around. There were fresh-baked muffins on the counter. I assumed they were for breakfast, so I had one. When Deanne came in from the garage, she started screaming at me about how those were for Trevor's Sunday school class, and now she had to bake a whole new batch because now she was one short and how I was so selfish, doing whatever I wanted without thinking about anyone but myself. She started throwing pots and pans around, I mean, it was scary. She just lost it. I know she wouldn't have gone off at me like that—"

"And over something so stupid . . ."

"—If Dad had been around. It was like her eyes rolled into her head and her head spun around a few times and she just revealed the monster inside that's been lurking under the surface all along."

"I can't believe she called you selfish. You're the nicest, least selfish person I know."

"It gets better," Sienna continued. "Have you gotten the bridesmaid pattern in the mail yet?"

"No."

"She's sending you the pattern and the material, and you have to go find someone to make it. She's talking about how nice it is of her to buy the material so all we have to pay for is the seamstress. It's like, hello, it's Dad's money. Anyway, the material is pastel flowers . . ."

"It is not."

"Oh, yes, it is, big ones. The pattern calls for a bow on the butt . . ."

"No!"

"Yes. I mean it's not huge. It's this kind of country look.

Country bumpkin really. And it has these puffy half-sleeves on the arms. The skirt billows out so it makes your butt look enormous."

"How could she?" Not that it was actually a surprise, or at least, shouldn't have been. But still, I was not happy.

I came home a few weeks before the wedding to help get things ready. Even though Sienna had told me about the house, I was blown away by how luxurious it was. Sienna and I had grown up in a modest two-bedroom. I couldn't imagine how they could afford this.

It was so strange staying with Deanne. I didn't know if I was imagining it, but every time Deanne looked at me, she did so with venom in her eyes. One night when Dad had to work late at the office, Deanne made dinner just for her and her kids. She didn't even offer me any. It was the weirdest thing. I said, "Well, I guess I'll make some mac and cheese," expecting her to say I could have some of the casserole with them, but she didn't say anything. I felt like such an outcast. I didn't feel I belonged at all.

Over and over I was reminded *this is not my home* by little things, like the fact the paper towels were kept under the sink instead of on the counter like they were when I was growing up, or how the brand of cereal she bought was something my family would never buy. In the weeks before the wedding, in my eagerness to do away with the awkward rift between us, I logged countless hours doing little things for the wedding, like assembling dozens of little bags of candy-covered almonds (which took *forever*), getting everything ready to get to the reception site, and running around doing other little last-minute stuff. She never thanked me for anything, and, in fact, she did her best not to talk to me. Even when I worked across the kitchen table from Deanne preparing a hundred bottles of bubbles for the guests to blow as Dad and Deanne exited the church, we worked in silence. And she never once said thank you. At that point, I was officially pissed off at how this woman was treating me, so I said, sarcastically, "You're welcome for the help."

"What do you want me to do, give you a medal? I think your father paying for your ridiculously expensive education should be reward enough."

Her comment took me aback. I started thinking defensive thoughts like, *Dad only* helps *pay for school. I've won scholarships . . . I work twenty-five hours a week . . . plus, I've taken out enough student loans to keep me in serious debt until well into my thirties . . .*

I told myself it was stupid to get defensive, but I couldn't help it. You don't grow up in a family where money ignited arguments daily and not know about the tension and quiet bitterness money can create.

I felt so acutely lonely after just a couple weeks there. It was very clear that Deanne thought of my sister and me as mooches siphoning money away that she thought should be hers.

It was an outdoor wedding. I followed Deb, Sienna, and Deanne's sisters down the aisle—step together, step together. We stood flanking the altar beneath the searing hot sun. In minutes, my makeup was melting, my hair was shellacked with sweat to my forehead and neck. I ran my tongue across the salty perspiration of my upper lip and looked over the expansive lawn at guests I didn't know, watching Dad in his plastered-on smile marrying a stranger, marrying a woman he didn't particularly seem to like.

I was there to see Dad into a new life. I certainly wasn't there because I was happy for them. I was there because I had to be. I was a prop in a flowered dress, wilting beneath the August sun.

Dad and Deanne didn't go on a honeymoon. She'd bought a brand new fifty thousand dollar car instead. I just wished them good luck and hightailed it back to the safe haven of college.

Over the next couple of years, my relationship with my father grew strained. He suddenly stopped paying tuition, and then the university would send me very bitchily worded letters threatening to kick me out of school if I didn't get money to them right away. I knew it was Deanne's doing. My sister's and my education had always been a huge priority for Dad. He hadn't let me work in high school, saying I should focus on my studies, which I did. He'd agreed to pay college tuition and rent for both Sienna and me, and it would be up to us to pay for food, books, utility bills, clothes, and everything else. Then Deanne came into his life, and suddenly he wondered if we shouldn't be paying for school entirely ourselves, despite the fact that we hadn't been able to save money because it had been his policy not to let us work in high school. Mom made peanuts at the time, so she couldn't help out financially, as Dad well knew.

Dad and I had made a deal on how I could finance my education, and now the rules were being changed. Now, with Deanne in his life, the mind games began. He always ended up paying the tuition bill eventually, but he always paid it late, leaving me constantly stressed out and terrified to open my mail. Because of this, and because our lives were in such different places, trying to maintain a relationship was a challenge. Every phone call was tense—trying to make conversation was hard. I would brag about the good grades I got—and I always got good grades, that one D in trigonometry my senior year being the only aberration on that score—and he would tell me about whatever carpentry work he was doing in his spare time, and then, after being on the phone less than five minutes, we'd give up and say our good-byes. That's when I learned that you should never count on a man to be the breadwinner. It's better not to rely on a man, especially when he can change the rules on you at any moment.

I can't say that when Deanne left Dad within two years of their marriage, leaving him for another man, I was upset to see Deanne go, though my heart broke for Dad.

It was just a few weeks before my graduation when Sienna called me to tell me the news. I'd been studying for finals all day and was distracted when I answered the phone.

"Hello?"

"They're divorced," she said.

"What?"

"Another man has already moved in."

"What are you talking about?"

"The whole thing only took three weeks."

"Why didn't you tell me about this earlier?"

"I only found out from Dad yesterday. You know how Dad can go for months forgetting he has daughters. I'm used to not hearing from him. But here's the deal, Deanne told Dad he wasn't good enough for her and she was in love with another man, and she wanted a divorce. Dad's been completely whacked out. It's like he's in a coma. Deanne took advantage of his shock and ravaged him financially. He was too stunned to fight back. She took everything. The house, the new car, most of the furniture—even the stuff he made. She's been dating this new guy for six months. Six months. Dad had no idea." Sienna broke down then. Her words came between jagged sobs. "He just looks so bad, you know? He's popping Prozac by the handful. He's got medication to help him sleep, but when I saw him earlier today, he said he hasn't slept in three days. He's blaming himself, saying he's a failure. I'm really worried about him. I think he might lose his job, he's missing so much work lately."

"Sienna, I don't believe it. I can't believe even Deanne could be that heartless."

"The one thing Dad wanted from the house was the fence. You know that fence he spent all summer on? I don't know if you ever got to see it, but it was super-detailed and intricate. He was really proud of it, you know? And she won't give it to him. She says it's part of the property."

"But he built that fence. She didn't even want it."

"I know. It's just so petty. Like she's deliberately trying to hurt him as much as possible."

When Dad came out for my graduation, he seemed even worse than what Sienna had described. He chain-smoked; he rarely spoke; he spent a lot of time staring at nothing in particular. He moved as if in a fugue, distant and lethargic.

Those weeks after Sienna told me about the divorce, I couldn't sleep. I was so furious. I cried countless tears of frustration and anger. I was mad about everything: Mad at Dad for marrying her in the first place; mad at Deanne for having such a poisonous effect on my relationship with Dad; mad about the way Deanne had hurt him. Somehow, what pissed me off the most was her refusal to give him that stupid fence.

It was the one thing from their marriage that meant anything to him.

But our family lost the war, and to the victor goes the spoils. The fence was, after all, just a thing. It's easy to forget that sometimes.

Watching my father go through the carnage of a second divorce only reinforced my belief that marriage isn't for everyone, and divorce, if at all possible, shouldn't be for anyone.

Chapter 14

By the end of the day today, the last of Will's stuff will be here. A couple of his buddies are helping him move the big stuff he couldn't get himself.

If you can judge a man by the friends he keeps, and I think you can, then I have even more proof that Will is a catch. Will's friends are all funny and smart, they tip well, and almost all of them have the good sense to agree with my political viewpoints. Will's friends tend to be computer geeks like him, but they aren't the kind of computer geeks that shouldn't be allowed into public. They are sociable computer geeks.

Will has a ton of friends, but many are married with kids, so naturally we almost never see them. We do get together pretty regularly with his friends Richard, Jerry and his girl-friend Abby, and James. James is married, but his wife is a med student, so we almost never see her, and when we do, she's usually propped up against a wall asleep and drooling. Richard and Jerry are the ones helping Will move. We now have two sets of couches between us, two large-screen TVs, and a ridiculous amount of plates, cooking utensils, and pots and pans. For now, we just put all of the duplicate stuff in my basement and talk vaguely of selling it at some point down the road when we can rouse the motivation to do so.

Moving Will's dresser into the master bedroom makes the room seem a lot smaller. The only other piece of furniture of his that we don't relegate to the basement is his liquor cabinet, which is a beautiful piece of furniture that could pass as modern art with its curved lines and sleek shape. We put that in the living room. It matches well with my couch and other furniture, but it does make the room feel a smidge crowded.

It takes all day for the three guys to move the furniture in. I help where I can, but most of the stuff is simply too heavy for me. I do stuff like carry the throw pillows. My presence here is sheer window dressing, but at least *I* won't have a sore back in the morning.

When we're done (and by "we" I mean "they"), Jerry turns down the offer of free beer and food in exchange for his labor, saying he has to get back home because he and Abby are going to her parents' tonight. But Richard is game, so he, Will, and I go to Mickie's Pub, our usual haunting ground for beer. Though ever since that fateful night when I ran across the *you are not the first and you are definitely not the last* graffiti, I've done my best not to use the bathroom while we're there.

Mickie's is a pub that Will and his friends have been going to nearly every Friday for the past two years, and when I started dating Will, I started joining them there for happy hour every week. It's a good bar with a wide selection of microbrewed beers brewed on site and good food at reasonable prices. It has an odd layout for a bar, with small rooms and an upstairs and a downstairs instead of one big room. It has a pool table and dartboard, wood tables and floors, and brick walls. The decorations are mercifully free of immature neon beer signs and scantily clad women. The lighting is kept dim. There is a small stage area where, on Friday and Saturday nights, local bands play at no charge.

We order beer and sandwiches, as usual. I take a big bite of my chicken sandwich, wash it down with a sip of beer, and ask Richard, "How's the love life?"

I pester him about this a lot. He's thirty-five years old and never been married, and it's something I just can't comprehend. He's good-looking, he's smart, he's got a good job, and while it's true he's a computer geek, he's not painfully shy. I've tried to convince him to try the personals (*Look how happy Will and I are!*), but he won't do it.

"It's dead. Completely nonexistent."

"When's the last time you were with somebody?"

"It's been, God, I guess it's been about eight months. That's depressing. Thanks for bringing that up."

"No problem. I just can't understand how you could possibly be single."

"I can't seem to meet anybody. It seems like all the women at work are married, and that's pretty much the only place I have to meet women. We come here every week, but I've never once met a woman here."

"Well, that's because you're sitting at a table with your friends. Maybe we need to start scouting the place for interesting women and sending you off on reconnaissance missions."

He shrugs. "A woman at work has been trying to set me up with her sister-in-law. I've seen a picture. The sister-in-law is pretty cute. Maybe I should go for it."

"Yeah, you definitely should. I wish I knew more single women I could introduce you to. Most of my girlfriends are coupled off. There is Gabrielle, the PhD student, but like I told you before, she's only five-foot-one."

"No good," says Richard, who's six-two. "It would never work. The taller, the better."

"You should at least meet her."

"It would never work."

I shrug.

"So, what's it been like living with Will? Are you sick of him yet?" he asks.

"Hello, did you notice, I'm right here?" Will says jokingly.

"Not a chance. I want to be with him every single second. Anyway, I've been so busy with work lately, we don't have as much time to spend together as I'd like. We've got house-guests coming next weekend, then I've got this wedding to plan. I feel bad for abandoning Will. Most nights I leave him on his own while I work."

"What do you do with yourself when Eva is busy?" Richard asks Will.

"Computer games, mostly."

"Have you tried the latest version of Dungeon Siege?"

And they're off, talking about games with names like Dungeon Siege and Demons of the Underdark or something like that.

This whole world of computer games is foreign to me. When I go into Will's study when he's playing on his computer just to give him a kiss or say hi, I'll pause a moment and watch him play. The games involve quests and spells and strange creatures that you have to kill to avoid being killed yourself. It rather boggles my mind how Will can spend hours entertaining himself in this way. I've never been much of a game person. Maybe it's just that I've never had the leisure time to learn how to play. Maybe it's that I feel guilty if I'm not doing something productive at all times.

There is a part of me that knows that the way I'm living is not sustainable. I need to find ways to relax. I would like to start doing yoga and do deep breathing exercises and maybe get into a routine of some low-impact aerobics a few times a week to destress. But I'm always much too busy and stressed to find the time to destress.

After dinner we thank Richard one last time for his help and go home to bed. Will is putting his house on the market tomorrow. Our lives are becoming more personally and financially entwined every day. It's thrilling and exciting and more than a little terrifying.

Chapter 15

I've spent the last month collecting data and crunching numbers, and I've put all the data in an eighty-page report for Woodruff Pharmaceuticals.

I have never taken on such a big project, and every now and then the thought hits me that—for the first time in my professional life—I may just fail. I was a straight-A student in school, and then I graduated to becoming the go-to colleague and dependable businessperson. I'm not brilliant, but I'm hardworking. If I study for the test, do the work and research that I'm supposed to do by the time I'm supposed to do it, everything works out. But with this project, I feel the stakes are just too high. I'm up to my eyeballs in financial analysts' reports, stock projections, and medical technology industry data. I can use all of these facts to bolster my report, but ultimately the test is going to come down to whether Ridan's new diagnostic tool, Exploran, is everything Ridan claims it will be. It doesn't help that both Kyle Woodruff and Michael Evans are hounding me relentlessly for status reports and updates. The fear of failure paralyzes me.

The next day I work my ass off all day in preparation for meeting with WP on Monday, and I don't look up from my

desk until I hear the door downstairs open and hear Will calling, "I'm home, sweetie!"

I look at the clock. It's after six. Shit, I'd meant to start
dinner before he got home.

I run downstairs, give Will a hug and kiss, and then I get
started on dinner. I love living with Will. He's neat, but not
so fastidious he makes me feel bad when I'm a little messy
myself. He never blares loud music. He wakes up naturally in
the morning so he doesn't need to set an alarm that would
also wake me up. It's so nice to be able to talk to him about
my frustrations over work at the end of the day. He really lis-
tens to me and he gives me smart advice about how to solve
problems I'm having. He helps me work through problems
when I get stuck. I'm afraid I can't really reciprocate. He tells
me about what he did at work. I'll squint at him with brows
furrowed in concentration as I try to understand what the
hell he's talking about. He goes on about prototyping web
pages and cascading style sheets and encapsulating page
headings and setting ASP.net user controls, but I don't understand a word of it.

The only thing that's hard about living with Will is trying
to feed both of us.

When I was single, I was happy to subsist on frozen pizza,
takeout, and mac and cheese, but now that there are two of us
who need to be fed, I feel like I should finally learn to cook.
Will would be the perfect guy if only he could cook. He can
make grilled cheese sandwiches and that's it. When we were
dating and going to one person's place or the other's every
night, we went out to dinner the vast majority of the time,
and I have the supersized waistline to prove it. Even though I
try to order healthy things off the menu when we go out, I
inevitably eat more when we go out than I would if we were
at home. I figure now that we're living together, I should try
to lose the weight that I always seem to gain when I fall in
love. Dating—it makes you fat.

The challenge is that Will and I have very different likes

when it comes to food. I love onions, tomatoes, and vegetables of all kinds. He hates all of these things. He likes spicy foods and red meats, and I don't. He likes fried foods and anything dripping with cheese and cream sauces, and while I like those things, my waistline doesn't. We both like lots of different kinds of pasta, but I'm thinking that the road to me getting me into shape isn't paved with noodles.

Tonight for dinner I make a three-bean enchilada casserole. It's edible, but not great, and I can tell Will isn't impressed. Though he thanks me for cooking, I can tell he has to force himself to eat the meal, and I feel like a domestic failure. I blame my mother for this. My mother was the queen of ground beef. Hamburger Helper, tacos, sloppy joes, meatloaf, hamburgers—if it was made with ground beef, it was on our dinner table. She was a busy working woman too, so I don't begrudge her cooking cheap, quick fare, but it didn't help me attain the slightest skill when it came to cooking, especially since today, in the era of mad cow disease, heart disease, and high cholesterol, none of my mother's favorite meals have much chance of appearing on my dinner table.

After dinner, Will goes into the living room to watch football. I look at the stack of unwashed dishes and will him to volunteer to do them. But all I hear is the sound of the announcer describing the plays as if one fumbled ball would be the end of the world.

I spend the next hour flipping through cookbooks, trying to figure out healthy meals we'd both like. It's not easy. I can get as far as finding a chicken dish and some sort of potato or rice side dish, but trying to think of vegetables he might actually like nearly does me in. Maybe I should just cook vegetables for myself and not worry about him? How is it that grown men don't get scurvy? If Will was left on his own, he'd eat peanut butter sandwiches, grilled cheese, or hamburgers—with the lettuce, tomato, and onion removed to ensure his sandwich was completely nutrient-free—at every meal.

I find myself opting for Easy Skillet Meals or Easy One-

Dish Baked Meals. Coming up with one dish to make is hard enough, let alone a meal with various side dishes.

After I construct a long list of ingredients to buy from the grocery store, I look at the stack of dishes one more time. I just can't face them right now. I just can't. I should go back to working on the project for WP, but the prospect is just too depressing. I need to escape. I go to the bedroom with a romantic suspense novel. I only read a few pages before I think, *he's retreating into football, I'm retreating into a world where the heroes never have potbellies and can be described with words like "swarthy." We're not even married yet and we've already become my parents.*

Chapter 16

On Monday morning, I meet with the execs from Woodruff Pharmaceuticals and give them a several-hours long presentation in a multimedia format that basically goes over the eighty-page report I sent them the week earlier. Highlighting what the report states in this way gives them the opportunity to ask questions and make comments as we go. I review the potential benefits and potential risks, and I tell them that, "While branching out into the area of diagnostic equipment could be a good move for WP in the future, at this time I believe the risks outweigh the potential benefits. The economy is just too rocky right now, and you don't have the cash reserves to get through tough times, if that's what it comes down to. I think the plan to acquire Ridan should be shelved until next year at the earliest."

"But look at these numbers," Kyle says, pointing to a chart that estimates what Exploran could yield the company in terms of revenue. "Look at that potential. I say we go for it."

"Haven't you been listening to a word she said?" Michael says.

In moments, the air in the room is like a wrestling match, with shouts and accusations being flung around like rotten fruit thrown at actors in a bad play.

I keep out of it. I've given them my opinion. It is possible that acquiring Ridan could be lucrative, but before it can become profitable, WP will have to expend a tremendous amount of capital that will severely strain their resources and could potentially be the ruin of the company.

I don't like Kyle Woodruff, but I almost feel sorry for him. He does not know what he's doing; he does not know how to run a business; but he feels like he *should* know what he's doing and that he *should* know how to run a business because his father was a savvy businessperson, as if this were the sort of thing that was passed on through genetics rather than experience.

After an hour or so of debate in which I'm silent unless asked a question directly, Kyle says he thinks they should take a vote. He finally gets the men in the room to state their opinion about which way they are leaning. One by one he goes around the room—after skipping Michael and Dr. Lyons, stating "we already know how you two feel."

Kyle starts with Brandon Donovan, a tall, forty-something guy full of arrogance and self-confidence. I suspect he was a star on his high school basketball team and never quite got over himself.

"So, Brandon, what do you think?" Kyle asks.

"Well, I'm concerned about what happens if the stock market takes a hit. With all the political unrest in the middle east . . . what if there comes another event like September Eleventh? Are we going to be able to survive if we outlay the capital we'll need to ensure Exploran is a success?"

"Obviously, Brandon, no one can predict the future," Kyle says. "Are you suggesting that we don't make any strides forward just in case there is political unrest or the uncertainty of terrorist activity in the future? Because if that's the case, we may as well shut our doors right now. I can guarantee that wars will continue raging in some corner of this planet and a few terrorist insurgents will continue to voice their unhappiness in violent and destructive ways."

"Of course you're right, I just meant—"

"I think the bigger question is, do you think Ridan can

take our company into untapped markets, thus bringing the potential for new growth and new opportunities?"

"Clearly, the numbers show that that's possible."

"So then what you're saying is that you're in favor of acquiring Ridan Technologies?"

"Ah . . . yes, that's what I'm saying."

If an executive or board member sounds like he is wavering in favor of holding off on making a bid on Ridan, Kyle keeps hammering away at him, asking questions until he at least *sounds* like he's agreeing with Kyle. Then Kyle says, "So you agree that we should move forward with the acquisition?"

Then the man, tentative and vaguely confused, will nod, "Yes, I think we should."

So okay, I take it back—Kyle does know what he's doing. Maybe not how to run a business, but he sure knows how to get his way because in the end, the vote is eight to seven in favor of purchasing Ridan Technologies and acquiring Ridan's primary technology, Exploran.

Basically, Kyle Woodruff paid me thousands of dollars to do the exact opposite of what I recommended based on several weeks of research.

The meeting breaks up. Some people leave, others cluster together talking. As I pack up my laptop and briefcase, Kyle comes up to me and says, "Eva, I just wanted to commend you on some exceptional work. As we discussed earlier, I told you this project had the potential to take on a life of its own and there might be several stages to it. I'd very much like you to be a part of the next phases. Specifically, we're going to need help communicating the news of this purchase with all the satellite offices, and we'll need assistance in planning our marketing and communication strategies for external audiences. I'd like you to help with that."

There is a large part of me that would like to say no. Why would I want to be a part of communicating what a great idea it is for WP to acquire Ridan when I don't, in fact, think it's a good idea? But I don't have any other projects lined up. I was too busy working on this project to generate other leads. So, I tell him I'll be happy to.

And then, as I leave WP World Headquarters, it hits me that I'm not happy to. Not happy one bit.

Chapter 17

I spend the few days before Dad and his new girlfriend arrive furiously cleaning the house and my car. It takes so much more time to really clean the house than to do the cursory cleaning I normally do. I have to clean *everything*, every nook, windowsill, closet, cabinet, appliance, and window. I do piles of laundry and clean the sheets and comforters. I vacuum with such vigor I break into a sweat. I wash and vacuum my car. And at last, I decide that, while it's still not perfect, my house is as clean as it's going to get.

I bought my home a year ago. It was the first time I'd ever owned my own place. My father has never seen it before, and since he's got a carpenter's eye for detail when it comes to homes and buildings, I'm worried about what he's going to think about it. When I first moved in, I spent a few weeks in a flurry of redecorating. I'd never paid the slightest attention to details like faucet colors, light fixtures, and door handles, but the moment I became a home owner, these seemed like hugely important details. There is no escaping it: When you become a home owner you are sucked into the Home Depot Vortex.

It started with little things: Shades for the living room and kitchen, a new lock for the door. The woman who'd owned it before me had painted the entire house in a pale, cheery yellow, and I decided I'd just do a little painting. Paint was only twenty dollars a can or so, right? And how hard could it be? I'd wrap it up in a weekend.

Two weeks, countless frustrations, and hundreds of dollars in primer, paint, and equipment later, the master bedroom, the guest bedroom, and the downstairs basement were delightful shades of pale green, rich blue, and medium rose, respectively.

It wasn't easy getting there. I may well be the worst painter on the planet. Because my walls have a bumpy pattern—knockout, I learned it's called—trying to get a straight line where the blue wall met the white ceiling was challenging indeed, as the paintbrush would bump along on the hills and valleys of the textured walls. I tried four different kinds of paintbrushes before I found one that worked just this side of miserably. In several places, I splattered the white ceiling with splotches of blue paint. So I took some white paint that had been left in the basement to cover it up. I didn't realize that I was using gloss paint against a flat white ceiling until the next day, when the paint was dry and shining patches of ceiling beamed out at me like stage lights.

Every ten minutes I would need to run back to Home Depot: I'd run out of masking tape; I'd need a different kind of brush; I'd need a lightbulb for the spotlight that lit my way. I began to hate Home Depot, its magnetic pull, its seemingly inescapable hold on me.

What was worse was that in the process of deciding what colors to paint the rooms, I'd flipped through dozens of decorating books and magazines for ideas. Looking at those beautiful homes in which every item in every room—every piece of furniture, every decoration, every floor and window covering—were perfectly coordinated and stunningly executed was like trying heroin for the first time and becoming instantly addicted. I salivated over the spacious kitchens, the stunning designs, the gorgeous furniture. The internal mantra began: I want, I want, I want.

I decided I simply couldn't tolerate the old carpeting. If I emptied out my savings account, I could get lovely new carpet. And it would help the resale value too, right?

Without hesitation, I eviscerated the remainder of my savings account and ordered the new carpeting.

I thought of several more expensive improvements I could not live without, even though my credit card was getting so much use I was developing ulcers.

I finally had to go cold turkey on the decorating magazines before I ravaged my finances any more. But right now, as I think about my father seeing where I live, I wish I'd done more. In fact, I wish I'd never bought this place to begin with. I hate everything about it.

Will and I pick Dad and his girlfriend Annabella up from the airport. Annabella is a beautiful woman. She's thin and has dark hair and dark eyes, great clothes, and funky jewelry. It looks like Dad's taste in women has improved considerably since Deanne.

Dad and I exchange hugs and great-to-see-yous. He congratulates me once again on my engagement and then says to Will, "So, this is the guy who finally convinced Eva to tie the knot, huh?" He gives Will a big handshake.

We pile into my car. The first thing out of Dad's mouth is this: "Have you *ever* cleaned these windows?"

Immediately, I'm embarrassed by my inadequate car-cleaning skills. I'd tried so hard to get my car into sparkly great shape, but I forgot to clean the inside of the windows and so, of course, that's the first thing Dad notices.

"I guess not." I laugh, but I'm mortified. "So, how was your flight?" (Notice my deft work in changing the subject.)

We make idle chitchat on the drive home. When we get to my place, I give them a tour of the house. They don't say any of the stuff they are supposed to say, like, how cute and homey the place is.

"So, what do you think?" I say, determined to get praise somehow, even if I have to beg for it.

"It's cozy," Dad says.

"Well, yes, I guess with all of Will's things here, we don't have any extra space really," I say.

"I couldn't bear to have all my walls bumpy like this," Dad says, patting a wall. When Dad makes the comment, I want to tear all the walls down and start over. But there's nothing I can do about it now, so instead I just get everyone something to drink and get started on making dinner. I'm making an asparagus and sundried tomato risotto recipe. I tried it out on Will the week before and we determined it was edible, which makes it one of the few dishes I've experimented with that we can say that about. As I chop vegetables and prepare the meal, Dad, Annabella, and Will sit at the kitchen table not ten feet from the counter where I'm working.

"How's work going?" Dad asks me.

"Great. I may get flown out to Germany next month as part of this major consulting project I'm working on for Woodruff Pharmaceuticals. I'll go with an interpreter, naturally."

"Everyone in Germany is miserable. The Germans all have unhappy marriages," Dad says.

I wish I could tell you I was making this up. You'll notice, if you haven't already, that my father makes sweeping generalizations based on no evidence whatsoever. My guess is that he talked to an acquaintance who has one unhappily married friend in Germany, and Dad has extrapolated this and decided it's a fact across an entire culture and country. When Dad talks, you can just hear the gavel coming down and the words "OZ HAS SPOKEN" bellowed in the background.

I used to think my father was omniscient. I thought of him as more or less as a superhero, someone who could protect me from all harm, the real and the imagined.

When he would go away on business trips, leaving me, Mom, and Sienna alone, I couldn't sleep. I was too worried about the burglar-murderers who'd slice my sister, mother, and me to pieces with no problem at all without Dad there to protect us.

Dad unknowingly cultivated my belief that he was omniscient and omnipotent. When I was young, no matter what I asked him, he always had an answer. He spoke with such unwavering authority, such absolute confidence, I really thought he knew everything.

Then one day when I was about seventeen, Dad and I were at McDonald's eating french fries, and Dad said something about how potatoes were a delicacy in Russia, a real treat, and weren't we lucky that McDonald's cranked fried potatoes out by the millions for us here in America?

"Wait a minute," I said. "Dad, I'm pretty sure that potatoes are like one of the main things Russians eat. I mean isn't that what vodka is made of?"

"You know," Dad said, nodding, processing what I'd said with a thoughtful look, "you may be right, I may have gotten that backward."

I sat there in stunned silence. The curtain had been pulled back, the wizard was just an ordinary man, and he was blithely eating french fries as my universe crumbled around me.

Of course, it was just the first of many times that would illustrate that my father was a mere mortal. The desire to believe that my father is omniscient still lingers, though. Even now, everything Dad says he says with such conviction, without the doubt or hesitation or I'm-not-really-sure-but-I-think sort of phrases that permeate my sentences. I still want to believe everything he says, but now I can't, I always have to wonder.

Chapter 18

The visit with my father goes better than expected, and I get through the weekend relatively unscathed. Just the two self-esteem hits about my inadequate car-window cleaning skills and my too-small house with textured walls. Dad and his girlfriend are only here for two days, but it seems like a lifetime. It's just exhausting trying to keep two people entertained twenty-four hours a day.

The good news is that I like Annabella a lot. She's sweet, and kind, and she treats my dad well. The four of us are eating breakfast at a restaurant called Bump & Grind, which has a Petticoat Brunch on weekends. That just means that all the waitstaff are men in drag. It's a fun place, with toys on the table for you to play with while you wait for your meal. There are also funny little hats and headbands that make you look like you have blond braids or springy alien antennae. Dad looks hilarious wearing the blond braids. He never would have put those on when I was a kid. He's mellowed considerably now that he's older. Maybe it's Annabella's doing. She is an amazingly positive, happy woman. She determinedly sees only the bright side of things. She's a jewelry maker, so she's got that artist flaky thing going for her. She's nice and smart in a vacant sort of way. Or maybe Dad's chilled out now that he doesn't have to worry about supporting two daughters anymore. The only duties required of him as a parent are a once yearly visit and the occasional phone call.

It's interesting to watch your parents grow and change. Maybe some people's parents never evolve, but that's not the case with mine. I've watched my parents date, fall in love, fall out of love, and have their hearts broken and their dreams crushed. I've seen the entire evolution of my mother's career from being the low man on the totem pole to having a stressful, powerful position making lots of money. And now I'm witnessing my stressed-out father learning how to enjoy life. I'm jealous. He's learned how to relax and I'm still stuck in basketcase mode.

"Are you two thinking about getting married?" I ask Annabella.

"We're actually talking about moving in together, but I don't want to get remarried," Annabella says.

"Really? Why?"

"There are just too many financial considerations. I've done marriage once. That was enough. But congratulations to you on your engagement."

I laugh. After she's just told me that she no longer believes in marriage, she congratulates me on my engagement. There seems to be a pattern here. "Thanks."

"Have you started planning it?"

I nod. "I've started checking out reception sites.

"Have you picked a date?"

"Nothing official."

"Well, I'm just excited to be able to walk one of my daughters down the aisle at last," Dad says.

"Oh, Dad, you're not going to walk me down the aisle." He looks at me. He's initially taken aback by that announcement, and then he looks hurt. "It's nothing against you or anything, it's just that I want Will and I to walk down the aisle together, hand-in-hand. I don't like that whole 'being given away' concept. I'm not being given away, Will and I are *choosing* to go into this thing together."

Dad smiles the kind of smile that is a mere curvature of the lips and doesn't extend to his face or eyes.

"I suppose you'll want some help paying for the wedding though. The bride's father paying for it—I bet that's a tradition you'll follow."

Ouch. The way he says it has a harsh tone of anger masked beneath the surface. "No, Dad. Actually, Will and I are going to pay for everything ourselves."

Now I've truly stunned him.

"I mean, Dad, if we'd gotten married in our twenties, then yes, we definitely could have used the help, but we're well-established in our careers. We have money in the bank. We'll take care of everything ourselves." I think back to what a struggle it was to get through college when I was so dependent on Dad's checkbook to help me achieve my goal of getting a degree. I never want to feel that dependent on him again.

Dad brightens considerably. "Really? Well, maybe I can pay for the rehearsal dinner or something." Everything is different now that he knows I don't expect his money. Now, he can pay for things not out of duty, but because he wants to.

"If you want to, that would be very kind. We don't have to figure any of this out now."

We stop by my house to pick up their luggage before I take them on to the airport. While Annabella and Will are busy in other rooms, Dad pulls me aside.

"I really like Will," he tells me.

I smile. "Good. Me too."

Chapter 19

After my father leaves, I get started on planning the wedding in full force. I buy a notebook with colored tabs and I begin making lists of everything I need to get done and timelines to do it all in.

I very quickly develop a pattern of working five or six days a week on the project for WP and devoting my Saturdays to getting this wedding planned. On top of all this, I'm also trying to learn how to cook.

Every Saturday morning I'll clean the house, then I'll spend time flipping through cookbooks, plan a week's worth of menus, and then go to the grocery store to buy everything on my list. By the time I get home from the grocery store it's already noon and I'm exhausted and I want to pass out, but instead I drive all over Colorado trying to find a reception hall to host the wedding and reception.

The first place I visit is relatively inexpensive. Not for what we're getting—a place to gather our friends and family for a few hours—but compared to what other reception halls are charging. It's a lodge in the mountains, which seems like it might be a romantic spot to hold a wedding. I drive through teeth-grittingly slow traffic across half of Colorado to get there, and when the person who works there shows me around, it becomes painfully obvious why the price isn't exorbitant—it's essentially a barn with an outhouse. The wood walls are decorated with horseshoes and hunting trophies: A stuffed elk and a bear head look at me woefully as if I personally cut their life short and turned them into decorations. If I held my wedding here, it would turn into some kind of celebration of the West—like my mom's—complete with hoedowns, line dancing, and perhaps a steer or two wrestled into submission for good measure. It wasn't quite the theme I was going for.

Sometimes I drag Will along with me to check out reception sites. He's easygoing and laid-back about it, but I can tell his heart isn't really into it. He wouldn't mind if we held our wedding at a McDonald's parking lot.

I drive Will bonkers deliberating about where I want to have it. On the one hand, I don't want to get sucked into wedding mania and go crazy spending money rather than sticking to a budget. But, of course, the places I love are ludicrously expensive because they have stunning mountain views in great locations. I can't bear the thought of holding our wedding at a place without any personality that performs wedding ceremonies in an assembly-line manner, with just a thin fake wall separating one event from another. A friend of mine had a wedding like that. Just as she and her fiancé were saying their vows, the wedding in the next room over was just kicking up into full swing. I couldn't hear a word the minister or my friend or the groom said. Their vows to spend eternity together were drowned out beneath the booming voices of Kool and The Gang belting out, "Celebrate good times, come on!"

Will and I end up putting a deposit down on a place that is too expensive, but very beautiful. It has a view of the mountains and an outdoor veranda where the guests can go outside, weather permitting. The wedding and reception will be held inside in a grand hall with a winding staircase and sumptuous chandeliers. It's official, we have a wedding date.

One task down. Four million more to go.

Chapter 20

Having goals is the only possible way to be productive when you work as your own boss, particularly on Fridays, when every fiber of my being longs for five o'clock to roll around, so I can turn off my computer and go downtown to drink beer.

Five o'clock finally comes, and I go to Mickie's to wait for everyone to arrive. There is a large crowd of men sitting next to me. I can't help overhearing their conversation. From the context, I gather that the men are all teachers at the local high school.

I take out my notebook that I carry with me everywhere and I jot down a to-do list of things to do this weekend for WP and for the wedding.

"Are you getting this all down?"

"What?" I look up from my notebook.

"It looks like you're taking notes on all that we're saying," one of the men says.

I smile. "Don't worry. You're safe. I'm working on something else entirely."

"No, no, you should get this down. This is a good line: 'They like to rename the wheel before they rebuild the wheel.' Huh? What do you think?"

I'm not actually sure what the hell he's talking about, but I say, "That's a pretty good line."

The men keep talking and laughing and including me in their conversation. I make sure to flash my engagement ring around a lot so they know I'm not available.

I know it's okay to talk with strange men at a bar, but it feels a lot like flirting, and I'm not even attracted to any of these men. I realize suddenly that my flirting days are over. I can't say I'm exactly upset about it. I never much cared for flirting in my single days. I always imagined that one day I'd somehow miraculously become a flirting machine, but it never happened. (Hence the reason I had to meet my husband-to-be over the Internet.) That life I imagined—where I am a sexy, courageous woman who can chat up a roomful of men— is never going to come to pass. That dream is over.

Abby and Jerry are the first ones to arrive and we stake out a table for six. Abby and Jerry, like many of our friends, have been together for years and have never gotten married. Abby would like to get married, but she's not dying to. She, just like me, is unsure about whether to have kids, and without kids in the picture, she's all right with doing the living-together thing without a ring on her finger.

Richard and James arrive a few minutes later, and Will arrives seconds after them. Richard is tall with dark hair and glasses. Abby and Jerry are both petite and thin; Abby is Korean with thick, long straight hair and Jerry has a thick swirl of dark curls kept under control by frequent haircuts. James has the thick neck and crushingly broad chest of a defensive lineman and the blond hair and blue eyes of an angelic-looking choirboy.

After everyone says their hellos and we have a very "Cheers" moment—being at a place where everybody knows our name—I ask Richard if he ever went on that date with the sister-in-law of his coworker.

"It was all set up for last Saturday," he says. "We'd talked on the phone a few times. We were going to meet at Marlowe's downtown. I went there and I waited outside for about fifteen minutes, and then I went inside and nursed a drink for twenty minutes. I called her on my cell phone, but there was no answer. Twenty-five more minutes went by. I called her again. No answer. I left another message, this time saying that I was leaving."

"Are you sure you didn't miss her? How were you supposed to recognize her?" I ask.

"My coworker, Mary, the one who set us up, she'd given me a picture of Brenda, that's how I knew what she'd look like. I didn't hear a word from her all day Sunday. I didn't know if she somehow got a glimpse of me and decided I was hideous and snuck away before we could meet, or if she chickened out. I don't know what happened. So I went into work Monday morning and Mary came up to me first thing looking all apologetic. She said, 'I'm so sorry Brenda wasn't able to make it.' I said, 'What happened? It would have been nice if she could have called me to tell me she couldn't make it.' Mary said, 'She only had one phone call, and she used that to call her lawyer, because she was *arrested and sent to prison*.'"

Richard can make a facial expression of the hapless, put-upon sap like nobody I know, and between his story and his beleaguered appearance, we all hoot with laughter, a pound-the-fist-on-the-table laugh riot.

"So that really didn't turn out as well as I'd hoped," he says when the laughter dies down.

"Poor Richard," I say. "What are we going to do with you?"

"I don't know."

"What happened with your last girlfriend? Why didn't that work out?"

"It was a long-distance thing. We met at a wedding. She lived in D.C. working as a lobbyist; I live here. It was fun for awhile, but it's hard. You visit each other on the weekends, and you feel like every single second has to be fun and sexy and exciting. It's not real life. But the main thing was that she wasn't going to leave D.C. and I wasn't going to move to D.C., so there was no way it could work out."

"Do you want to get married some day?" I ask him. One of Will's friends had been so soured on the idea of commitment after his divorce that he told me he didn't believe in sticking around in a relationship for more than three or four months. Then, seconds after he told me that, he asked me if I had any single friends I could set him up with. I told him the truth: For you buddy, I don't think so.

Richard nods. "Sure. Some day."

I nod my approval. I know some women over thirty think there aren't any more good men out there, but the world is full of guys like Richard. Guys are out there, they're just not out at bars hitting on women. Instead, they're at home playing computer games, like Everquest and Dungeon Siege, and hence you have no way to find them.

James, Jerry, Will, and Richard have worked in the computer industry for the last ten years. The programming community is small enough in Denver that they have all worked together at one point or another. When Will first got out of college, he worked at a company with James. At his next job, he worked with Richard. Then Richard left that company and took a job working alongside James and Jerry. You get the idea.

Computer games, current events, movies, and politics make up the bulk of our happy hour conversation. We always laugh a lot when we're together, mostly because the guys tease each other relentlessly. They'll give Will a hard time about his increasingly bald head or James a dig about his weight or torment Jerry about being "a cheap Scottish bastard" or taunt Richard about his lack of a girlfriend. If someone teased me about my appearance, weight, character flaw, or pathetic love life, I'd burst into tears and hide under the covers for a week. But when guys do it to each other, it's gut-bustingly hilarious.

"My brother is having a white trash party in a couple weeks," Richard says. "Maybe I'll meet someone there."

"A white trash party?" Will asks.

"You have to dress up in your finest trailer trash garb, and you'll be expected to eat hot dogs and potato chips, that kind of thing."

"Sounds great."

Will and I get our email invite to the trailer trash bar-beque the next day. Moments after I mull over the email, which instructs us that we have to dress up, the phone rings. It's Gabrielle.

"Hey, Gabrielle, what's up?"

"Nothing. Is something wrong? You sound distracted."

"No, sorry, I was just reading email. Sorry. Will and I just got invited to a white trash barbeque."

"What's that?"

"I'm not really sure. I just know we have to dress up and bring food like Cheez Whiz and crackers or Jell-O or franks and beans, that sort of thing."

"Who's hosting the party?"

"Friends of Will's. He's got a group of married friends that I never see because they're too busy being married and rais-ing kids and living far, far away in the suburbs. Apparently, they like to throw theme parties."

"You're not really going to go to this party, are you?"

"Um, I think so. Why?"

"Don't you realize how classist that is? You wouldn't go to a party that made fun of black people, would you?"

"Of course not."

"Don't you see how working class white people are the last group it's socially acceptable to mock? You wouldn't engage in racist or sexist behavior, but this kind of classism is okay?"

"Ah . . . I see what you're saying. Let me ask you this: Would you have a problem with us dressing up like rich peo-ple and pretending we liked opera and caviar?"

"That's different. There's a striking power differential with the upper class . . ."

Gabrielle and I argue about this for awhile longer. "Argue" isn't really the right word. "Discuss" is more like it. I like Gabrielle for just this reason. When I talk to her it's like being an undergraduate student again—I question things I normally wouldn't think twice about.

Gabrielle talks about stereotyping and prejudice and fear of the "other," whatever that is. I see Gabrielle's point, but I think it sounds kind of fun to drink cheap beer and eat crackers with Cheez Whiz. Anyway, I want to meet these friends of Will's. I don't want to refuse to go to the party for political reasons and have them decide I'm a politically correct lunatic before we even meet. I have to pick my battles, and I just don't think this is going to be one of them. I end our conversation by agreeing to disagree with her and then asking what's new with her.

"I've got a date," she announces.

"That's great. With a guy you met online?"

"With a woman."

"Um, excuse me, what?"

"With a woman. Her name is Cara. I met her through Bev. Bev is that really cute bisexual meat-eater who thinks she is a lesbian vegetarian who sometimes slips up. She has blue eyes and short black hair?"

"Yeah, I remember Bev. What I'm stuck on here is the part about you going out on a date with woman. A date-date?"

"A date-date. I believe that sexuality is artificially constructed by society, you know that."

"But you've just happened artificially to choose men as your sex partners up until now?"

"I was married for seven years, dating women wasn't an option. Anyway, so I met Bev and her girlfriend, Ashley, for lunch last week, and they brought along Cara and right away I was attracted to her and I thought, why not? Later I called Bev to find out the story with Cara, whether she was dating anybody, whether she might be interested in me, you know. So Bev set up a sort of group date for us Saturday night, and I want you to go. Just you. No boys allowed."

"Why me?"

"It's my first date. I'll just feel better if you're there."

"Ah, okay, I guess I could come."

"You're the best. Thank you."

That afternoon Will gets home from playing basketball with Richard, James, and Jerry. His skin is still damp to the touch, but his sweat has mostly dried.

He leans in to give me a kiss, and the visor of his baseball cap hits my forehead, keeping our lips several inches apart. He smiles and lifts his cap and readjusts it so it's on backward, and there is something so boyish and cute and sexy about that simple move, with his forearms flexing ever so slightly, and it reminds me that even when I want to plonk him on the head, I'm still hopelessly attracted to him. We kiss, and the kiss leads to groping, and the groping leads me to take him by the hand up to the bedroom, where we make love, slowly.

Afterward, our naked bodies lying entwined, I tell him about how Gabrielle has a date with a woman and I'm going with her.

"Huh," he says.

"Would you ever want to have sex with me and another woman at the same time?"

"No, of course not."

I smile. I love this man so much, even if he is a complete and utter liar.

I used to go to gay bars a lot in college, mostly because they had better music than most of the straight bars. But it's been awhile since I've been to one, and as Saturday dawns, I'm feeling apprehensive about fitting in.

Thus begins Operation-Pass-for-a-Dyke. This involves going sans makeup, of course, and wearing copious amounts of flannel, obviously. I pull my curly hair back into a loose ponytail and inspect my visage. Verdict: I'll never pass. They are going to know.

Gabrielle picks me up and we drive down to the bar.

"Do I know any of these women?" I ask.

I've met many of her lesbian friends at various parties she's held over the years, mostly women from her sociology program.

"Yeah. There's Susan, that cute Latina."

"Was she the one that was in the total standard, cliché lesbian attire, the Doc Martens, the bad attitude?"

"Yeah, but she can surprise you. When she takes those combat boots off, her toes are painted bright red or orange."

"No way."

"Way. I completely love that about her. Then there's Ashley."

"I remember Ashley." Ashley had bleached white hair with two-inch black roots. She worked at a coffee shop and reveled in her poverty. She was always talking about being a member of the working poor. She still hadn't gotten over Ani DiFranco getting a boyfriend.

When we got to the club, Susan, Bev, Ashley, and Cara are already there.

"I need something to eat. Where's the waitress? I'm famished," Susan says.

"I can't believe this drink cost five dollars. That's sinful," Ashley says. "Three dollar cover, five dollar drinks. This place is exploitive. I mean, really."

"Did I tell you guys I bumped into my ex-girlfriend Gina last week?" Bev says.

"You didn't tell me," Cara says.

"Ooh, Gi-naaa," says Susan.

"Who's Gina?" Ashley asks.

I keep alternating my gaze from Cara to Gabrielle, trying to see if I can discern any chemistry between them. Nothing seems obvious to me, but then, the entire situation feels surreal.

"Gina is this woman that I was madly in love with in college. She's the sexiest woman on the planet, no question. I was just crazy about her. So was every other lesbian in New England."

"Bitter, party of one," Susan says.

"I'm not bitter. So here's the deal, I was at lunch last week with some clients, and I see her there. Even though I'm totally over her," she gives Susan a look, "she's still a babe. I excuse myself from the table and walk up to her. She tells me she's living in New York now. She didn't know I was living in Denver. I tell her I'm a graphic designer, and she tells me that she's still doing the photography thing, but now she's also modeling. Turns out she's in town promoting the 'Women Only' calendar."

"Oooh sheeet." Susan chuckles.

"'Women Only'?" I say.

"It's a lesbian porn calendar," Ashley says. "*Très* scandalous."

"Oh."

"We had a nice conversation. Unfortunately, she was only in town for that one day, but we promised to keep in touch. I was in a rush because my clients were waiting, so I just gave her my business card. I don't know if you've ever bumped into the lust of your life, but let me tell you, it messes you up. I returned to my clients a totally dysfunctional, babbling idiot. I mean she's in town one day and we just happen to go to lunch at the same place? That's crazy."

"That is so bizarre. Fate," Ashley says.

"I haven't even gotten to the best part. So yesterday, I get the calendar in the mail, at my office."

"Whoa," says Susan.

"So, I get my mail, I sit down at my desk by the door, and open this calendar, my heart leaps, my jaw drops, the works."

"That calendar is fucking hot. Which one's the famed Gina?" says Susan.

"She's March. She has dark, olive skin and dark hair that goes like this," Bev takes her finger to indicate bangs that fall across one eye. "In the picture she's topless and her eyes are closed and these thin pale arms reach from behind her and undo her jeans."

"Yum. I love that picture," Susan says.

"Any you don't like?" Bev asks.

"No. You're right, I like them all."

"I have the calendar open to Gina when my phone rings, and the phone is way on the other side of the room. I have a pretty big office because I have drawing tables and a lot of computer equipment. I have this chair with wheels, so I fly across the room and answer the phone. I get all into this conversation with a client, yada yada yada . . . I'm jotting down some notes, writing down what my client is saying, I've totally forgotten about the calendar, when my very conservative manager walks in. I wave him in, smile, gesture to let him know I'll be done in a minute, then I go back to what I was doing. I'm still on the phone when I notice he's checking out the calendar. Now, I'm not closeted at work exactly, but I'm not out either, and this is one of those guys who can really break my career. I scream into the phone, 'Doug, I'll call you back!' I slam the phone down, zoom across the floor in my chair, and come barreling into my desk, I just crash into it, I start babbling, trying to explain . . ."

"You, Ms. Calm and Collected?" Cara says.

"Yeah, well first, it is totally unprofessional to have porn at the workplace, unless you work at an automotive garage or something. Second, I really hadn't wanted to out myself in this manner. So anyway, I'm trying to explain that an old friend of mine is in the calendar and she sent me a copy, which is why I have it at the office; I just opened it a second ago. I hold up the envelope as if that's the proof I need to get me off the hook. I'm brandishing this envelope like a 'Get out of jail' card, like it's my key to freedom or something. He says, 'Are these lesbians?' I'm like, 'Ah, yeah.' He just kind of nods, all casual. Then he asks about how Ashley and I are doing, do I think it could lead to wedding bells. Under my breath I say, yeah, if it were legally recognized. I have no idea what he's talking about. I'm so confused because I figured I've been outed for sure. Not only had I been gawking at naked women, I had been gawking at naked lesbians. Then he says something referring to Ashley and uses 'he.' He thinks I'm straight. Despite the considerable evidence at hand, nothing can dissuade him from the idea that I'm straight."

The waitress stops by as we're all laughing. "What's so funny, girls?"

"My boss," says Bev. "He's a wee bit dense about certain things."

"How are you all doing on drinks?"

Bev nods and indicates that we are ready for another round. When the waitress turns to get our drinks, Bev finishes her story. "Just as my boss is about to leave my office he says, 'I think it's great that you're friends with a lesbian. That's so like you to embrace diversity like that.' I say, 'Well, you have to keep your mind open to all the possibilities.' My voice is dripping with irony, let me assure you. I mean what the hell do I have to do to let people know I'm a dyke? I could be eating Ashley out on my desk and they'd be like, oh Bev, you are just so sweet to lesbians, you're such a humanitarian. I mean, how much more evidence do you need? I'm looking at lesbians fucking each other. Clueless."

They keep me laughing the whole night. At one point Gabrielle and Cara go off on their own to the dance floor. They dance a number of slow dances, so I take it that things are going well.

I have fun talking with the other women and after I've had enough drinks they even manage to get me out on the dance floor with them. When a slow song comes on, I want to hide my engagement ring to see if any women will ask me to dance (just out of curiosity's sake, of course), but ultimately I chicken out.

I've completely lost track of time when suddenly we're being urged out of the place by the waitstaff.

"We shut the place down?" I say drunkenly. "I haven't stayed 'til a bar closed in years."

"It's a new, more exciting era in our lives, Eva," Gabrielle says.

As she drives me home, I grill her about Cara. "Do you like her? Do you want to sleep with her? Do you think this might get serious?"

Her answers are yes, yes, and maybe, respectively.

I keep rambling on until we get to my place.

I simply can't wait to hear the details from the rest of her night.

Chapter 21

Email and the telephone are simultaneously the greatest friends and worst enemies of the independent contractor who works from home. All day I check my email approximately a jillion times, awaiting news on how the rest of Gabrielle's date turned out.

To: gabileveska@hotmail.com
From: eva@lockhartconsulting.com

So?!?

To: eva@lockhartconsulting.com
From: gabileveska@hotmail.com

So, we have a date to go out to a comedy club tomorrow night, just the two of us.

To: gabileveska@hotmail.com
From: eva@lockhartconsulting.com

Did you kiss, have sex, anything?

To: eva@lockhartconsulting.com
From: gabileveska@hotmail.com

A girl never tells.

To: gabileveska@hotmail.com
From: eva@lockhartconsulting.com

Don't you dare pull that shit with me. I want details.

To: eva@lockhartconsulting.com
From: gabileveska@hotmail.com

I'm joking with you. There are no details to tell. A
chaste kiss. *C'est tout.*

Chapter 22

After three months on the market, Will finally sells his house, which is a huge relief because now he can help me with the mortgage payments on my place. I mean *our* place.

I spend my entire Saturday doing research on caterers and wedding menus. I didn't sleep well the night before and I'm beat. The work is utterly exhausting. I think back to Mom's suggestion that we just fly to Bermuda to get married. Suddenly that seems like a really good plan, and I toss the idea out to Will.

"Will, what would you think about eloping in the Bahamas? We could invite our closest friends and family to see us get married. They could have a mini-vacation and seconds after we exchanged vows we could get started on our honeymoon."

"I'd love to, hon, but how important is it that my mother sees our wedding?"

"What kind of crazy question is that? It's critically important. She's like the third or fourth most important person, right after you and me."

"Well, then, I'm afraid the Bahamas are out. My mother doesn't fly."

"What? Never? Can't we just knock her out with some kind of drug and drag her on the plane with us?"

"She's never flown in her life. I don't think she's going to start now. We can go to Vegas. That's within driving distance."

"You know I hate Vegas." I took one weekend trip to Vegas. I enjoyed the first day of checking out the kitschyness of it all, but since I'm not much for gambling, the last two days of the trip were an exercise in surviving the torture of excess and ringing bells and twinkling lights. I vowed I would never set foot in Vegas again, much less get married there.

"We can just go to the courthouse or something," he says.

"Did you have a big wedding when you got married the first time?"

"We eloped."

"At the courthouse?"

"In Vegas."

"So you thought you could do the exact same thing with me? Just another bride on the assembly line?" Is it wrong of me to want to kill him right now? Is my irritation with him reasonable or a product of my lack of sleep? I'm not sure, but I scowl at him anyway. How else will he learn how not to piss me off, right?

"No, Eva, I was just throwing out some ideas."

I can't believe he'd take me to Vegas like he did with his last wife. Now I really have to throw the wedding of the century, God damn it. I'm not really a superstitious person, but if he went to Vegas the first time and that wedding failed (how many Vegas marriages last for more than a few years, that's what I want to know?), then we have to get married in the opposite sort of ceremony to placate the capricious gods of fate.

"Come on, Will, let's go taste wedding cake." I sigh. I'm still irritated with him, but I still want to marry him anyway.

"Wedding cake?"

"Yeah. I asked Mom where she got her wedding cake for her wedding to Frank, and she told me about this pastry shop in Arvada. They give free tastings on Saturdays."

"Free cake? I'm there!"

Deciding on a wedding cake is probably the least pressing thing on our to-do list, but it sounds like the most fun, so I've moved it up on the priority list. I've printed a map from MapQuest on how to get to the pastry shop. Will and I get into Will's car and begin the journey to the suburbs.

It will never cease to amaze me just how long it can take to get from some place in the city to some place in the suburbs. On a map, it doesn't look that far away, but then you start driving down the endless streets and getting stopped at stoplight after stoplight, and you may as well take a detour on foot through the Serengeti to get there, because it would take just as long.

As we drive, a wave of exhaustion nearly knocks me flat. Coffee, I need coffee. I look around hopefully for a coffee shop, but I don't see a thing. Starbucks are located every four feet in most places, until you really need one.

"Where do I turn next?" Will asks.

I read from the directions I printed out from MapQuest.

"That's like seventy blocks away. Are you sure that's right?"

"That's what it says. Hey, why does that street sign say fifty-fifth? We were supposed to turn on sixty-fourth."

Will turns around at the next light. In addition to being tired, I realize I'm dying of thirst. *When are we going to get to the stupid cake shop? I need coffee. I need water. My needs aren't being met. Wah!*

Will and I drive in circles for fifteen minutes before it occurs to me to call the cake shop and get directions from them. I hand the phone to Will since he's driving.

"Yeah, I know where that is. Okay, thanks," Will says, then hangs up the cell phone. He turns around once again. "We were going in the completely opposite direction. It's a good thing we called. I don't know where MapQuest was taking us, but it wasn't to the cake shop. It's like they left out a major street for us to turn at."

I look at the MapQuest directions again and realize that

MapQuest didn't leave a street out, my tired eyes simply skipped from one step to another without even noticing. I decide not to tell Will this. I'm going to let MapQuest take the blame for this one.

When we get to the cake shop, a friendly young girl points to a list of cake options and tells us we can choose to taste as many samples as we'd like. We choose several and she cuts us thin slices of each, then we sit down at a table, and she brings us coffee and water. I'm so happy to be able to quench my thirst and drink coffee and eat cake that my irritation quickly evaporates and I decide wedding planning is pretty fun after all.

The tiny cake shop is simply hopping with young couples. Will and I flip through photo albums of cake ideas and we walk around the shop looking at sample wedding cakes. There are a couple really cool ones, like one three-tiered cake decorated with a marine theme. Each tier is separated by a glass fish bowl, and within the fishbowl are fake seashells and starfish and plants. It's not the right look for our wedding, but it's fun and different nonetheless.

"I like the more colorful designs as opposed to plain white," I say to Will.

"Cool," he says. "That's fine with me."

"Maybe we could get the fondant frosting in a deep pink color with red ribbons and flowers or something."

"Sure. Whatever."

"What flavored cake do you like? We need to pick three, one for each tier. I definitely like the chocolate lovers."

"Me too."

"I also think we should get a plain vanilla cake, maybe with fresh strawberries in the center."

"Sounds good."

It occurs to me that I asked him for his opinion and then went on to not listen to his opinion but to impose my own. I need to stop being a dictator about this. This is Will's wedding, too, after all. "How about for the last cake? You pick the flavor."

"I like the orange blossom."

Ick. "Um, but that's a dark orange color. That won't go with red and pink frosting."

"Sure it will."

"No. No, it won't."

"Nobody will see the cake anyway."

"As soon as it's cut open they will."

"It'll be fine."

Compromise. That's what partnership is. So I smile. "Okay. You're right. That's fine."

Why on earth did I ask Will's opinion? Men don't know anything about weddings or tasteful elegance. Note to self: Only *pretend* to solicit Will's opinion in the future. Orange wedding cake. I mean really.

Chapter 23

It's going to take several months for the accountants to do the due diligence work necessary to purchase Ridan. Still, I'm frantically planning marketing strategy and drafting a communications plan, both to communicate the purchase internally and to the public.

At a meeting with Kyle and other executives, Kyle tells me that I have to tell the regional directors around the country the news of this acquisition forcefully.

"We want to make sure everyone is on board with this change in focus," he says. "I don't want any dissension. We have to go in and set the mandate that this is the priority. If they had different sales and marketing goals, well, they are going to have to push those aside and revamp their plans. We have to go in and vehemently state that Exploran takes precedence over everything else. We can't be wishy-washy about this."

"Kyle, I absolutely see what you're saying," I say, choosing my words carefully. When you encounter a wild animal, you need to show no fear and proceed cautiously. That's the tactic I'm taking here. "Let me just throw out this idea, and you let me know what you think. The deadline you've set on sales goals for Exploran is very aggressive, as you know. I think that before we go into the branch offices and dictate the change in focus, what might be helpful would be to get buy-in from our regional directors. What I'm saying is, that our approach could be simply to let them know what an exciting opportunity this is, and how much potential there is for everyone to make money. I think if we went in there and set this down as a mandate from above, there might be some initial resistance. But if we point out what a great opportunity this is, they'll see that this change is to their benefit."

Kyle's brow furrows and his lips purse. My heart stops for a few moments as I wait for him to bite my head off, fire me, or some combination of the above. Instead, he takes a deep breath. "I see what you're saying. What are you thinking exactly?"

Oh, thank God. I exhale and go on to tell him my plans. It seems to me that Kyle is genuinely grateful to get some management advice, no matter what the source. He wouldn't thank me directly, but I can see the relief in his expression.

I routinely put in twelve-hour days working for WP. I'll work from seven in the morning till six at night, then I'll take a break to make dinner, then I'll go back to work for a few hours. While I'm killing myself, Will watches football or plays computer games or plays around on his guitar. It's not his fault that the WP project is really too big for me to handle on my own, but I can't help envy his leisure time. I can't wait until I'm done with this contract. After WP, I'm going to do a better job picking projects with reasonable timelines, so I don't have to bust my ass to meet the deadlines. I'm so jealous that for Will, after he's put in an eight-hour work day, that's it; his time is his own to relax and do with it what he wants. Plus, he gets two full days off every weekend, while I'm working my tail off to plan a wedding. And yet I'm still the one cooking dinner every night and doing the bulk of the housework.

If I ask Will to do the dishes or the laundry, he'll do them without complaining, but he never, not once, has gone and done a domestic chore on his own volition. One important lesson I have learned in this life is this: Boyfriends and husbands need to be strictly project-managed when it comes to household tasks.

On Saturday morning, I want desperately to spend the day at a spa doing nothing but getting massages and facials and sitting in a hot tub whiling the hours away in leisure. But that fantasy is not to be had. Today I have meetings with two caterers to try to plan a menu.

Before I have to go meet with caterers, I try to clean up around the house. I have very low standards when it comes to housecleaning. Even so, it boggles my mind how much time it takes to maintain even a low standard of cleanliness.

As I scrub the toilet, I call Gabrielle on my cell phone. I always have to be doing eighty thousand things at once. I don't even know how to live another way anymore.

"How are things going with Cara?" I ask.

"I don't know. We slept together."

"Holy shit!" I drop the toilet brush. This new development is worthy of my full attention. "How was it?"

"It was good. It was soft and slow and sensual. But I think I'm going to break up with her."

"Why?

"It's her friends I can't bear. They all smell like patchouli and smoke pot all the time. Is this the price of lesbianism? Having to fraternize with patchouli-smelling pot-smokers?"

"I'm sure there are non-patchouli-smelling lesbians in the world."

"Maybe. I can't seem to find one. I can't seem to find anyone who fits quite right."

"You'll find somebody."

"I know. I'm not going to give up or anything. But I foresee a hell of a lot of miserable dates in my future."

"But eventually you'll get lucky."

"Yeah. I know. I've decided something."

"What?"

"I'm going back to working on my dissertation. I figure since my social life is in the toilet, I may as well spend my evenings and weekends working on something worthwhile. It's been my goal forever to be a professor."

"Of course. Why else would you spend ten years in college? I'm happy for you. That's really great. How long do you think it'll take?"

"I think if I work really hard, I can get far in the next nine months. Then I was thinking I'd take three months off of work to focus on finishing it up and get ready for my defense. I'd already written big sections of the dissertation before I quit school, so I just need to finish writing it."

"Gabrielle, I think that's wonderful. Good for you. Look, I should get going. I have to go interview caterers."

"You don't sound exited."

I worry about that myself. I fear I'm not bridal or blushing enough. I'm finding this whole planning a wedding thing to be more work than fun. "Actually, interviewing caterers isn't that bad. I get to eat a lot of free food. Honestly, you could save a ton of money on food by just pretending you're having a wedding and letting them feed you."

"That's a good idea. I will be an impoverished grad student again soon, so that could really come in handy."

"Glad to help, babe."

That night, Will and I drive to the Denver Tech Center area, where Richard's brother lives. Richard's brother and his wife are hosting the white trash party. Will went to Kmart and bought a black Metallica T-shirt and a Nascar baseball cap and flip-flops for his costume. I tease my hair and put on excessive amounts of makeup and wear overalls with one of the straps undone over a white T-shirt.

I don't know most of the people at the party. Really, I don't know anyone except Richard. The women are all in the kitchen, and the men are all outside drinking cheap beer and pretending they're not middle-class yuppies. The music being blared, Will informs me, is Iron Maiden. The music makes my ears bleed.

I attempt to befriend the women. I go into the kitchen to get a beer and approach the table where they're talking only to discover their conversation is about training for marathons. One woman is talking about how she trained for running a race up a mountain *while she was pregnant*, and how she continued racing while she was breast-feeding. I sit around the table drinking my beer, quite certain I have nothing to add to the conversation, although if anyone asked me what I thought of training for a marathon, I would say, "You're trying to train yourself to run for several hours *in a row*? Are you mad?" But this is Colorado. Any party you go to in Colorado, you'll be able to find somebody who's in training for a marathon. Coloradoans are a sick people as a rule.

At some point, the conversation on marathons stalls, and one of the women asks me which guy is mine. I turn to point him out through the kitchen window, and that's when I find Will, in his Metallica T-shirt and Nascar baseball cap, playing air guitar to Iron Maiden.

"He's mine," I say humbly.

There comes a time in every relationship when you find your man doing something—say, for example, playing air guitar to Iron Maiden—and you think to yourself, just who the fuck *is* this man I'm thinking of marrying?

The women all offer expressions that I think are supposed to mean, "Oh, how lucky you are" when in fact what they mean is, "We're so sorry."

A little about me: I'm of the opinion that there is simply no situation that warrants playing air guitar to Iron Maiden, white trash party or no white trash party. Let me repeat: No situation.

I smile stupidly and bid a hasty retreat outside where all the guys are. I tell Will about how I pointed him out at the exact moment he chose to play air guitar to Iron Maiden. He looks suitably chagrined.

I stand around outside drinking beer with the men for the rest of the night because at least I have things in common with Will and Richard.

"So, Richard, no luck with the single ladies tonight, huh?" I say.

"They're all married. Just my luck. I did go on another blind date, though."

"That's great! How did you meet?"

"She plays online games. When you play online, as you go along, you can instant message the other players, and so we flirted via email, and then decided to get together in person. I wanted to make it just a really quick lunch because I've been really busy lately. So we meet, and she's attractive, so I'm thinking, 'Okay, this is promising.' And then she starts to talk about her evil ex-husband and her teenage daughter who is addicted to drugs and the child-support battles she's waging with her ex and how much debt she's in. She didn't stop complaining for three hours straight. When it was over I wanted to charge her for the therapy session."

I snigger. "Poor Richard." But secretly I sort of enjoy hearing the dating traumas of my friends. It makes me feel even more grateful for having met Will.

Chapter 24

"**H**ey, stranger," Rachel says.

"Hey," I say into my cell phone. I'm on my way to the grocery store, stopped at a red light.

"Have you fallen off the face of the earth? You never come by the store anymore."

"I know. I'm sorry. I'm a terrible friend. Between planning the wedding and working on this consulting project, I don't have time to eat or sleep."

"Come over this afternoon. Please?"

"I really need to look at wedding dresses today. I just cannot find a dress that I like. I swear I think I've tried on every dress in the Denver/Boulder area, and I just don't like any of them."

"You just don't like how you look in them or how the dresses themselves look?"

"A little of both, I guess. I'm sort of thinking I want a really untraditional dress. Something very not-bridal. Like a red dress."

"Red? That is unusual. Why red?"

"I don't know. The thing is, I'd always vowed I'd have a nontraditional wedding. Something unique and not like those boring cookie-cutter weddings I've gone to all my life. And so far, the only unusual thing I'm doing is walking down the aisle hand-in-hand with Will instead of being given away by Dad, and even that isn't that unusual. I know lots of brides who go down the aisle with their mom *and* dad or whatever. I vowed I wouldn't spend too much money, and then the next thing you know, I see this beautiful, overpriced reception hall, and I fork over a chunk of my money to these people as fast as I possibly can. And I hate how everyone is trying to screw me over, you know? Like the way bridal shops charge such ridiculous amounts of money for a dress just because it's white and called a bridal gown, and then they have the audacity to purposely make sure it won't fit you so you have to spend another two hundred bucks to have the damn thing altered. So I feel like I have to rebel in some way, hence I'm open to dresses of any hue. Anyway, even though I hate it all, I need a dress. I don't think it would be good to walk down the aisle naked."

"That would be different. It would be very nontraditional."

"True. But I'm afraid it wouldn't quite set the reverential, serious tone I'm going for. Ugh, I don't want to think about wedding plans. You know what, I *will* come over this afternoon. I'll look for some dresses and then I'll come by."

"Awesome. Come over around one, okay?"

"See you then."

I pull into the grocery store parking lot, throw my cell phone into my purse, and walk through the lot to the door. As I walk, I realize just how completely exhausted I am.

I haven't been sleeping well lately. I've always had trouble sleeping because I'm a worrier, and between the wedding and work, my anxiety is through the roof.

As I approach the store, a mob of boys dressed in baseball uniforms descend on me like a pack of wolves bearing chocolate bars. They plead with me to help support their baseball team. Every time I come to the grocery store, there are throngs of schoolchildren trying to get me to buy something. When did the entrances to grocery stores become *the* place to attack strangers to buy overpriced candy in the guise of charity? (Well, besides the office place in corporate America where I was always getting hit up for money by parents working as mobsters for the Boy and Girl Scout Cookie and Popcorn Mafias.) I know that my irritation is overblown. All I have to do is smile and say, "No thanks," but today, it just grates on my nerves. Or maybe I was already irritated and this just gives me something to focus my irritation on.

I buy just a few things and go to pay at the self-checkout line. It seems like everyone in front of me has decided to pay with check or cash, and I have to say, I just don't get this at all. You can pay with a credit card in ten seconds. Cash or check seems to take eons by comparison. Don't these people know about cash-back rewards and mileage points? I guess there are people who can't seem to pay off their credit cards every month, and so they have to avoid using their cards. But can't these people go to the regular "Ten Items or Less" line and get the hell out of my way? Debit cards anyone? I watch a middle-aged woman write out a check as minutes of my life pass by in staggering, obstinate slowness. And that's all it is—a few extra minutes—but I'm so impatient I could explode. There are so many ways I could be spending this time in more profitable pursuits.

I think I get my inability to be idle from my father. When my parents were separated and then divorced, Dad would see Sienna and me every other weekend. We'd do stuff like go to the art or history museum or drive to one of the forest preserves in Illinois to hike or go to the Chicago River and canoe. For the entire drive to whatever the event of the day was, Dad would test Sienna and me on things like the state capitals. It would be something of a contest between my sister and me to see who could shout out "Concord!" fastest after Dad said, "New Hampshire!" Then when we would hike through the woods, Dad would point out various plants, trees, and shrubs, giving us their Latin names and a little trivia about how we could identify them in the future, like by the color or shape of the leaves. Or as we strolled through the science museum, he would ask us questions about the exhibits we were reading about to ensure we were truly absorbing all there was to learn. We had to be learning and improving our minds at all times. His dedication to our education worked—Sienna grew up to graduate summa cum laude and I got my MBA—but there are times, like now, when I just wish I had an easier time relaxing. I wish I didn't constantly feel the need to be productive. I wish I could wait five extra minutes in a grocery store line while the slowest employee on the face of the earth called for a price check and not want to spontaneously combust.

After I get home and put the groceries away, I go to a bridal shop downtown and try dresses on with maniacal determination. I need to get this task out of the way. I have so many other things to do. But it's no good, I just don't feel right about anything I try on.

I somehow get stuck at the bridal store until nearly two o'clock, and then it takes me a half hour to drive over to Rachel's.

Rachel only has two children, but when I get there, it seems like there are about forty kids running around because the place is so loud and chaotic. I do a quick head count. Not forty. Four. Rachel's kids and two neighbor kids.

"I'm so sorry I'm late, I got stuck trying on dresses."

"Any luck?"

"No. None. Is this a bad time?" I ask. "I'm sorry. Maybe we should reschedule."

"No, now's fine. I have to get the kids ready to go to piano practice, but we don't have to be there for half an hour. Julia, come here. Let's get your shoes on."

Her three year old hands her two tiny gym shoes and climbs up onto her lap.

"Is that a new outfit?" I ask Rachel. She looks adorable today, as always. She knows how to fill out a pair of jeans like nobody I know. I could spend the rest of my life searching and I would never be able to find a pair of jeans that fit that well. On me, jeans are always just a little too saggy in the butt or else they are so tight in the butt my underwear lines play a starring role in my ensemble. She's wearing a sleeveless top in retro black-and-white stripes. There is a silver hoop above her cleavage and it's from there that straps hook the front of her top to the back of her top. I will always be jealous of the ways thin, flat-chested women can get away with looks that women who need to wear bras could simply never pull off.

"It's a new design of mine," she says. "Do you like it?"

"Very sexy, very stylish. It's a great look."

"Thanks. What's going on with you?" Rachel asks me as she begins prying Julia's foot into one of the shoes.

"Nothing much. What are you up to?"

"Well," she says quietly, a conspiratorial smile on her face, "Shane and I have been emailing back and forth. Harmless flirtation you know, but it's been fun."

Julia has wriggled her way down so she's lying on her back on Rachel's thighs. Julia kicks and flails her legs every which way. Rachel seems not to notice or care and just goes about the business of putting her daughter's shoes on, even when Julia has slid backward down her legs so Julia is upside down with her head on the floor. Mother and daughter look like World Wrestling contestants.

"Rachel, are you sure that's such a good idea?"

"It's fine. I've got everything under control. Anyway, it's really mostly all business. He's been giving me some ideas on how I can improve operations at my shop."

"If you need a business consultant, that happens to be what I do for a living."

"Nothing's going to happen. Don't worry."

But I do.

I hear the door open. It's Sandy, who's used her key to come in instead of knocking. Rachel gives me a pointed look that says, "Do you see? Do you see what I have to put up with?"

"Hey, Sandy," I say.

"Hi, Eva. How's it going?"

Sandy has always had a sad, wounded look. She's frighteningly skinny and her skin is so pale it seems translucent.

"I've got to take Jim and Becky home," Rachel says, referring to the neighbor kids, having successfully wrestled her daughter's feet into a pair of shoes. "I'll be right back."

I nod at Rachel, and then to Sandy I say, "Things are good. I got engaged."

"Let me see the ring."

I extend my hand.

"Wow, it's beautiful."

"Thank you. I think so, too. Life has just been really busy. I'm busy with work and trying to plan a wedding. I'm trying to learn how to cook. There aren't enough hours in the day, you know?"

"Yeah. I know how it goes. You do look a little tired."

"I'm exhausted. I can't get enough sleep and even when I go to bed I can't rest because I'm too wired."

"I have something that could help you with that."

I give her a confused look. "What do you mean?"

"I have something that can help you feel more awake."

"What is it?"

Sandy digs through her purse and pulls out a tiny bag of white powder.

"Cocaine!" I cry.

"No, no, nothing like that."

"But I'm supposed to snort it?" I laugh, the idea is so preposterous. "I don't think so."

"No, it's no big deal. It'll just help you stay alert. Take it. Just try it."

I *would* like to stay more alert. I look at the baggie Sandy is offering and imagine it must be like a hyped-up version of

NoDoz or something. I remember a lot of my college friends taking NoDoz to stay awake and it was hardly a big deal. But still, I tell Sandy "thanks but no thanks."

"Just take it. If you want to try it, fine, if not, no biggie, right?'"

I take the bag with the idea that I'll just toss it in a garbage some place after I leave. It seems easier than having to argue with her. I wonder if I should mention to Rachel that her sister-in-law seems to be around drugs again, but I don't want to create any more stress for Rachel than she already has, so I decide to hold off, at least for now. I put the baggie in my purse nervously.

When Rachel gets back from walking the neighbor kids home, she has to get going to take her own kids to their piano lessons, so I say my good-byes and head home.

I'm starting on dinner when my mother calls me to grill me on my wedding plans.

"How are things with you?" I ask.

Mom goes off on one of her typical rants on how Frank is being a lazy slob and how work is killing her. When I was growing up, she worked as an administrative assistant. After I moved to Colorado, Mom moved too and got a better job, and then she got promoted, and then she got promoted several more times, and was ultimately offered the high-paying, stress-packed job in California that she has now. The people she works with all have MBAs, and my mom doesn't even have a college degree. But she's good at what she does. And she likes her job, most of the time, despite the long hours and frequent travel.

Will comes home from work and I give him a kiss. "Mom," I mouth to him. He nods.

"What do you think we should do for Christmas?" Mom says. "Have you spoken to Sienna? I'm assuming she and Mark will want to come to Colorado since that's where Mark's family is. You wouldn't mind us staying with you, would you?"

Oh, my God. The holidays. How dare the holidays descend upon me when I have a wedding to plan? Gifts to buy and wrap, a house to decorate, food to make, and, most dire of all, having to share my home with my mother and stepfather and sister for an entire week. I want to pass out just thinking about it.

I think about how much work I have to do for WP and how I still haven't booked a DJ or a videographer and any number of other tasks my wedding planning book told me I should have gotten done by now but I haven't.

I think about the stuff that Sandy gave me. I haven't thrown it away yet. I didn't want to throw it in just anyone's trash in case somebody stumbled on it. I didn't want some poor stranger to get in trouble with the cops or anything.

I realize I could just flush it down the toilet. But there isn't any rush. Instead, as I wait for our dinner to finish cooking, I take my purse upstairs and take the baggie out of it. I wrap the powder in a pair of my old sweats and stuff the sweats at the back of the bottom drawer of my dresser. It would be sort of nice to have a little more energy, a few more hours in the day . . . what am I saying, I'm not going to do drugs. I'll throw it away right after dinner.

I go downstairs and give Will a smile. "Dinner should just about be ready."

Chapter 25

My life is one giant to-do list, and it only gets worse as December approaches.

Will and I go to Thanksgiving at his mother's house. It's Will, his mother, me, and two sets of couples who are his mother's friends. Dennis and Elaine and John and Peggy all have kids who are grown up and married with new families to celebrate the holidays with, so together we comprise a sort of ad hoc family—the young childless couple and the older couples in their second stage of life.

I expect Will's mother to forget any hesitation in regard to her feelings for me now that Will and I are engaged, but I don't get the flood of warmth I was hoping for. Instead, the first thing she says is, "Let's see the ring."

Smiling, I offer up my hand, fully expecting to be reassured that it's gorgeous. Instead what she says is, "It's big." And not in an impressed, "Wow! It's big!" sort of way, but in a "You really are just after my son's money, you trollop" sort of a way. Oh dear.

Over dinner, I compliment every single item of food in a ridiculously gushing manner, hoping to stroke Will's mother's ego. Like me! Like me! I may as well be shouting. The one dish I don't go near is the Jell-O with fruit and marshmallows. I have never been a fan of Jell-O. There is something about translucent, neon-colored, jiggly food with fruits trapped in it like prehistoric bugs frozen in amber that makes me queasy. Apparently, I'm not the only one. No one else takes any of it either.

"Doesn't anyone like Jell-O?" Will's mom asks.

I've had three servings of green bean casserole! I want to shout. Doesn't that count for anything!

"I wonder if Jell-O was on the menu of the first Thanksgiving in November long ago," Dennis jokes.

"Actually, the first Thanksgiving was in October to celebrate the pilgrims' first harvest," I say. "Thanksgiving was first officially celebrated during Lincoln's presidency, but it didn't get its November date until FDR. He moved the date and made it a national holiday." Oh God. They think I'm some uppity know-it-all. Backpedaling is in order! "I was a history major. I retain useless trivia like that." I try to laugh. Oh God! Please like me despite the fact that I'm smart!

"How did you go from being a history major to being a business consultant?" Dennis asks.

"I got sick of being poor, so I went back to school to get my MBA," I say. Thankfully, I get a few polite chuckles out of that.

Dennis and John ask me about my work, and then the conversation comes around to the wedding. I decide no one thought I was showing off after all. It was just my overactive imagination rearing up.

The rest of the day goes all right. I'm constantly on edge and I can't wait for the day when I can relax around Will's mom to come along, but I expect I'm just going to have to log a lot of awkward hours with her before we get to know each other well enough to feel comfortable together.

With Christmas looming, I try to streamline to the best of my ability. I buy as many gifts as possible online and have them shipped to their future owners, and then I go to the mall and finish buying whatever gifts I couldn't buy online. I descend on the mall like an attack commando buying up presents and spending money as quickly as I possibly can.

On top of wearing my credit cards out buying Christmas presents, I buy some new sweaters and jeans to wear for my mother's and sister's visit. I tend to either wear sweats or business suits, and I don't do well with fashion that falls between super-casual and business chic. The truth is, I've always hated shopping. It seems to me that fashion designers are always trying to foist impractical fabrics in unflattering cuts that will be out of fashion in about twelve minutes, and the fact that they refuse to acknowledge how real women live pisses me off. I feel like I'm hunting for buried treasure trying to find clothes that don't require lots of ironing or trips to the dry cleaners. Plus, when you have a big bust, wearing a sweater or blouse that is remotely formfitting means walking a very fine line between sexy and slutty. I never intentionally buy sexy tops, but I tell you what, you add a set of 36Ds to just about any shirt, and you've got yourself a sexy shirt. It's truly amazing how wearing a top that reveals just a little cleavage can turn a normally polite and courteous male into a salivating idiot savant who is unable to pry his eyes from my breasts. It is a kind of power to turn men into lust-crazed lunatics, but most men are seconds away from sex-induced dementia anyway, so it's not much of an accomplishment. I don't like feeling like merchandise on display, so trying to find clothes that fit my figure isn't fun. It's nearly impossible to find fabrics that don't cling to my ample ass and thighs in a provocative manner and yet don't make them seem any bigger than they need to be. I think it pains Rachel how little I care about fashion. She's tried several times to get me to try on cute little outfits that come into her store, but I'm just not much of risk-taker in fashion or in life. I started my own business, which is a huge enough risk that I think I'm absolved from having to parade around in the latest poufy skirt fashion for at least several years.

Probably one of the reasons I'm not big into clothes is that I'm not in love with my body. I don't hate it either, you understand. I've made peace with it. My body is the relative I know I'll never really click with, but I'll be as friendly as possible toward it because there is no use fighting. We're stuck with each other after all.

Though I'm not a fashion hound, it does boost my confidence when I finally find a few cute outfits. Laden down with new clothes for myself and an extravagant array of gifts for the people I care about, I go home hell-bent with the intention of decorating my home in Yuletide cheer as fast as humanly possible. Will helps me wrap gifts, thank goodness, and he puts the entire fake tree up and puts all the ornaments on, and I'm so grateful for him taking over that chore for me that I give him a toe-curdling blow job in thanks.

I remember when I was a little kid, putting up Christmas tree decorations and baking Christmas cookies wasn't a chore, it was fun. It was something to look forward to, but now I always feel so busy that there's no time to admire the pretty ornaments or twinkling Christmas lights. Right now I'm just too tired to enjoy that sort of thing.

My life isn't all work, though. One Saturday night, Will and I go out to a nice dinner and then go hear a band play in a dark, smoky bar. I stand in front of him and we sway to the music. He puts his hand on my waist, his fingers touching my bare skin beneath my T-shirt. I can feel his hard-on pressing into my ass. He slides his fingers up my shirt to my rib cage, just beneath my breasts. I take a quick look around. No one seems to notice or care what we're doing. It's dark and everyone is just enjoying the music, watching the band on stage. Will inches his fingers a little higher. My nipples harden in anticipation of his touch.

For an hour or so we keep this up, him grinding his erection into my back, me grinding right back, exchanging covert and not-so covert gropes, driving each other wild with lust.

I turn to face him and say into his ear, "Wanna go home and fuck?"

He nods yes.

We drive home, whip off our clothes, and kneel on the bed, facing each other. We move together in a frenzy of searching kisses and passionate touches. Then Will lowers me so I'm lying on my back. He slides his fingers inside me, then out, then circles his finger on my clitoris, faster and faster . . .

My orgasm is powerful, but he doesn't stop, his fingers keep going, sustaining my orgasm for what feels like hours, but can probably only be a minute or two until I'm breathing so hard and so fast I feel like I might pass out from too much pleasure.

"Fuck me," I say.

There is nothing better than that moment when he first plunges himself inside me, that first delectable thrust.

It's times like these I'm astonished at my body's capacity for pleasure. I may be out of shape and overweight, but god damn if my body isn't an amazing thing.

Will and I are tubby, wrinkling, balding, orgasm *machines*.

The next morning when I wake up, Will is already awake and out of the shower, padding around our room with a towel wrapped around him, his curly hair not yet combed and thus springing out in a Troll Doll sort of look.

When he turns to fish something out of the dresser, I see his back, which looks like it's been attacked by a saber-toothed tiger.

"What happened to your back?"

"You happened to my back," he says with a smile.

"Oh, sorry."

"Don't worry about it."

"Did I hurt you?"

"In a good way."

I smile. I am a sexual animal, even if I can't pull off wearing a merriwidow without feeling like an idiot. He wraps his arms around me. I feel safe and cherished and happy.

Chapter 26

It turns out I don't have to go to Germany, at least not for a few months, but in the middle of December, as if I weren't stressed enough, I have to go to California to meet with WP executives in their office there.

There is something so exhausting about have to wake up at an ungodly hour to catch a flight and then have back-to-back meetings all day. It's a productive workday, but I feel like I'm running on fumes.

At the end of the day, I go back to my hotel room and change into my pajamas. I pull the sweats out of my suitcase and the plastic bag of speed tumbles out. My heart goes crazy—I can't believe I transported illegal drugs across state lines. Moreover, I can't believe I transported illegal drugs across state lines—and didn't get caught. I examine the baggie for several seconds, then put it down again. I had completely forgotten I had the drugs . . . obviously I wouldn't have taken it on an airplane with me if I had. I wonder how much I would even take? I know nothing about drugs. I wonder if it would really give me more energy like Sandy said . . .

I shake my head at the ridiculous idea and hide the baggie beneath another pair of pants and try to find something else to occupy my thoughts.

I look around the room and realize I feel lonely. I check my email, willing contact from other human life. I send out emails to everyone I know in hopes of drumming up some email in return.

To: gabileveska@hotmail.com
From: eva@lockhartconsulting.com

So have you given up on dating entirely? Are you still even looking at the personals?

I order in room service and stare at my computer screen, waiting for Gabrielle to get back to me. I send an email to Sienna asking what's up with her, and an email to Will telling him I love him. I flip through the channels on TV, refresh my email, turn off the TV, refresh my email, pace around the room, refresh my email. I give Will a call, but he doesn't answer. His phone is probably downstairs and he's probably upstairs playing computer games. He checks his email frequently, but I'll have to wait until he isn't busy saving the universe from bad guys before I hear from him.

Finally my dinner gets delivered and as I sit at the desk eating, I get a return email from Gabrielle. I feel like a little kid at Christmas, I'm so ridiculously excited to have human contact, even in electronic form.

To: eva@lockhartconsulting.com
From: gabileveska@hotmail.com

I think I've given up on the personals. You know how you can select what age range you're looking for in a date? Every guy who's around my age says he's looking for a woman age nineteen to whatever a year younger than he is. So if he's thirty-four, he wants a woman who's between the ages of nineteen and thirty-four. So here I am, a thirty-three year old, and I feel ancient. The personals are too depressing.

To: gabileveska@hotmail.com
From: eva@lockhartconsulting.com

That is creepy. I certainly don't want to be dating a
nineteen year old when I'm thirty-four. I didn't want to
be dating nineteen year olds when I was a nineteen
year old. I bet when they put that age thing in there,
it's not a hard-and-fast rule. Will's first wife was older
than him. You never know who you're going to fall for.
You need to be open to the possibilities.

To: eva@lockhartconsulting.com
From: gabileveska@hotmail.com

I was open to the possibilities and look where it got
me. I dated a woman for a few weeks, we slept
together a few times, and now she's essentially stalk-
ing me and telling me I've broken her heart. It's so
hard. I know exactly what she's going through. I was
going through it myself a couple months ago. I think
it's easier to break up with guys because you can get
yourself into one of those, "All men are scum"
moods. You can't do that with another woman. So, in
case you're thinking of dating women, you have been
warned . . .

To: gabileveska@hotmail.com
From: eva@lockhartconsulting.com

I don't think Will would appreciate me dating other
people, but thanks for the insight.

Before Gabrielle can write me back, I get an email from
Sienna.

To: eva@lockhartconsulting
From: sienna28@hotmail.com

I gave up coffee in my quest to make my stomach happy and live a pure existence. But I have to say, life is so much less interesting without coffee. I feel calm and capable and my belly is no longer distended, but I'm sleepy and the colors just aren't as bright. I was only drinking one cup a day, but it was mine and I liked it.

I finally got a desk chair that's not meant for a seventies kitchen table! It's amazing. My life has changed. You see chairs every day, but I don't think you can really appreciate them until you've spent eight hours a day for six months fashioning pillows and blankets and broken cardboard shoeboxes to create the guise of ergonomics. (Why couldn't I have at least found an *unbroken* cardboard shoebox to prop my feet on?)

How are things with you?

To: sienna28@hotmail.com
From: eva@lockhartconsulting.com

I'm glad to hear you're making bold strides to ensure your ergonomic health.

As for me, I'm stressed. Really stressed. I'm stressed about work and I'm stressed about the wedding. I'm not spending as much time with Will as I would like. On Saturday morning, we woke up and made love, and I actually kept looking at the clock and at the ten-minute mark, all I could think was, you're not done *yet*? Come on! I've got things to do! A house to clean! A wedding to plan! A major merger to work on!

Afterward, Will wanted to hold me in his arms and
just snuggle for awhile. At first I was like, are you kidding me? I don't have time for this. Then I reminded
myself why it is I'm killing myself to plan this wedding
in the first place. Because I love Will. Because he
makes me laugh. Because he makes me feel safe
and loved. I actually had to remind myself that Will is
the most important thing in the world to me. More important than a stupid wedding or a stupid merger.
Does that make me a horrible person? Anyway, how's
your life?

To: eva@lockhartconsulting.com
From: sienna28@hotmail.com

You're not a horrible person. You're just human.

As for me, life's been okay. It turns out that working
as an assistant to a young adult fantasy author has
transformed me into a fantasy geek. I have to read
all of my boss's books so I can answer fans' questions, so I take her books with me wherever I go. I
realized just what a nerd I was the other day when I
caught my reflection in a department store window. I
had my hair in pigtails and I was wearing a bright orange poncho, a backpack, and sneakers; in my
hand I carried a small book with a blue dragon on
the front and a young girl smiling up at him as if to
say, "Together we can do it!" I couldn't help but feel
that people were looking at me and judging me, or
just feeling very sad for me. "Oh, that's so sweet,
she's in her twenties and she's just learning to read.
She's *so* strong." Or: "Oh, that's so sad; she must
be mentally disabled."

I had a stand-up spot at the Patio the other day. I was so excited for the show. I felt really solid about my material. I practiced sufficiently over the weekend instead of cramming it in on the day of a performance like I normally do. But then the show got started late, and I started yawning and then there were four awful comics in a row, and then one good one right before me, and I felt myself fading. I tried to boost myself up and focus and remember back to when I was on the speech team in high school, when I would grow sleepy and tired of all the dramatic performances and think about what I had to offer and how I wanted to make the other people in the room not want to sleep anymore. It didn't work. I got solid laughs, but I didn't feel connected to the audience. It's like having sex without the orgasm. It's nice, but, come on, we all know why we step up to "the mic" in the first place. Release! There is no peace without RELEASE.

Last weekend was really cool though. Mark and I house-sat for Mark's aunt and uncle, who have this gigantic compound in Rye. They had a karaoke machine and Mark and I sang all the best cheesy songs to each other for about two hours straight. Then in the morning we bounced on the trampoline until our brains felt like mashed potatoes. Trampolines are the best toys EVER. I can't wait until I'm incredibly wealthy and can buy a trampoline. I'll put it in my living room. (I'll have vaulted ceilings, obviously.) Mark and I felt so amazingly in love. We couldn't get enough of each other—we swam, we sang, we had lots of sex and cuddled and laughed and talked. What a gift that we have each other in this life.

I'm desperate for some sleep. I love you. I know it doesn't do any good to tell you to relax, but try anyway, okay?

I think about Sienna and Mark singing karaoke and bouncing on a trampoline. Will and I would never be silly and goof around like that. When did I become so hard-working and goal-oriented that I lost my ability to have fun? I used to be a fun person, I swear. Don't get me wrong, I was never the life of the party, but I remember doing silly things with friends when I was younger. Like in college, I remember having a huge crush on a guy who lived in my dorm. My girlfriends and I would do childish things, like making crank calls and writing him elaborate love letters in various colored inks and then slide them under his door. Being on the guys' floor was strictly illegal, so that proves just what a risk-taking party animal I was. Okay fine, it doesn't. The truth is, I've always been a hopeless good-girl geek. But my antics were silly and fun and I remember laughing a lot with my girlfriends and having a ton of fun.

How do I regain my ability to be silly again? (Even in a G-rated way?)

To: eva@lockhartconsulting.com
From: WillCummings@leviathsoftware.com

When I was driving into work this morning, I had a very erotic daydream about you . . . I kept picturing slipping your panties off, spreading your legs, and sliding my tongue inside you. I kept glancing up at your face, and watching you while I touched you . . . I was hard all the way to work.

I love you.

His email puts a smile on my face. Thank goodness for email enabling me to keep up with everyone even when I'm all alone out here on the road.

To: WillCummings@leviathsoftware.com
From: eva@lockhartconsulting.com

I love you, too, Will. I love you because of your sexy guitar-playing. I love how smart you are. How kind you are. How sexy you are. How you always make me laugh.

To: eva@lockhartconsulting.com
From: WillCummings@leviathsoftware.com

What I love about you:

—that you like my friends (and that they like you)

—your ambition

—your taste in books and art

—that you'd want to spend your days and nights with me (I am still astonished, frankly)

I love:

—the feel of your nipples between my fingers and their taste on my tongue

—to fondle your clitoris while I kiss the sighs straight out of your mouth

—the fact that just thinking about touching you makes my cock hard as a rock (like it is right now)

I smile. Then I think about how much work I really should get done for my meetings tomorrow. I think about the baggie again.

The truth is, there is a part of me that has been wanting to try it since Sandy gave it to me. I've been trying to kid myself, but I would have gotten rid of it right away if there wasn't at least a part of me that wanted to try it out.

What the hell. I've always been such a good girl. Maybe it's time that I broke a rule or two, at least once. Just this once.

I retrieve the baggie from my suitcase and I put a little powder on my finger and snort it. It stings my nostrils a little. For a few moments I don't feel anything. Then I feel sort of a soft, warm feeling. A general feeling of contentedness. It's a wonderful feeling. I take a little more.

I feel energized and happy and raring to go. It's a feeling I could get used to.

Chapter 27

I had hoped that Will's mother would join us at our place for Christmas. I'd been looking forward to her coming to see Will's new home and to meet my family. But she says she's not ready to do holidays with other people—she's still getting over the death of her husband. I can understand that getting over the death of someone you were married to for forty years would take some time, but there's this part of me that worries she's not coming to meet my family or see what kind of life Will is making with me because there is a part of her that hopes my relationship with Will is temporary. I fear that she's hoping Will and I will break up and he'll find a woman who wants kids.

The day before we're supposed to pick up Mark and Sienna from the airport, I get my Annual Christmas Cyst on my forehead. It's one of those unpoppable zits that grow to the size of a grape beneath the skin, managing to be both hideously unattractive and incredibly painful at once. A holiday bonus of added stress. I try to ice it to get the swelling down, but it's there when I pick up Sienna and Mark and it's still there in all its throbbing glory the next day when I'm supposed to pick up Mom and Frank from the airport. I can't bear to see my beautiful mother for the first time in a year with a giant tumorlike growth on my face, so I poke at it, turning my Annual Christmas Cyst into a bloody, scabby lesion protruding in a pulsating, enormous mass on my forehead. Charming.

Will and I pick them up from the airport together. As always, my mother looks drop-dead gorgeous. Her skin has a youthfulness that makes her look considerably younger than she really is.

After we hug enthusiastically, the four of us pile into the car. I turn from the passenger seat to face Mom, who's sitting in the back with Frank. "Mom, you look great. How do you keep your skin looking so good?"

"I moisturize. A lot."

I moisturize, too, and I still have more wrinkles than she does. I give her an incredulous look. There has to be something more to her routine.

"Oh, and I bought this product called the Facializer. You put it on your face like this." Mom inverts her fingers in two upside down A-Okay signs, encircling her thumb and index fingers around her eyes. "And then you do your Facializer exercises." She demonstrates by raising her eyebrows up and down, like someone suddenly terrified and then not terrified. Terrified, not terrified.

I watch the odd look Will is making as he watches her performance in the rearview mirror.

"Mom? Mom?" I say. Terrified, not terrified. Terrified, not terrified. "Mom? You've only known Will for three minutes. Let's not make him believe he's marrying into a family of lunatics right off the bat, okay?"

"Marrying into the family!" she gushes. "A wedding! It's all so wonderful. I'm so excited for you two. Welcome to the family, Will. Oh, Eva, I saw my psychic the other day, and he assured me that you're going to get pregnant this year. I know you've thought you didn't want children, but really, you do. It's going to be a boy."

"Mom, every psychic you've seen in the last four years has been telling you that I'm going to get pregnant right away. Do you know why? Because that's what you want to hear."

"No. Do you know what it is? It's that when you're close to people, their energy mixes with your energy. Sometimes the psychic reads the other person's energy off you accidentally. So for the last few years, my psychic was inadvertently forecasting the birth of my girlfriends' grandkids. But this is my year to become a grandmother. I know it."

I watch Will stifle a laugh. "Mom," I say, "you do realize that any crap psychic could use that excuse about other people's aura rubbing off on you as the reason they're completely wrong about all their predictions."

"Oh," she says, ignoring me, "and I visited a pet astrologer a few weeks back to see why Schroeder is so aloof." Schroeder is the cat that Mom and Frank got from a pet shelter about six months ago. "She told me that Schroeder's astrology sign isn't a good match with mine, so that's why he's so withdrawn."

"Mom, Schroeder is aloof because Schroeder is a *cat*."

But, of course, there is no talking sense to my mother. She goes off on a new conversational tangent, pretending like she didn't hear me.

We've covered the Facializer, psychic readings, and pet astrology all within the first ten minutes of my mother meeting my betrothed. I have a sneaking suspicion it's going to be a long, long week.

The few days before Christmas are a whirlwind. Mark and Sienna shuttle back and forth from my family to his family's. Mom and Sienna have to buy last-minute gifts, because they didn't want to have to ship everything or drag it on the plane with them. I'm torn between wanting to work and wanting to spend time with them. I opt to spend time with them, but as I walk around the mall while they shop, all I can think about is how this is a waste of time and how I should be working.

Having three extra people staying at my place makes me feel overwhelmed. Mark stays at his family's house most nights, but Sienna sleeps on the couch, while Mom and Frank have taken over the guestroom. With all of their luggage and all the gifts they've brought, there simply isn't enough room for all of us, and it makes me feel claustrophobic. Plus, I simply can't believe how many dishes five people can use up in a day. I feel like all I do are dishes, even though Sienna, Mom, Frank, and Will all help out. I have no idea how families with kids manage the endless dishes, but I'm really not used to it.

On Christmas Eve, Frank and Will stay home wrapping gifts while Mom, Sienna, and I battle mobs of people at the grocery store buying food for Christmas breakfast and dinner. Over the course of the last month, the three of us have been emailing each other back and forth, trying to plan the meals. I enlisted their help as I did not want to be responsible for making dinner an inedible fiasco.

It's not easy to be around my mother because my mother and I are so much alike. We are two strong women who like to have things our way. The problem arises when her way is different from my way. Sienna is much more go-with-the-flow. She always wants to make everyone else happy, even if it means she gets the shaft. It's why Sienna wanted to become a comedian. She wants everyone to like her. Neither Mom nor I give a shit as long as we get our way.

Mom and I bicker about what to make for Christmas dinner. Mom is voting for steak now, even though we originally talked about Cornish game hens, since I'm not a fan of red meat. Mom ultimately gets her way, and I'm secretly triumphant when it costs her forty-five bucks for a steak for each of us and she blanches at the cost.

When we get home from doing the shopping, Will and Frank have taken over the kitchen. Tape, wrapping paper, and ribbons are everywhere. I've got heavy bags full of groceries cutting off the circulation in my fingers, and Frank is shouting at us that we have to get out of there or else we'll see our unwrapped gifts. One of the bags I'm holding breaks and the cider vinegar, which is in a glass bottle, slips out and breaks on the kitchen floor. My anxiety level goes into the stratosphere, and it gets worse when I reach down to pick up the shards of glass and cut my hand. I'm bleeding all over the place, while Frank is still shouting at us to get out of the kitchen. Mom starts talking about some decoration she brought me and is insisting that I come look at it *right now*, and meanwhile I'm trying to do my best not to bleed over the entire house.

"Just a minute!" I shout to Mom. "Will, can you please get me a Band-Aid?"

"Sure, babe."

Will gets me a bandage, helps me clean my wound, and fixes me up. As he takes care of me, I calm down. Thank God I have him.

"I just cannot bear to battle the mobs at the grocery store again to replace the vinegar," I say.

"You need it for some recipe?"

I nod.

"I'll go to the store and pick some up."

"Really? I would be forever grateful. Thank you."

Sienna and Mark spend Christmas Eve night with Mark's family while Mom, Frank, Will, and I go out for a fancy, quiet dinner, just the four of us. After a couple of glasses of wine between us, Mom and I start snickering about the funny memories we have from her wedding. To wit: Mom had her wedding ceremony in the early evening, followed by the reception. The wedding was outdoors, and to get outside, the wedding party came down a spiral staircase from the second floor of the reception hall. As the bride and bridesmaids and groomsmen waited until it was time to descend the staircase, we enjoyed a few glasses of wine. Unfortunately, Mom's matron of honor, Helen, had one or five too many glasses on an empty stomach.

Mom had bought all of her bridesmaids dressy purses that matched our dresses—so all five of us had the exact same small clutch purse.

The wedding processional music began and we all walked down the stairs onto the patio where the veranda was. When we lined up, groomsmen on one side, bridesmaids on the other, Helen realized that she'd left the groom's ring in her purse, which was back upstairs. This little newsflash was whispered down the row of bridesmaids until it got to me. I covertly snuck out of line and tiptoed to where guests were watching and entreated Anne, one of Mom's friends, to miss some of the ceremony, sprint upstairs, grab the purses, and retrieve the ring. Anne did as she was asked, bringing all five clutch purses down from upstairs with her. As the ring-exchange portion of the ceremony grew ever closer, Anne went through one purse after the other, shifting through lipsticks and tampons and coming up empty-handed until at last she found Helen's purse, which contained nothing else besides three packages of cigarettes (Three! For a four-hour wedding!) and the all-important ring. Anne handed the ring to me, I handed it to Sienna, who handed it to Mom's sister, who handed it to Helen just as the preacher was asking them to exchange rings and repeat after her that this ring was a symbol of their enduring love.

Later, after the dinner, everyone at the bridal table took a turn passing the microphone down and recollecting fond memories of Mom and Frank and offering their good wishes. When Helen, who was still trashed, got the microphone in her hand, she wished Mom and Frank, "Rainbows and rainbows and rainbows. Rainbows and rainbows and rainbows." We all began clapping hysterically to shut her up and have her pass the microphone on, but she wouldn't give it up. "Rainbows and rainbows and rainbows and rainbows and rainbows . . ." Ultimately somebody had to tackle her to wrest the microphone free from her iron grip. Now, the phrase "rainbows and rainbows and rainbows" could have Mom, Sienna, and me on the floor in convulsions of hysteria in about ten seconds flat. There were, of course, the usual Funniest Home Video moments at Mom's wedding—the guy slipping and falling on his ass on the dance floor, that sort of thing. Mom and I have a riot reliving it all and wondering what debacles lie in store for my wedding. This is what family is. One moment your mother can make you so insane you're gritting your teeth so hard your jaw hurts and you're worried that the veins in your forehead are going to explode in a stressed-out fury, and the next minute you are hooting with laughter together at the memories of the life you've shared.

Christmas Day we have a nice breakfast and open gifts, then we watch a couple of videos. All day Mom complains about how cold it is. She's wearing just a thin blouse, while the rest of us have the good sense to wear sweaters, since we are in Colorado in the middle of winter.

"It's so cold here," she gripes.

"Mom, this isn't Los Angeles. This is Colorado in December. Do you want to borrow a sweater?"

I get her a sweater, and she puts in on, but only for a little while, because as we slave over the hot stove, we get warmer. I get hot and peel off my sweater, too. Me, Mom, and Sienna buzz around the kitchen all afternoon making appetizers and getting dinner ready. I tell them my trials and tribulations of trying to learn how to cook, and they share recipes and their cooking war stories as well.

By the time dinner is ready, I'm melting. I'm sweating as if I've been detoxing in a sauna. We get dinner on the table, pour the wine, and I actually have to rub my napkin covertly across my forehead to wipe away the sweat.

After dinner, we retreat to the living room to watch a video of one of Sienna's recent performances that she brought with her from New York. As we sit on the couch, I literally feel so hot I'm faint. I'm having hot flashes at the age of thirty-one. I crack open the window, feeling blessed by the breeze.

When my mother asks Sienna to pause the video so she can go to the kitchen to get another glass of wine, I get up to look at the thermostat to make sure nothing has gone haywire.

And that's when I learn that my mother has changed the temperature from the moderate 72 degrees I keep my home at to a tropical 82 degrees. My home. *My home.* Would she go into anyone else's house and render their residence the temperature of molten lava? I think not.

It is at this time that I decide I'm ready for my mother to leave my home and return to California.

"Such audacity! I can't believe the nerve!" I mutter angrily under my breath as I turn the thermostat back down to where it's supposed to be.

My nerves are fried completely. I run up to my bedroom and call Sandy. "Sandy, hi. Merry Christmas."

"Who is this?"

"Oh, sorry, this is Eva, Rachel's friend?"

"What's up?"

"Um—" I sigh. It's one thing to have used what she gave me. It's another to call her up and ask for more. The stuff definitely made me awake, which is a plus. But what Sandy didn't mention is that it also leaves you with an incredible sense of well-being, a feeling I have in short supply in the best of times, and am craving desperately right now.

"Did you want some more?"

"Well, if you have some handy. It's just the holidays, you know. Family get-togethers . . ."

"Meet me in front of Rachel's store in half an hour."

"Half an hour?" I'm elated. That's no time at all. I don't have to wait. Thank God. "That sounds perfect. I'll see you then."

Rachel's store is only a ten-minute walk away. I wait as long as I can, then I tell my family I want to get some fresh air and walk off a few of the holiday calories I've been packing in these last few days.

"I'll come with you," Mom says.

"Um, no, if it's okay, I'd like a little alone time."

"Oh, sure." She looks a little hurt, but the concept of alone time is a popular one in our family.

As I wait in the cold for Sandy to show, there is a part of me that thinks about my family back home and how I'm buying drugs on a street corner like some common addict, but I quickly push the thought from my head. I can't think about that right now. I just need to get through the holiday—I just needed a little help.

I also realize that I have no idea how much Sandy charges for this. I have a stack of twenties in my wallet. If what she's asking is too unreasonable, I'll tell her never mind.

Sandy arrives only a few minutes late, but in those few minutes I've managed to go from mildly impatient, to irritated, to about to explode with anger—doesn't she know my entire family is going to wonder where I am? But then she shows up and I simmer down. She asks what seems to me to be a reasonable price, although truth be told, I have no idea what the going rate for this sort of thing is. I can afford it anyway.

"Thanks, Sandy. Thanks a lot."

Chapter 28

I have two more days of having my family here. On the day after Christmas, Mom and Frank get together with some friends of theirs and Mark spends the day with his family. Will has to go back to work, so I have Sienna all to myself.

Sienna is a huge fitness buff. She's thin and is extremely disciplined about what she eats. In her line of work, it's important to look good. She's dedicated to working out, and she asks me if I'll join her at the 24-Hour Fitness gym, so I do. I've been a member of the gym for years. It only costs me fourteen dollars a month, but since I work out so infrequently, I figure this one trip to the gym is costing me about three hundred bucks or so. We exercise for about an hour, and it feels good, but I know my out-of-shape muscles will punish me tomorrow. After our workout, we go into the Jacuzzi. I pray the healing waters will stave off the worst of the soreness that is sure to hit me. We have the Jacuzzi to ourselves.

"Are you dieting?" Sienna asks me as we ooze into the hot bubbles up to our shoulders, the tips of our hair getting wet.

"No."

"You've lost weight. You look good."

"I don't have time to eat. That's all," I say. "How are things going?"

"What do you mean?'

"I mean how is your life? How are things with Mark?"

She sinks down into the water, down to her chin. She stays there for a moment. "Things are good, mostly. On Christmas Eve, when we were at his family's house, I'm pretty sure every last member of his family asked us when we were getting married."

"Yeah? So when are you?"

"I don't know. I think he might ask me this year."

"Really?"

She smiles. "Maybe."

"What kind of wedding are you going to have? God, your wedding is going to be full of comedians. It's going to be way more fun than mine."

"It will be a lot of fun, for sure."

She talks about the sort of wedding she envisions. Since she is an artist, she's got friends who are photographers, filmmakers (for the wedding video), and perform in a band. She'll just have to pay for the wine, food, and a place to have it, and her friends will do everything else pro bono. She's even got a friend who's a comedian who is certified (or whatever you call it) to perform the ceremony itself.

"But, of course, he has to actually ask me first," she says.

"How do you think he'll do it?"

Since both Sienna and Mark are performers, I imagine it will be some hopelessly romantic and creative way. Sienna and Mark are the rarest kind of couple that actually write each other love poems talking about how their love for each other grows more and more each day, that kind of thing. It's really disgusting.

"I don't know. I told him I don't want him to ask me in public."

"Why not?"

She shrugs. "I don't know. I guess because so much of our lives are spent up on stage entertaining the public, I just don't want it to be another show."

"Well, your wedding will be a blast. You'll have it in Colorado, right?"

She nods.

"I think Mark is perfect for you. I'm glad things are going so well for you guys." Her face flinches, just a little, but there is something about her facial expression that gives me pause. "Things are going well for you guys, aren't they?"

She pauses. "Yeah. It's just hard, you know. We work all day and then we go to these bars and then after we perform we stay out late drinking and talking and . . . it's exhausting. And he can spend his entire weekend playing video games while I'm working out at the health club or working on new material, and there's this part of me . . . I don't know, I guess I resent it."

"I know! I work six days a week, twelve hours a day, and then on the seventh day, instead of resting, I bust my butt planning a wedding, and he can spend hours, *hours*, playing computer games. It boggles my mind. But I think there is something wrong with me and you. I think we need to learn how to be able to relax and do nothing."

"We're American. It's the American way to be working all the time."

"I think it was the ethic Dad taught us. That you always have to be doing something productive."

"Yeah, he did believe that, definitely. Even when we were doing so-called 'leisure' activities, we always had to be learning and improving ourselves."

"We're relaxing right now," I point out.

"But I'm thinking of a billion people I should call while I'm here in Colorado and trying to figure out how I can schedule seeing all my friends before I leave again."

"And I'm thinking of all the work I have to do and all the wedding plans I still have to take care of. Are we hopeless?"

"I hope not."

I try very hard to push all the thoughts of other things I should be doing out of my head and just relax. The hot water and pulsing jets do feel good.

Neither of us says anything for a moment. In the silence

of the whirling bubbles, I flash on a memory of my father. He was at work in his workshop, and I wanted some attention. I went into his workshop even though it was strictly off-limits.

"Hi, Dad. Guess what? I got an A-plus on my English assignment."

"What are you doing in here? You're not supposed to be in here. Shoo, shoo."

He made this hand gesture, this dismissive wave of his hand telling me to get lost. I remember thinking how much it hurt my feelings to be shooed away by my father like I was a gnat or a flea or something. Even my A-plus wasn't enough to impress him.

All through high school and college, I killed myself to get good grades to impress him. I stopped sleeping. I began getting sick all the time, and I started this terrible habit of tearing the skin around my fingernails to shreds. My hands were literally a bloody mess, but I couldn't stop ripping away at the skin, a nervous habit. One night before a final exam, I had the flu, but I was studying anyway. My mind was fuzzy from illness and exhaustion, and I actually passed out walking from my bedroom to the bathroom, just fainted on the hallway floor like a Hollywood starlet. The last words I thought before keeling over were, "If I'm not perfect, he won't love me. If I'm not perfect, he won't love me."

Chapter 29

After the Jacuzzi, Sienna and I go out for a light lunch of sushi. I'm so happy to be hanging out with her. I didn't always like my younger sister. When I was three and she was a brand spanking new baby, I decided I'd had quite enough of the little crying marauder and I marched into the kitchen, put my hands on my hips, and told Mom I wanted her to return Sienna to the hospital. At the time, Sienna seemed like a broken appliance: She wasn't doing a damn bit of good and she was taking up a bunch of space. I was extremely disheartened to learn that you can't return a baby sister like a dress that doesn't fit or a pair of pants you decide you don't like after all. But it worked out because a few years later, not only did I start to like the cutie, we became best friends. The two of us were each other's life support during our parents' rocky marriage. There was many a night when we were kids that our parents' screaming would wake us from sleep. Sienna and I would meet in the bathroom, both of us needing tissue because we'd been bawling our eyes out. Our faces would be red and soaked with tears; snot puddled above our upper lips. We'd hug each other, clinging together for reassurance as the world we knew raged in turbulent seas of accusations and recriminations around us.

Sienna started to get the performing bug in high school.

She was in just about every school play there was. She also made the sketch comedy team for the yearly variety show. Before her first performance, I had been so nervous that she would stink. I actually worried about having to lie after the show about how good her performance had been. Then she got on stage, playing the lead role as only a sophomore, and she rocked my world. I actually cried with pride, thinking, *Jesus Christ, that's my little sister up there!* Then, when she went to college, she heard about a contest for the USA network that was taking comedians from colleges around the country. The contest was Friday, and she heard about it on that Monday. She'd never done stand-up before, but she cranked out a five-minute routine in just the few remaining days, got up on stage that Friday night, and won. She was flown to New York and performed and actually appeared on TV—the very first time she tried her hand at stand-up. When she moved out to Colorado, she regularly performed at the amateur nights at Comedy Works. Sometimes she bombed, but most of the time she killed, and by the time she was ready to leave for New York, she'd built a loyal following and was the opening act for bigger name performers. I couldn't believe she was brave enough to get up on stage to try to make people laugh. But then she'd always been fearless, even as a little kid. We couldn't have been more different in that way. I was scared of everything. I couldn't watch scary movies; Sienna loved them. I was too afraid of getting hurt to ski; she was an extreme sports junkie. I'd always taken the predictable path in life, getting good grades and going to college like I was supposed to; Sienna abruptly quit a stable life and took off for New York to pursue an impossibly tough career. You'd think that her talent and ambition would be enough for her to succeed, but it wasn't. She also needed luck, timing, and the relentless persistence to keep going despite the challenge of working a full-time job and staying up late several nights a week to perform.

As we're waiting for our meals to arrive, I ask Sienna about what material she's working on for her stand-up routine.

"Well, remember how when I first moved to New York I used to temp for magazines like *Glamour, Vogue,* and *GQ*? I start out my new bit talking about that, then I say: I liked working for the magazines; it was pretty exciting to see into the world of high-fashion publishing. For instance, when I worked at *Glamour*, it was indeed very glamorous and everyone who worked there was also glamorous, as if in order to work at the magazine, you also had to be able to model in it . . . just in case! At *Vogue*, they made very important phone calls all day long, like the one I overheard regarding a photo of one of the models: 'Hillary! We can't use it! Her nipple is HUGE!' *Click!*" Sienna pantomimes hanging up the phone. "When I worked at *GQ* it opened up a new world of career options I never knew about before. For instance, I answered phones for the 'Director of Grooming and Fragrance,' and the 'Director of Wine and Spirits.' These options were never listed at my high school Career Day. I like wine! I like spirits! What degree was I supposed to get for this position?"

Sienna keeps going over bits of her act until I'm snorting with laughter.

When Sienna and I get home, my mother and her husband are bickering. Mom is downstairs in the living room and Frank is upstairs in the guest room. This is how the conversation goes: *Mom*: "Can you hear me?" Long pause. *Frank*: "What?" "I said, have you finished packing?" Long pause. "What?" "You said you'd be done packing. Are you done packing? Why do I always have to watch your every move? Why?" Long pause. "What?"

This goes on for several minutes, until any relaxed feelings I got by working out and sitting in the Jacuzzi are long gone.

My family leaves the next day. I love my family very much, more than anything, but all I can say is, *Thank God they're going home!*

At a happy hour after Christmas, Will and I meet up with Richard, James, Abby, and Jerry at Mickie's Pub.

"Eva, you are looking so skinny these days," Abby says to me as we join them at the table. "You're not dieting for the wedding, are you?"

"No. I've just been too busy to eat."

"Well, you're looking good, but don't lose any more weight, okay? Anything more and you'll get to that creepy skinny level."

Abby is extremely slender herself, but she has a completely different build than me. I'm all curves, while she's all angles. She's right, I am losing too much weight, and I'm not even trying. I just can't always remember to eat these days.

"So, how were all of your Christmases?" I ask.

"Well, Clarice and I went to her parents for the holiday," James says. Clarice is James' wife, the medical student. I've met her a couple times so I know she's not a fabrication of James' imagination, but for all the hours she puts in at the hospital, she may as well be.

"How was it?"

"Let's put it this way. You know that I'm something of a wine snob, right?"

"Of course," I say.

"Well, Clarice's parents are wine-from-a-box kind of people."

"Really? Ick. Well, I guess somebody has to buy that stuff," Abby says.

"So not only is all they're serving wine-from-a-box, all they're serving from the box is pink Zinfandel," James continues.

"Gross," says Will.

"Yeah, apparently they thought they were serving twenty-two-year-old women and not thirty-five-year-old men. At first, I was too much of a snob to drink the stuff . . . and then the fighting began. Clarice's mother started fighting with Clarice, and Clarice was fighting with her sister Margaret, and Margaret was fighting with her husband and her father . . . and soon I was basically just drinking from the tap of that box of Zin the entire weekend." He pantomimes lifting the spout to the box of wine and just drinking straight from the tap, making glug-glug-glug noises. "It was awful, but it was the only alcohol available to me, so I sucked it down like water."

"How about you, Rich? How was visiting with your family in Albany?" I ask.

"I was there for an entire week with my parents, my brother and his wife, their two loud kids, and my grandmother. I stayed intoxicated for seven days straight."

"Did you get any good gifts?" I ask.

"My favorite was from my grandmother. Apparently my grandmother thinks I'm a ten-year-old girl," Richard says.

"How do you figure?"

"She got me a doll for Christmas."

"A doll? What kind of doll?"

"A boy-doll with overalls and a backward baseball cap."

"What are you going to do with a doll?"

"Bring it home and put it in my bedroom to ensure I never, ever get laid again. What do you think? I gave it to my niece."

I laugh, appreciating just how much I need these weekly happy hours. For one thing, much of the time I'm working home alone and I don't have any contact with the outside world, and for another thing, it lets me forget my stresses and worries, at least for a little while. The problem with destressing is that you can re-stress about ten minutes later.

It's a never-ending battle.

Chapter 30

I spend the month of January going to meeting after meeting with Kyle Woodruff and the other execs from WP. I secure a caterer and a DJ, but every time I look at my spreadsheet of "to-do" items for the wedding, it seems to get bigger rather than smaller. I rarely get much sleep, and the exhaustion is getting to me.

The worst thing about taking drugs is having to buy them. It's something of an ordeal to figure out a way I can sneak out of the house to meet Sandy without making Will suspicious. Then when I meet her, we have to do this ridiculous small-talk thing where we pretend like we're old friends when, in fact, I barely know her.

In mid-January, I call her again to get more, just to help me get through my meetings with WP. We meet in front of Rachel's store at night. It's dark out and the entire experience is terrifyingly awful. I keep imagining police lights and sirens pulling up.

"How are you doing?" Sandy asks.

"Fine." I look around for the twentieth time in sixty seconds. I'm as subtle as a bull in a china store. Hurry up! I want to get out of here!

She hands me a brown paper bag; I hand her cash. "Thanks," I say.

"Thank you."

This is absolutely going to be the last time. I don't like lying to Will. I don't like the sneaking around. And there is no way I want to get dependent on drugs. I'm way too smart for that.

Chapter 31

Today is a typical workday for me. I slurp down so much coffee my arm muscles actually get sore from raising the mug to my lips so often—I wish I were kidding about this. I prepare feverishly for my next meeting for WP.

Kyle Woodruff calls me dozens of times. I avoid as many of his calls as I can because otherwise I'd just be talking to him all day and I'll never be ready for the meeting, but even so, I spend the bulk of my day on the phone with him.

I'm sure you've worked for someone who tells you that he wants one thing and then, when you do it, he claims no knowledge of ever having asked for what he asked for, and instead pretends he'd wanted something else all along. Well, Kyle Woodruff isn't the first boss to do this to me, but just because I have experience with people like this doesn't ever make it easier or less frustrating to deal with. Every time I email him over a copy of the reports or Excel documents or PowerPoint presentations I've prepared to his specifications, he calls me with accusations about how I didn't do what he asked and tells me to start everything over from scratch, despite the fact that I've been working on this stuff for weeks and the meeting is tomorrow.

Then at about three o'clock that day, less then twenty-fours before the meeting, he tells me he'd like me to play around with the current logo for Exploran and the logo for

WP to show how the looks could be integrated. That type of thing is so out of my realm of expertise and I'm so shocked that he'd even think it was appropriate for him to ask me to do such a thing, I'm literally speechless for several long seconds.

"Ah, Kyle, I think that's something better handled by a graphic designer when we're at the branding stage of this process. That's not my area at all," I finally manage to say.

"I know, I know, I just want to give the board of directors an idea of how we can integrate the marketing of Exploran and WP."

"I appreciate that, Kyle, but I can't start fooling around with logo treatment for a meeting that's scheduled in about eighteen hours. I don't have any graphics software, for one thing, and I have no experience or skill with graphic design."

"I know, I'm not saying you need to design a new logo, just give an example of how the logos could work together."

I finally give up the fight. How this man could think someone who does the financial and marketing strategy for new products could just whip a brand new logo design out of her ass in a few hours' time is beyond my realm of understanding. To placate him, I add a slide to my PowerPoint presentation in which I import the Exploran logo with the WP logo as a brief talking point about how part of the branding process will be integrating the two looks. I don't know what else I can do.

The meeting the next day goes well. Or at least I think it does, until the meeting adjourns and Kyle pulls me aside to scold me on my "superficial" coverage of the logo issue. I try to defend myself, but Kyle is not a man of reason. I'm not sure of the exact definition of the word "psychopath," but I'm pretty sure it means someone who is completely out of touch with reality, and thus, distressingly, I think the word describes Kyle Woodruff nicely.

When I leave WP headquarters, my heart is pounding ferociously. I try to think about how many cups of coffee I've had today. My pulse rate is going crazy.

I pull over to the side of the road. For a moment, I wonder if it's possible that I'm having a heart attack, but then I realize that's ridiculous, it's just stress.

My cell phone rings. I check the caller ID. It's my mother. This is the fifth time she's called me in the past two days. She keeps hounding me for details, like whether I've finished planning the menu or picked out the invitations Why can't she leave me alone?

I start tearing up. I'm so tired. I'm so stressed. I can't do this anymore.

Moments after I let my voicemail take my mother's call, my phone rings again. The caller ID lets me know it's Will.

"Hello?" I say, blinking back tears.

"Hey, you. I was just on my way home from work and I wondered if you needed me to pick up anything at the store for dinner."

"No."

"Is everything okay?"

"Fine. Everything's fine. How about you? How was your day?"

"Nothing interesting. I'll tell you about it when I get home. I'll see you in half an hour or so, okay?"

"Bye. Will. I love you."

I get home and make a vegetable lasagna for dinner. It turns out pretty well, if I do say so myself. Will and I talk about our days and then he goes upstairs to his study to play computer games, and I go up to my office and pound away at work for WP for several hours.

I come downstairs around midnight. I'm exhausted, but I can't sleep. Will, of course, is sound asleep. Unlike me, Will never has trouble sleeping.

I get started on doing the dishes, and as I'm doing them, I actually feel like I might faint from exhaustion. I'm in this trance as I work. I may well be partially asleep. I feel a flash of vertigo, and I'm brought back to that time in high school when I was so ill from killing myself by studying so much that I fainted. Back then, I worried that if I wasn't perfect, my father wouldn't love me.

Thirteen years have passed since that night I fainted, and as I wash dishes, woozy with exhaustion, I think about how I'm killing myself working twelve-hour days and yet cooking dinner every night and washing the dishes and keeping the house clean and trying to plan a wedding and having sex with Will nearly every day and I realize I'm doing it again. I'm trying to be perfect, but this time, it's not my father I'm trying to impress, it's Will. I'm trying to be perfect because I'm worried that if I'm not, he won't love me.

It's the last thing I think before I collapse, the water still running, the plate I'm washing splintering into a million pieces when it crashes to the floor beside me.

Chapter 32

When I come to, it takes me a minute to figure out where I am. I'm lying down on a gurney being wheeled down a hospital corridor. Above me are doctors and nurses and bright lights on the ceiling overhead. If I look straight ahead, ceiling and lights would be all I could see. I look around, and I see Will walking along side the gurney as the doctors push me along the hallway. There are tears in his eyes.

"She's allergic to peanuts," he's saying. "We had lasagna for dinner, but maybe there were nuts, I don't know, in the noodles or the sauce or something."

"Not nuts," I manage to say. My chest is exploding. I feel like my heart is going to burst. "Purse," I say, gesturing to my purse, which Will is holding, probably for my health insurance card that's in my wallet. "Purse," I say again.

The doctor, a young, good-looking man, takes the purse from Will and looks through it. He finds the drugs.

"We've got an overdose. Methamphetamines," the doctor says.

"What?" Will says

"Your fiancé is using speed."

Will stops dead in his tracks. I will never forget the look on his face as I'm wheeled down the hallway. Shock. Betrayal. Disbelief.

The look on his face confirms all of my worst fears.

I have lost Will forever.

Chapter 33

I don't know how much time has passed when I awake, look around, and realize that I'm in a hospital bed. Will is beside me. He looks like shit. His eyes are swollen from crying, and he looks exhausted. He's staring at his hands, which lie limply in his lap.

"Hi," I say in a voice that's quiet and unsure. Guilt threatens to swallow me. Fear of how Will will react terrifies me.

"Hi."

"I'm sorry."

"You're sorry."

"I'm sorry."

He says nothing for several seconds. "Do you know what the doctors told me, Eva?"

"No."

"You could have had a heart attack. A heart attack. You're thirty-one years old."

"I'm sorry."

"What the fuck, Eva. Why? Why did you do this?"

The truth is, I'm not even sure. I don't have the words to express how jumbled I feel about my life. So instead I just repeat sentiment again. "I'm sorry."

"Those words are meaningless. Why? How long have you been—"

"About a month."

"How did you get the drugs?"

"Sandy. Rachel's sister-in-law Sandy."

"Why? Why would you poison yourself with something like that?"

"There weren't enough hours in the day. I had so much to do. Work . . . the wedding . . . I wanted to be perfect . . . I wanted to cook nice meals . . . I just wanted you to love me."

"I do love you, Eva. You don't have to be perfect. I . . ." he tosses his hands into the air and shakes his head. Clearly, he can't begin to fathom my actions.

"I'm so sorry, Will. I'll make it up to you."

"I don't understand how you could do that to yourself. I don't understand . . . were you unhappy? Are you unhappy with me?"

"No. No, that's not it at all. It was a stupid mistake."

"You could have been arrested, Eva. The doctors could have gone to the police."

"Why didn't they?"

"I told them you'd never done anything like this before. I told them I'd make sure you went to Narcotics Anonymous."

I sigh. I do not want to live a life filled with twelve-step plans and NA meetings. Will is completely overreacting. He's just had a shock, that's all. I only used it a few times. It was a stupid mistake, but it's not like I've got a problem.

"Will, it's not like I'm some junkie. I made a mistake. It's not a big deal. I mean, it is a big deal, but I can stop. I promise. There isn't going to be any problem."

Chapter 34

Before releasing me, the doctor gives me a big speech about how using a drug cooked up in some drug dealer's kitchen means I don't know exactly what dose I'm taking of the drug—which could lead to an overdose—and it means I don't really know what chemicals I'm willingly ingesting into my body. I know he's right. I sit there feeling idiotic and ashamed as the gorgeous young doctor points out what a moron I've been. He also goes on to tell me about how addictive meth is, and how low the success rates are for people who want to quit for good—a staggering number go back to using.

"Chronic use can cause permanent damage to the nerve endings of your serotonin and dopamine neurons. Those are basically your pleasure receptors," he says. "Imagine a nest full of baby birds squawking for food. Those are your dopamine receptors that will loudly clamor for more of the drug. But the more you take, the more you wear down the neurons, and thus the more drugs it takes to get that same high.

"I know you think you had the power to decide whether or not to use, but with drugs like this, very, very quickly, it's the *drug* that tells *you* to use. When the little voice inside your head says, 'Hey, wouldn't it be nice to use some meth right now? Go ahead, do it. It's not a big deal. It's not like you have a problem,' you think it's you talking, but in fact, it's your addiction. Your addiction will use any excuse to get you to use. It's very manipulative and opportunistic."

I think he's being melodramatic. Addiction! How ridiculous. I just used it a few times over the course of a month. Hardly anything serious.

"With meth, Eva," he continues, "people rarely overdose after just a few uses. But what happens with repeated use is that your blood levels can gradually accumulate to toxic levels. You can develop an increased heart rate and heart palpitations and eventually you could develop paranoia or have a stroke or heart attack or seizure."

"I'm sorry."

"Don't apologize to me, Eva. Do you want to go back to using?"

"No. Of course not."

"Are you sure?"

"Yes, I'm sure."

"What did you like about using?"

"What do you mean?"

"You used speed more than once, right?"

I nod.

"So there must have been something you liked about it. What did you like about it?"

"Well, I guess . . . I felt energized. I felt euphoric."

"So when you go home, today or tomorrow or the next day, when you're feeling a little run down and wish you had extra energy, are you going to use? There are a lot of pleasurable things about speed, you said so yourself."

"No, I'm not going to use again."

"Why not?"

He's confusing me. "Because like you said, I don't want to ingest mysterious substances cooked up in somebody's kitchen. I don't want to get arrested. I don't want to have a heart attack. I don't want to become an addict."

He nods. I think he's finally satisfied with my answer.

"Next time you need help, Eva, ask for it. Okay? When life starts getting crazy again, and it will, ask for help."

"I will. Thank you."

I'm released later that day. At home, Will and I are all awkward with each other. He keeps watching me. He doesn't trust me. He has reason to doubt, but I still don't like it.

"Are you ever going to take any kind of illegal substance again?" he asks me.

"No." He eyes me, unsure whether to believe me. "No, Will. I promise."

"I just don't understand how you could put those poisons into your body."

"Will, I've had an incredible amount of things to get done lately. I haven't been able to sleep, so I was always tired. I just needed a little help staying alert."

"You've got to figure out a way to reduce your stress. Taking drugs is not a logical solution. Maybe you should see a therapist. Someone you could talk to about your anxiety and inability to sleep."

I laugh. "Yeah, right, like I have time for that."

"Eva, you have to do something. I think we should talk to your mother."

"No! Are you crazy? She'd freak."

"And with good reason. I just don't know how to deal with this. I think you've got some emotional issues that a therapist might be able to help you with. You said yourself you have a lot of anxiety. Maybe somebody could help you with that."

"You're overreacting. I made a mistake. A serious one. But everything is going to be fine."

"I'm just scared."

"What are you scared about?"

"I'm worried about you. I want you to be healthy. And . . ."

"And what?"

"And I'm worried about us. Do you think I want to marry someone who abuses drugs? No thanks."

This hits me with a stinging slap. "I mess up once and you're just going to leave me? Just like that?"

"I didn't say that. I just . . . I don't know how to be sure this isn't going to happen again."

"It's not going to happen again. I'll look into going to therapy, okay? I'll take a little time off work. I'll figure things out."

We order Chinese for dinner, absently sit in front of the television for a few hours without paying any attention to it, and then we go to bed in silence. We sleep on the opposite sides of the bed, as far from each other as we can.

In the morning, I wake before Will. I watch him sleeping and begin to cry. I love him so much it hurts. I move to him and lay my head on his chest and wrap my arms around him. He wakes and returns my embrace.

"I'm sorry, Will. I love you so much."

"I love you, too. You really scared me."

"I know. I'm so sorry. Please say everything is okay between us."

"Everything is okay."

"Do you still want to marry me?"

"Of course I do."

Relief floods me. I begin kissing his chest, his nipples, his neck, his lips. We make love together as if discovering each other's bodies again for the first time, appreciating just how good we have it that we have each other.

We shower together, and as we're toweling off, Will says, "I don't have to go to work today. I can call in sick."

"I'll be fine. I promise."

"Are you sure?"

I nod. "I'm sure."

After I kiss Will good-bye and he leaves for work, I call Kyle Woodruff and tell him I had a bad reaction to some medication—which is sort of the truth—and I need a few days off. He makes it sound like he's just disgusted that I could make anything a bigger priority than WP.

"I actually had to be hospitalized," I say, feeling a deep-seated hatred for this man.

"Oh," he sighs, "well, I hope you feel better," but he sounds like he couldn't care less, and I'm sure he couldn't.

Next I call Gabrielle and tell her about what I did.

"Oh, Eva. I'm so sorry you're going through this. Is there anything I can do?"

"Will wanted me to talk to someone, a therapist or someone, about my stress, things like that. I don't know, he might be right. You liked that therapist you went to after your divorce, right?"

"Yeah. She was great. I'd definitely recommend her. Do you want me to get her number?"

"Yeah."

The therapist is a woman named Anne Braithwaite. After I get off the phone with Gabrielle, I call Anne. Anne says she had a cancellation and I can come that afternoon, so I agree, but in the back of my mind I'm thinking that after this week off from work, I won't have time to do things like go to therapy.

I spend the hours before my appointment researching meth online, and I have to say, what I read humbles me.

I learn that meth is one of the few drugs used by both men and women about equally. (Most drug addicts are male.) Men take it for the high, while women take it so they can lose weight (it's a derivative of amphetamine, which was once prescribed for depression and obesity) and so that they have the energy to work long hours and still have enough to be a good mother to their kids. The problem is that it's a drug that's harder to quit than crack cocaine and it can set people off in violent rages. Because meth can be made with chemicals found at any drugstore or from materials handy on farms, it's becoming extremely prevalent in rural areas. But it has found its way to the more affluent as well.

I read several women's stories of addiction. I read about professional women who got so caught up in addiction that they lost their jobs. Several women said it was so hard to stop using that they thought seriously of suicide because it seemed like an easier solution than quitting. I read about successful women who ended up in jail because the drug made them lash out in violence, not to mention the fact that being caught with drugs is illegal. Meth contributes to memory loss, aggression, psychotic behavior, and potential heart and brain damage. Unlike cocaine, which quickly metabolizes and thus is removed from the body, meth lingers for a much longer period of time, making the dangerous effects even more destructive.

How could I have risked imprisonment so I would have extra energy to plan the perfect wedding? How could I have been so stupid?

Anne Braithwaite is an attractive woman in her early fifties. She's a blonde with a prodigious bosom and a warm, comforting smile.

"It's nice to meet you, Eva."

I clear my throat. "It's nice to meet you, too."

She gestures for me to take a seat. Her office is small and very plain. The carpet is worn and the furniture is old—thousands of troubled people have parked their butts on the very cushions of the loveseat I sit in now.

Anne has a large desk with a thick mahogany clock facing my direction. That's really the only decoration in the room except for books. Books are everywhere. Thick, serious-looking books that jam shelves that reach the ceiling on two of Anne's walls. Books are stacked on her desk and on the two end tables on either side of the loveseat where I sit and there are piles of them on the floor, too.

"What brings you here today?" Anne asks.

"A friend of mine, she was a former patient of yours, and she recommended you."

We stare at each other for a moment. We both know that's not what she meant.

"I'm not really sure where to begin," I say. I start where I think it starts, one year ago when I fell in love with the man I want to spend my life with. I tell her about the project with Woodruff Pharmaceuticals and about planning the wedding and trying to be the perfect domestic and sex goddess to Will, and how there wasn't enough time in the day for it all. "And when Sandy gave me the drugs and said it would give me energy, I—unbelievably, stupidly, idiotically—I just took it. And what happened was that after I used it, I loved it, and I wanted more, and I didn't particularly care about what it was exactly that I was putting into my body. I'm feeling very stupid right now. And ashamed. I'm a smart woman, and yet somehow I managed to convince myself that it was better to poison myself with an illegal drug than to waste time being tired.

"I think," I continue, "that at the base of all this, I struggle with self-esteem. In my teens, I really had serious problems with it. I wrote over and over again in my diaries that I was fat and ugly and boring and not worth loving. Then I got to college and I discovered feminism. I was surrounded by other feminists and reading these authors who told me about how the diet and fashion and makeup industries fueled our insecurities to sell products and that it was a bunch of bullshit and we were wonderful just the way we were, and I believed that. I stopped hating myself. I stopped counting calories. I stopped putting myself down all the time, and I came to believe that I was okay just as I was. I don't mean to say that I never suffered from self-doubt, because I did, but I stopped thinking things like I didn't deserve to be loved just because I was a little overweight. And then I started succeeding at my career, and I really began believing in myself, believing that I had talent and worth. Then, when I met Will, I fell for him so hard. I was out of my mind in love with him. I'd never loved anyone like that, and it kind of scared me. I started worrying that I would lose him. I worried that he would think I wasn't as sexually adventurous or fun as his first wife, and that he would constantly be comparing us in his mind. I worried that even if we did get married, I'd mess it up because I have a hard time communicating my emotions. I worried that he'd leave me for a woman who could cook. It was just this downward spiral of self-doubt."

I pause to take a breath. I look at the clock. I've been talking nonstop for forty-nine minutes of our fifty-minute session.

Anne smiles at me. "You certainly make my job easy, Eva. You're very self-aware."

"Is that a good thing or a bad thing?"

"It's a good thing, but I think that because you're so self-aware, you beat yourself up too much. I'm going to give you a homework assignment."

My homework is to pat myself on the back three times every day for something I've done well, even if it's as insignificant as making a good cup of coffee. Any time I start to beat myself up over something or put myself down, I'm supposed to banish the negative thoughts from my mind immediately.

It's much harder than it sounds. I have no trouble picking on myself for things I don't do well, but I have a much harder time thinking of things I do right.

Chapter 35

For the first several days after I get out of the hospital, Will watches me in a way he never did before. When we go out for beer at Mickie's with our friends, he studies me taking every sip of beer, as if I'm some junkie who can't be trusted with any mind-altering substance, even something as innocuous as beer.

This is what fucking freaks me out. On Sunday night, I suddenly, out of nowhere, get this incredibly intense desire to get high. I think briefly about all the terrible things about taking drugs. The heart attacks, getting hooked, getting thrown in jail, and I think, *no, no, that's not going to happen, I just want to get high tonight.* I can't stop thinking about calling Sandy and seeing if she can hook me up. I try to think of lies I can tell Will to get out of the house so I can meet her.

But I get through the night sober. Several more times over the next couple weeks, my craving for drugs nearly over-whelms me. The craving is so intense that things like getting thrown in jail don't seem like that big of a deal. Jail? Bah! A trivial detail. And it scares the shit out of me to find myself thinking this way. I think about what the doctor said about how it seems like I'm the one thinking I want to use, when really it's the drug addiction telling me to. I get through these nights white-knuckled with my craving to get high. All I can do is not use. I can't read, or watch TV, or concentrate on anything. I just don't use drugs. It takes everything I have. All my energy, all my mental faculties. It's exhausting. I only used a few times. How could it possibly be this hard to quit?

After three weeks of staying sober, Will begins to believe me that I've learned my lesson. He stops watching my every move like a hawk. We start to build trust again. On the nights when I don't have the strength or courage to stay sober for myself, I find the strength and courage to stay sober for Will. I want ours to be a relationship based on trust and honesty, and if I'm using, that's not possible.

Seeing Anne is helping me, too. I've talked to her about how all my life I tried to succeed to make my father proud of me, and how I always strove to be perfect and beat myself up when it turned out I wasn't.

I've also told her about all the stress in my life. She tells me to think of creative ways of how to reduce it. I talk with Will, and we decide we'll hire a maid to come once a week to clean the house. We also agree that he'll do the dishes on the nights I cook, and I ask him to be in charge of dinner three nights a week, whether he makes grilled cheese or frozen pizza or takeout, I don't care, I just don't want to have to worry about feeding us. I'll cook dinner the other nights of the week, but I'm going to stop killing myself trying to plan perfect meals. We may eat mac and cheese every night, but I just don't have it in me, at least not right now, to worry about achieving perfection.

The work I've been contracted to do with WP will be over in a month. Kyle Woodruff will likely want to renew my contract and have me consult on the launch of their new product line. I'm undecided about whether to turn him down. If I did, it would mean I'd very probably never get work from WP again and Kyle would likely bad mouth my work to other execs in the area, which would potentially damage my career. My other option is to agree to do more work, but only if Kyle agrees to let me bring in a partner or lets me map out more reasonable deadlines. Whatever happens, I can't worry about it right now.

My efforts to finish planning the wedding are halfhearted. It's t-minus four months until we're supposed to get hitched, and I've pretty much stopped planning the thing.

The only thing I'm still doing is looking for the elusive perfect dress. Something that will transform me. I don't mean just some dress that will make me look beautiful, although I want that, too, but a dress that somehow gets me feeling like having a wedding will be the most exciting thing in the world for me. I go into boutiques and try on dresses, and I just feel hollow. I feel bored with all the work it takes to plan a wedding. I just want to be married and not have to bother with all this other stuff.

It occurs to me that I could just hire a wedding planner, but when I think of how quickly the cost of this wedding could escalate. I feel torn by genuinely wanting a gorgeous, perfect wedding and not wanting to get sucked into the expense and hype of having a gorgeous, perfect wedding.

So rather than deciding what it is I really want, I do nothing.

Chapter 36

I'm nervous about meeting Gabrielle and Rachel for lunch. I take extra care with my hair, makeup, and clothes, trying to look as healthy, happy, and normal as I can. I haven't seen them since I landed in the hospital, but I've spoken to them on the phone so they both know about what happened. Rachel is already sitting at a table when I get to the café. I take a seat across from her.

"How are you?" Rachel asks me. She looks at me like I'm a china doll with a hairline fracture threatening to split into a million pieces in the slightest breeze. I want to die of embarrassment.

"I'm doing okay. Work has been really stressful."

"I wasn't talking about work," Rachel says.

"I know, but I mean . . . that was a big trigger for . . . what happened."

"Why don't you quit then?"

"I signed a contract. It would be hell to get out of now. This phase of the project is almost done anyway."

"You're used to dealing with stress. What's different about this?"

"It's the man I'm working for. Did you hear that Warren Woodruff, the founder of Woodruff Pharmaceuticals, turned the company over to his son when he retired about a year ago?"

"That sounds vaguely familiar, but I can't say I really stay on top of business news," Rachel says.

"Well, it's one thing to turn a small family business over to your son, but it's another thing to turn over a huge company to your kid. It wouldn't have been a big deal if Kyle had experience, but he didn't. It's unfortunate because I really liked Warren. Warren was an unpretentious self-made man. I learned a lot about business from him. But his son . . . Kyle doesn't really know what he's doing, so he's got this personality that's a cross between being arrogant while at the same time craving approval. He's kind of a dictator. He's a rich kid who is used to getting his own way, not through consensus, but by demanding it or manipulating it. So anyway, between that and the wedding, I just, I . . . What am I saying? I don't have a good excuse. I'm going to shut up now."

"I want to murder Sandy."

"It's not her fault."

"Yes, it is. She got back together with her loser boyfriend, and how does she make a living? By selling drugs. To my friends. Drugs her idiot boyfriend cooks up in his kitchen."

"I didn't realize she'd gotten back together with him."

"It's still an on-and-off thing. Right now it's back off. But yeah, that's where she got it. It's just so infuriating. Do you know how much all of us chipped in so she could afford to go to rehab? A lot. I feel like she owes it to us to stay clean."

I look up to see Gabrielle pulling out the chair next to Rachel, so I'm now facing both of them.

"How are you?" Gabrielle asks.

"I'm good. I'm fine. I'll be fine."

"How's therapy?"

"It's good. Who knows, my little brush with drugs could actually turn out to be a good thing. It's making me face a lot of things I didn't want to face."

"Like what?"

"Like my lack of self-esteem. I have such a warped sense of self-worth. My therapist wants me to work at complimenting myself on all the things I do well. I can't even tell you how hard it is. All I can see is what I don't do well. I have such a hard time believing I'm beautiful and worthy. How could I have such a low opinion of myself? What kind of feminist am I?"

"You live in a culture that doesn't value anything women do," Gabrielle says. "It doesn't value child-rearing, or cleaning, or cooking. And it values sexy women at the exact same time it degrades them as sluts and whores. We're constantly barraged by images of eternally young and surgically enhanced women that we compare ourselves to. It's very hard not to let all that patriarchal bullshit get to you."

"'Patriarchal.' I've heard that word before. What does it mean again?" Rachel asks.

"Patriarchy is Kyle Woodruff being named chief executive officer of Woodruff Pharmaceuticals, even though he's not qualified for it, just because his father started the company," I say. "Patriarchy is children and women taking the man's surname. Patriarchy is when sons get elected to office not because of their intellect or ability, but because their dad is wealthy and well-connected in political circles."

"Ah. Got it. But what if the daughter of a wealthy politically connected family gets elected to office? What's that?" Rachel asks.

"That's a simple case of nepotism and class warfare," I say with a wink.

"Patriarchy also expresses itself in the fact that we're endlessly subjected to gorgeous young women in movies and advertisements," Gabrielle says. "That's because, by and large, men still have the money in Hollywood and business, so they're the ones deciding what movies get made and what products get sold and how, and we're constantly subjected to images of women most of us can't possibly measure up to. So we feel bad about ourselves and will go to ridiculous lengths to feel pretty. All these girls on those *Girls Gone Wild* videos, I just want to pull them aside and say, Girlfriend, men hooting at you will never fill the holes you seek to fill. You need self-esteem and self-respect. Come on!"

"Yeah, you know, I remember when the movie *Troy* came out," I say. "And all my male friends got all blustery by how distractingly good-looking Brad Pitt looked in that movie. I mentioned how I'd read that Brad had been kind of put out because he'd had to add on ten pounds of muscle for the role, and the guys were all like, 'Oh yeah, poor Brad Pitt, his normal Adonislike body isn't enough.' I remember thinking, 'Ah-ah! That's a small taste of what it's like to be a woman. Now just multiple that by a thousand percent, three hundred and sixty-five days a year, and you'll get the full picture."

"Plus, when you live in a world where men are valued more than women, it's really hard not to let that get to you," Gabrielle says. "You feel like you can never quite measure up because you'll never be a male."

"I don't feel like things are quite so dire," Rachel says. "I mean, yes, women don't make as much money as men and we don't have nearly as many women in government as men, but I don't think things are unequal. Well, I mean, not exactly—"

"Back in the days when women couldn't vote or work or own property, they didn't think things were unequal either. They thought that's just the way things were and always would be. They thought it was natural. Inequality is even more dangerous when it's subtle. It's easier to kid yourself that things are okay," I say. The three of us pick at our food in silence for a moment. I think about mentioning how in China and India there is a huge disparity in the number of men to women because female fetuses are aborted and female babies are abandoned. The implications of this for the future are significant, but I decide that I don't want to talk about this anymore. Reality can really just be too much of a drag. I decide to change the subject instead. "Anyway, how are things going in your life, Rachel? Still sending steamy emails to Shane?"

She smiles. "I know it's terrible, but it's been really fun."

"What if Jon found the emails?" I ask.

"I've been saving them in an obscure folder within a folder. He could never find them."

"You're not deleting them?" Gabrielle asks, eyes wide.

"I like rereading them."

"What do you say in the emails?" I ask.

"Sometimes we just talk about our days. But other times . . . he tells me how beautiful he thinks I am and how sexy I am. He tells me the things he'd like to do to me if I weren't married. He tells me about the tropical paradises he'd take me to and how he'd make love to me for hours and basically worship me. It's a nice fantasyland."

"But it's always just going to stay a fantasy, right?" I say.

Rachel pauses a moment too long.

"Rachel?" I prompt.

"Yes, yes, of course, it's just going to remain a fantasy."

"Rachel," Gabrielle says, "I've got to tell you, as someone who's been cheated on, it's the most painful thing in the world to experience. You really need to think this through."

"Yeah, Rach, think of this from Jon's point of view. What if you found out he was flirting with a woman via email?"

"He's already done it."

"What are you talking about?"

"There was this little chippy he worked with that he flirted with through email."

"When? How did you find out about it?"

"A couple of years ago. We never use passwords or anything on our email, and then suddenly I noticed that he'd password-protected his email account, so I immediately got suspicious and hacked my way in."

"How'd you do that?" I ask.

"Because I know my husband. I know he doesn't have a great memory, so I knew he wouldn't use anything complicated. I tried several combinations of the kids' names, his age, the dog's name, until I finally figured out what his password was."

"What was it?" I ask.

"Mr. Happy, of course."

"Mr. Hap—? Oh."

"Yeah, men are sooo predictable. Anyway, it was this really flirty stuff, it really pissed me off. I nearly tore his head off. He vowed he'd stop, but I caught him at it again and again. We ultimately ended up in couple's therapy because of it."

"But now you're doing the same thing," I point out. "You're not trying to get back at him for what he did, are you?"

"No, of course not."

"Maybe it's time to get back into couple's therapy," Gabrielle says.

"Maybe. I don't know. I just can't stop fantasizing about a weekend away with Shane in the Bahamas. I just want to have fun and sex and romance with someone who isn't Jon."

"So, do you want that more than you want to keep your family together?" I ask.

"Of course I don't want to tear my family up. I just . . . want it all. And as long as this stays a fantasy, what's the problem?"

"You're not addressing the real problems in your marriage by running away into this other world," Gabrielle says. "How are things at home between you?"

"It's been hard lately. Really hard. We just snap at each other and go around with very short fuses."

"What about the sex?"

Rachel rolls her eyes. "We actually had sex last night, and the whole time, all I could think about was those damn garage shelves."

"What are you talking about?" I ask.

"Don't you remember? Months and months ago, back on Jon's thirtieth birthday party, instead of helping me get ready for the party, he spent the day buying supplies to build garage shelves. And he still hasn't put the damn things up. I've asked him to do it a million times. Every week he promises he'll do it this weekend, and then the weekend comes and goes, and he has all these excuses for why he didn't get around to it."

"You don't want to destroy your marriage over garage shelves," I say.

"Don't you get it? It's not about the shelves. It's about how I bust my ass to keep him and the kids fed, the house cleaned, the dog walked, and I want Jon to show me that he values me and loves me and appreciates the work that I do to keep our family safe and happy. So if I ask him to put up some shelves, he should put up the fucking shelves."

"Have you talked to him and put it that way or have you just been nagging him?" I ask.

Rachel pauses a moment. She takes a deep breath and looks off at nothing as tears fill her eyes. She quickly brushes the tears away. "I'll talk to him."

"Are you and Jon going to make it through this?" I ask.

"Yes. We love each other desperately. Marriage really is a good thing, Eva, I swear. I'm sorry I'm just showing you the tough side of marriage. That's just where things are at for me and Jon right now. But it really is an amazing thing to build a life with someone, I promise. How are wedding plans coming?"

I can't tell them that my wedding is supposed to be four months away and I've stopped planning it completely. I've secured three big things—the reception/ceremony site, the caterer, and a DJ. I'm not going to use a florist, so I'm okay there, but I haven't chosen a dress or shoes or selected wedding invitations. I haven't booked a photographer or done anything about a rehearsal dinner or a million other details. I don't know how I expect any of this will get done, but I can't seem to bring myself to do it. I wonder if it means that I really don't want to get married after all.

"I can't seem to find a dress. According to this book I got on how to plan a wedding, I should have gotten a dress months ago, but I just can't seem to find something I like."

"What are you looking for exactly?" Rachel asks.

"That's the problem, I don't really know. Sometimes I think I want something really different, a beautiful gown that wouldn't necessarily have to be considered a bridal gown. Then then other times, when I'm flipping through the bridal magazines, I'll see these dresses on these gorgeous models and become convinced that's the dress I want, so I'll go to the store and try it on and as it turns out, I look nothing like the model. I don't know, I want a dress to reach out and grab me by the collar and shake me, announcing that this is it! This is my dress!"

"If you want help shopping for dresses, I'll be happy to come with you. Or maybe I could draw a few designs for you, and I could sew it myself," Rachel says.

"I couldn't ask you do to that."

"It could be my wedding present to you."

"No way, all that material would be much too expensive."

"Okay, well the gift could be my labor. You can pay for materials."

"Maybe." I don't want to talk about weddings or dresses or failing marriages anymore. After I swallow a bite of my sandwich, I say, "Gabrielle, how is your research going?"

"Good. I've gotten the okay from the Human Subjects Committee to go ahead and conduct my interviews. That was my last big hurdle, besides finishing the damn thing. So I'm crafting an online survey, and then I'll do some face-to-face follow-up interviews."

"Will and most of his friends are all into computer games, so if you want to interview any of them, I'm sure that they'd love to talk to you. They can talk about gaming for hours."

"Yeah. I'd like that."

"We get together at this bar called Mickie's every Friday night. Any time you want to come, let me know."

"I will, thanks."

"Rach, how are the kids?"

"The kids are good. You know how my friend Lisa is pregnant?"

I wonder if she's talking about Evil Bitch Woman Lisa. "No, I didn't know that," I say.

"Well, she is. She's really big now. She came over yesterday and Julia put her hands on her hips and asked, 'Why are you so fat?' I said, 'Julia, honey, she's not fat, she has a baby in her tummy.' Julia got all big-eyed and said in this shocked tone, 'Lisa! Why did you eat a baby?!'"

I smile. "She's such a cutie."

"I know. And then my eldest is being his usual brilliant self. He goes to a charter school," she tells Gabrielle. "It's very academically rigorous and it starts kids on foreign languages in second grade instead of waiting until they're in high school. But with the budget cuts, they're talking about shutting the school down. So there was a public meeting the other night to discuss this, and some of the students wrote speeches about why their school shouldn't be closed down. A ton of people came to this meeting—we filled the rafters of the kids' gym. The committee head said there were going to be too may kids speaking to applaud them all, so we had to do the silent kind of applause where you just wiggle your fingers." She demonstrates by putting her hands out with her palms facing us and then wriggling her fingers. "So kid after kid went, and, you know, they're kids, their speeches tend to ramble and go off on tangents and the kids tend to not be the best public speakers. So after each kid, all the parents do the silent finger-wiggling thing, and then my Isaac gets out there, and he reads a speech that's so well-written it sounds like the speechwriter for the president penned the thing. He wrote the entire thing himself, with no help from Jon or me. And he did such a good job of presenting this heart-wrenching talk on how the school has changed his life and how the teachers are passionate about teaching and the students are passionate about learning that when he finished, despite the mandate not to clap, the entire audience burst into thunderous applause. I was crying my eyes out, I was so proud of the kid, and I leapt up and started shouting, 'That's my kid! That's my kid!'"

"Rachel! You didn't!" I laugh.

"Yes, I did. But here's the best part. After the meeting was over, there was a reporter interviewing the kids for their reaction about the school being shut down. Isaac answered the reporter's questions and then he turned to me and said, all serious and matter-of-fact, 'I just don't know if I can handle all the fame.'"

Gabrielle and I hoot at this. As I laugh, I realize that if I never have children, I'm never going to have a moment like that, being filled with so much pride that I jump up and start hollering that that's my kid to a huge audience of people.

I feel suddenly sad and nostalgic about a life I may never have.

Chapter 37

In the first few days after I quit using, I felt irritable and depressed, but for the last few weeks, I have felt like a dynamo of health and productivity. I feel positive about my life and my future and I'm feeling good about myself. I barely even think about drugs.

So when my pink cloud of happiness and illusion pops, it happens abruptly and unexpectedly. I get an urge to take speed that's so overpowering it overwhelms me. I feel stressed and anxious and I crave it so badly I feel I would gladly do anything to get it because if I don't, I'll go crazy. In that moment, I don't try to do anything to talk myself out of using. I don't want to talk myself out of it. I want to use. I call Sandy on her cell phone and she agrees to meet me in an hour at a coffee shop close to Rachel's shop.

As soon as I've gotten the wheels in motion, my anxiety lifts. I feel happy and secure. I just need to get through the next hour, which is totally doable.

I get to the coffeehouse early and get a cup of coffee to go. I take the coffee outside, have a few sips, and dump out the rest. Then I take the empty cup inside to the bathroom with me, rinse it out, and pat it dry with a paper towel. Next I fold up the bills and put them in the cup and put the lid back on. It feels very James Bondish.

I wait for Sandy in a booth. She hands me a brown paper bag.

"This is for you," she says.

"And this is for you." I slide the coffee cup across the table. She takes it without opening it.

"How are things with you?" she asks.

"Better now. And you?"

She shrugs. "Same shit, different day, right? Look, I've got a bunch of shit I need to do. Call me if you need me."

"Sure. Thanks, Sandy."

On the drive home, I feel excited and at peace.

When Will finds my stash of drugs, he freaks out. He starts screaming so loud it scares me. I'm not scared in the sense that I'm worried about my safety, I mean it's scary because I hadn't known he was capable of such ferocity. He's usually so gentle. It also scares me because it reminds me uncannily of the way my father yelled at me sometimes. My father, like Will, rarely got angry, but when he did, the way his booming voice thundered through the room made me want to hide under the bed for safety.

I'm not proud of what I do next. I get defensive. "I've been doing really well. So I slipped up. You think someone who is trying to quit smoking never sneaks a cigarette here or there? It takes time to change!"

"Meth is not the same thing as a cigarette. It is an illegal drug that can land you in jail and can kill you not in years but in a matter of weeks."

"I'm trying! Change isn't easy."

"Why did you do it? Why couldn't you have told me that you wanted to use?"

"It was late. You were asleep. I couldn't sleep. I had too much work to do, so I just thought . . ."

"Eva, you can wake me up at any time of day or night. I

just don't understand why you didn't feel like you could come to me."

"It's not that I didn't think I could come to you. I—" The truth is, I didn't want to be talked out of using. I just wanted to get high. I just thought, *getting high would be great right now*. And without any internal debate, I called Sandy and got the wheels rolling. "I'm sorry. Next time I think about using I'll come to you."

I go to the appointment I had scheduled with Anne the next day and tell her what happened.

"You do realize that if you keep using drugs, you're going to lose Will," she says.

I nod my head. I do know that. It's just a question of exactly how much time it will take for Will to get fed up with me.

"Are you having doubts about Will?"

"No. I don't have any doubts that I want to spend my life with him. But the whole marriage thing is freaking me out a little."

"I want to address your relationship with Will first. You're sure you love him?"

"Yes. I'm absolutely sure. Why are you asking me that?"

"I just want to be sure you're not purposely trying to sabotage things with him."

"No. I waited my entire life to find someone like Will. I know it makes no sense. I dream all of my life of finding true love, and then I finally find it and I do everything I can to screw it up."

"It might be that you're testing his love for you. You have trouble loving yourself so you have a hard time believing someone could love you."

"At least I pick sweet men who treat me right, you know? I may not have any self-esteem, but I don't have abusive boyfriends." I realize I'm being defensive again. I want a medal because my fiancé doesn't beat me? Jesus, I'm in bad shape.

"Drugs are kind of like an abusive boyfriend who you keep going back to, aren't they? You know they aren't good for you, but you keep going back anyway," Anne says.

"I don't even know why I used the other night. It was so stupid!"

"Don't say that. Then you're saying you're stupid."

"I'm not saying I'm stupid, I'm saying my actions were stupid."

"Don't beat yourself up. Just think about why you used. What were you thinking and feeling before you used? This is a good opportunity for self-discovery."

Don't beat myself up? How can she say that? I betrayed Will, broke the law, and put my life and health in danger. I'd say a little bit of whipping my ass in shape is in order. "I wasn't *thinking* about anything. All I thought was, gee, it'd be nice to get high." I study my fingernail and begin using my thumbnail to poke back the cuticles on my left hand. "I don't know. I guess there was this part of me that felt like I was getting away with something. Like I thought I could use without Will knowing. Not using made me feel sort of, I don't know, like I feel when I diet. I feel deprived or something. But that's ridiculous. We can't give in to any urge or craving we have. Otherwise, we'd all be stealing from each other and we'd all weigh a thousand pounds and we'd all owe millions of dollars in credit card debt. You have to practice a little self-control."

"Eva, have you suffered from depression?"

"I've had bouts of depression, sure. Who hasn't?"

Anne just nods. "Depression is anger turned inward. I think you have anger you're not expressing, anger you can't face, and that's why you're getting high—when you're high you don't have to feel those emotions that make you uncomfortable."

I shrug. Anger turned inward? What do I have to be angry

about? My good job? My education? My two parents who love me?

"Let's talk about your memories of your parents when you were a child."

"Like what kind of memories?"

"We have to uncover where your anger comes from."

"Look, I can buy that I have issues with my parents, but I need to stop using drugs right now. I need help changing my behavior now."

"Your behavior will change once we heal the core issues. The fact that you used the other day gives us an opportunity to explore these issues."

We spend the rest of the time talking about my childhood and my relationship to my parents. It's painful to dredge up memories of when my parents were less than perfect, but even so, their "crimes" against me seem really minor. So my father had extremely high expectations of me and he had a hard time expressing his love for me. That must describe a huge percentage of fathers in the world. So many other fathers abandoned their kids or molested their kids or were abusive alcoholics, my father's failings seem pretty damn minor by comparison. But I keep telling Anne any memories that come into my mind. They all seem like small incidents. I almost get the sense that Anne wants me to reveal that my father molested me or that I was raped when I was twelve or something. As if once I could deal with a huge traumatic event, my anxiety and anger that seem to come from nowhere could suddenly be explained and everything would magically fall into place. But I don't have one big traumatic event. I just have two imperfect parents. To me, it's not my relationship with my parents that I think we need to talk about, it's my reaction to the daily stresses of life that needs to change.

Anne tells me that psychological health takes time and can't be rushed, and I understand that I can't order self-esteem at the drive-through window of a McDonald's. I am fully willing to work hard at improving my mental health for my sake and the sake of the people who care about me, but I feel frustrated with Anne for not seeing that, in addition to this long-term goal, I need a short-term solution for keeping me away from drugs.

Four days later, it's three in the afternoon and I'm exhausted from a shitty night of sleep the night before. I lie down to take a nap, but after ten minutes I get up again because there is no way I'm going to be able to sleep. I think about how Anne said that when I used the other day, I shouldn't beat myself up about it. I just needed to examine why I did what I did. I decide to take her comment as permission to use again. I am doing much better after all. The important thing is that I'm cutting down and that eventually I'll quit altogether. When I admit to her that I used again, I'll just explain that I was exhausted and I didn't have the energy to fight the craving. I understand that I have to quit and I *want* to quit, but later, not right now. Maybe after the wedding. That would be a much better time to quit.

Once again I call Sandy and once again we meet at the coffee shop, but this time I can't wait to get home. I duck into the bathroom at the coffeehouse. My nails aren't very long, but they will do. I stick my pinky finger in the bag of powder, then I bring the finger to my nose and snort.

I walk home from the coffee shop feeling my anxiety lift like fog passing.

When Will gets home from work, we eat dinner together and then watch TV together, and the whole time, all I can think is that I'm wrecked out of my mind and Will doesn't know it.

He goes to bed, but I can't because I'm wired. I start freaking out and feeling restless and I'm worried about how if I don't get to sleep, I'm just going to be tired again tomorrow and my productivity will be in the toilet once again but I don't want to use because I promised Will and if I keep using that will mean I really do have a problem after all.

So the sensible thing to do is to have a drink or two, something to calm me down. We have a few bottles of wine on our wine rack, but I don't want a whole bottle of wine. I go to Will's liquor cabinet. I've never really checked out what's in it before, so I open the cabinet to find that we basically have a fully stocked bar. I could make anything out of this stuff. I'm trying to think of what I'd like to drink when I remember I have a bottle of raspberry vodka in my freezer from a party I had awhile back. A cold, fruity drink sounds perfect right now, so I go to the freezer, pull the nearly full bottle out, and pour myself what I estimate to be a couple of shots.

I put the bottle back and go into the living room. I sit on the couch and wait for my heart rate to slow down and for me to start feeling more relaxed.

I feel restless. I don't know what to do with myself. I look at the clock. Only two minutes have gone by, so of course the alcohol hasn't kicked in yet, but I'm impatient.

My heart feels like it's pounding so hard it's going to cannonball out of my chest. Maybe one more shot will help me calm down more quickly . . .

Chapter 38

When I wake, the first thing I feel is an intense pain in my right wrist. I groan when I feel the throbbing headache making my brain feel thick. My mouth feels mossy and tastes awful, as if something died in it. I shift slightly and an intense pain shoots through my upper left arm. I pry my eyes open and see that I have a gigantic bruise on my arm. In the center of the bruise is a small cut, but it's insignificant compared to the giant purple blob of a bruise that nearly extends from my elbow to my shoulder. It looks like a particularly hideous Rorschach inkblot.

I raise my right hand to touch the bruise and that's when I see that I've bruised and scraped my inner right wrist as well. I stare at my injury for a moment and then I feel eyes on me. I look up. I'm lying in bed and Will is awake and lying next to me, watching me. Turning sets off a maelstrom of hangover malevolence, but I look at the clock. It's 5:42 in the morning. For several moments, I can't remember what day of the week it is.

The cruelly bright sun is barging its way into the room.

"What happened?" I ask.

"You got wasted last night. You woke me up when I heard a crashing sound in the bathroom. I'm not sure exactly what happened, but the shower curtain had been torn down and all the shampoo bottles had been knocked off the edge of the tub. I think you grabbed the shower curtain to keep you from falling, but it didn't work."

"I'm sorry."

"You've been saying that a lot lately."

"I know."

"I love you, Eva, but I don't know how to help you."

"I know."

"I'll do anything I can to help you. If you want me to look into rehab programs for you or go to Narcotics Anonymous meetings with you, I'll do that. Just let me know how I can help you."

"I'll call Mom. I'll ask her . . . I don't know, I'll tell her I need help."

"Good. I think that's the right thing to do."

"I'll call Sienna and tell her, too."

"Okay."

He watches me for another hour. I am in so much pain I want to die. I have never had a hangover like this before. I can't believe I willingly ingested so much alcohol that I could do this to myself. It's insanity.

"Are you going to be okay? Should I call in sick from work?" Will asks.

"I'll be fine."

"Are you sure?"

"I'm sure. Go to work."

Will leaves for work and I just stay where I am in bed, unable to escape into sleep. All I can do is feel like shit and like an idiot for doing this to myself. At around ten in the morning I muster the energy to reach my hand out and pick up the phone to dial Mom.

"Hi, Mom."

"Eva? What's wrong? You don't sound well."

"I'm not. I have something to tell you. A few weeks ago, I landed in the hospital."

"What! Why didn't you tell me this? Why didn't you call me? Why didn't Will call me?"

"Will didn't call you because I asked him not to. Mom, the reason I didn't tell you was because I was embarrassed."

"Embarrassed about what? You can tell me anything."

"Let me finish, okay? I was embarrassed because the reason I landed in the hospital was because I had a bad reaction to methamphetamines."

"Oh? A diet drug? That's nothing to be ashamed of. A lot of women want to lose weight before their weddings."

The fact that my mother finds no problem with the fact that I would take drugs to lose weight is several therapy sessions' worth of mental turmoil for me to work out at some point, but right now I don't have time to deal with it. "No, Mom. It's a derivative of a diet drug, but meth itself is actually illegal. I could have landed in jail."

"What? Eva, I don't . . . but why . . . how . . ."

"It can help you feel energized and with the wedding plans . . ."

I tell her the whole story, about how dangerous the drug is and how I vowed to stop and how I thought it would be no problem. I tell her about seeing Anne and how I thought I was doing better, but then I woke up this morning after having battered and bruised myself up as if I were a crash-test-dummy, and now I'm beginning to see that kicking this thing isn't going to be as easy as I thought.

Telling my mother that I cut and bruised myself, but have no memory of doing it, helps her to understand how serious this really is. She cries. She asks if my problem with drugs is her fault. I assure her that it's not.

"You know what it is? Why you're abusing drugs?" she says at last.

I sigh, not looking forward to my mother's armchair therapist interpretation of my problems. "Why?"

"You always had so much anger that you didn't know how to express."

"Oh, my God, that's so weird, that's exactly what Anne said. But what would I have anger about?"

"You had two dysfunctional parents in a very dysfunctional marriage."

"Everybody has dysfunctional parents. The whole planet isn't battling drug addiction. I don't buy it."

"Eva, when you were growing up, I had a lot of anger. Your father expected me to be a stay-at-home mom, and I wanted to want that, because I thought that's what I was supposed to want, but the truth was, as much as I loved you and your sister, I was going out of my mind with boredom. I made up reasons to go to the grocery store every single day just to get out of the house. I was so lonely, so unbelievably lonely. Your father would work all day and then he'd hide in his workshop building furniture at night. I felt like I had no one to talk to. When I finally got a job, that didn't make me happy either because my bosses treated me like I was some stupid housewife just because I never got a college degree. And the work was boring, too. It was just a different kind of boredom. Then there was your father. He was emotionally absent for you and Sienna, too. You tried so hard to get his attention but it was nearly impossible. You suppressed your anger over that. You need to speak with him and tell him what's going on with you. Tell him about the drugs."

"Mom, I talk with Dad two or three times a year. What's the point? Even if I did confront him about how I think he failed me when I was growing up, what would that change? Do you think Dad and I would suddenly become close after all these years? Do you think Dad is suddenly going to change and listen to what I have to say and magically see the error of his way? Dad and I could talk 'til we were blue and things might change for about ten minutes and then we'd both go right back to being the same people we always were."

Mom sighs. "You may have a point about that."

"Anyway, regardless of the fact that I obviously learned some really poor coping skills for dealing with anger when I was growing up, I don't see how that has anything to do with what's happening to me now. I have a wonderful man whom I love, I have a good job, I'm financially secure. Why would I suddenly decide now to start hiding my feelings with drugs?"

"Maybe because until now you were so busy working and trying to get your career on track that you never had time to think about serious issues like whether you were happy. Now that you're not struggling with basic survival, you have time to think about bigger things. Not to mention the fact that you're planning to commit to spending your life with someone. You're getting in touch with some of the emotions that you've kept buried for a long time."

"Maybe."

"Eva, I'm so worried about you. Do you want me to come out there? Do you want to come out here and stay with me?"

I love my mother more than anything, but if there was anything that would drive a person to substance abuse it would be hanging out with my mother for any stretch of time. "No, Mom, that's okay. I'll be okay. I think what happened last night finally helped me to figure out that what I'm dealing with is more serious than I was willing to admit before. I think I have to face the fact that . . ." The possibility seems too awful to verbalize, but I do it anyway. "That I'm a drug addict."

Even as I say it out loud, the idea seems outlandish and ridiculous. I'm a successful business owner! I have an MBA! Drug addicts are sickly looking people who can't hold down jobs and have boyfriends with prison records, people like Sandy. I'm not a lazy person. I'm not a bad person. I don't fit my own stereotype, so how could *I* be one of *them*?

I know life isn't a fairy tale, but wouldn't it be nice if life would cooperate for just a little while so you could pretend like it was? I finally fall in love and instead of being able to just be happy about it, all these self-esteem demons and personal issues rear their ugly heads and demand attention, forcing me to confront things I'd really prefer not to confront.

* * *

In reaction to what happened, I do two things. I book an appointment with my doctor to discuss my anxiety problems
and I look online for classes for substance-abusers and find
one that's held every Tuesday night for two hours a night for
eight weeks. I call to get more information, and the woman
who answers asks me whether I'm required to take level one
or level two classes.

"Required? I don't know what you're talking about."

"The courts didn't mandate that you enroll in outpatient
treatment?"

"What? No, I want to. I want some help."

"Oh," she says, her surprise evident. I could have told her
I was a magic fairy and I think I would have gotten approximately the same reaction.

We work out the payment fee and she tells me I can join
the next class.

I continue seeing Anne and my mother calls me every day
to check up on me. Sienna calls or emails every day. The constant phone calls help remind me that I am loved and my
problem isn't just about me, it impacts all of the people I
love. Even so, a couple times I get really intense cravings.
One time it happens in the middle of the night when I've had
a stressful dream. In the dream, I'm lost in a house and I can't
find the way out. I keep walking up and down stairs and in
and out of rooms but I can't find any way out, I just keep
going and going and going. I come into a dimly lit room and
there is a man in there, and for a moment I feel relieved,
thinking that he can help me find my way. Then I realize this
man has his pants down around his ankles. He's jacking off
and smiling at me with a leering smile. I turn and run away. I
run and run, but I can't find any way out of the house, not a
door, not a window, not even a vent to crawl through. I turn
a corner and as I run down the hall, I realize the surface I'm
running on has changed. I hear crunching noises and I finally
look around me and realize that every surface is covered with

black crickets so thick the walls and floor writhe like ocean waves.

When I wake up, my heart is pounding and I'm completely stressed. All I can think about is how I want to escape from what I'm feeling and how getting high would be a great way to do just that.

The other time I crave getting high is after Will and I run into a friend of Will's from college when we're at a restaurant. We ask Will's friend, Brant, to join us. Brant is a middle school teacher, and when we ask him about his job, he tells us about all the twelve- and thirteen-year-old girls who get knocked up each year and about the girl whose father had to admit he was raping his daughter after she came to school with hickies, and about two boys who attacked a girl in the hallway of the school, tearing her skirt down and thrusting their fists into her so hard they bruised her pelvis. They only got ten days of suspension and the boys' parents thought that was too harsh a punishment. That's the part that makes me so upset I can't bear to feel what I feel. That there are parents who think publicly raping a twelve-year-old girl with a fist isn't a very big deal. That's the kind of thing that makes me hate the world I live in. But I don't get high because I know my using isn't going to help that poor girl. My running away from anger and frustration isn't going to help a thing.

My doctor prescribes me Lexapro for my anxiety and Trazadone for the nights I'm having trouble sleeping. I notice a difference right away on the Lexapro. I actually find myself smiling and feeling happy instead of feeling anxious all the time.

As I feared, it does have an effect on my sex drive. I can still have orgasms, but it takes longer to have them than it used to. On the weekends, it's no problem to prolong foreplay to get me where I need to be, but on mornings when we have quickies before Will has to high-tail it to work, it's simply a lost cause. For the time being, that's a sacrifice I'm willing to make.

When the night of the substance abuse support group comes, I'm scared out of my mind. I keep telling myself that everything is fine and my problem isn't that bad and this has all been a terrible misunderstanding, but then I look at the bruise on my arm that still hasn't gone away. It still looks terrible. If anyone saw the bruise, they'd think I had an abusive boyfriend for sure.

I'm not exactly sure what I expected from the people in the group. I guess maybe I was expecting an emaciated group of people that could fit right in with the cast from *Trainspotting*, but the five other people in the group don't look at all scary.

The man leading the group is named Tad. Tad is in his midthirties and is cute in a tall, skinny, nerd-with-glasses sort of way. There is a black man who looks to be in his late thirties and four other Caucasian women ranging from about twenty years old to about forty-five. It seems odd that there are so many more women in the group than men when the stats say men and women battle addiction in equal numbers. Maybe it's just a coincidence, or maybe it's just that women are more willing to admit they have a problem that they need help with.

Tad begins the class by discussing how you go about making a change, whether it's quitting smoking, changing your diet, or getting off an illegal substance.

"The first thing you need," Tad says, "is to believe that you can change. If you think that you are an addict and that's just the way you are and you'll never be able to quit, well, then, you're right, you're never going to be able to quit. But if you can imagine yourself getting through hard times sober, if you can imagine why making that decision will ultimately make your life richer and more fulfilling, then you are off to a great start. The second thing you need to do is unlearn learned behavior. Maybe you associate relaxing with drugs or a drink after a stressful day at work. Well, you need to learn a new way to unwind after a tough day. The third thing you need to do is to make a conscious decision to change. Often we'll make promises when we've landed in jail or we're going through withdrawal. But if you're serious about changing, your heart needs to be in it, not just when you can remember the pain of addiction, but when all you can remember is what you liked about using. Fourth, you need to cope with cravings. I wish there were an easy way through this step, but whether you crave chocolate ice cream or crack cocaine, the only way to get through the cravings is to buckle down and wait them out. Last, you need to find something to replace the old habit. If you used drugs when you were feeling bored or lonely, you're going to find a new way to kill time when you're lonely. Maybe you can take up a hobby or join a book club or take a pottery class, but you'll need to do something because when you quit abusing drugs, you'll find that you have a whole lot more time than you used to."

Every word he says makes a lightbulb go off in my head, that undeniable PING! of recognition that *that makes sense*.

After Tad talks about what we need to make a change, the rest of us talk about what we think the hardest of these steps might be and how we can overcome the challenges we're going to face. One of the women, whose name I learn is Robbie, short for Roberta, also used crystal meth. She is a very attractive, fit woman with curly hair and bright eyes, so when she says that she used to save and dry out her urine so she could resmoke the meth, it's too shocking for me to even begin to believe. *How could this cute woman be so desperate as to do something so vile? Could that happen to me?*

"So, Eva," Tad says when the class is wrapping up. "This was your first time with us. What do you think?"

"I think I learned a lot. I'm glad I came."

"We're not scary people who live under bridges," Robbie says.

"No. That's the scariest part," I say.

*   *   *

As time passes, I still have cravings, but they aren't nearly as intense as they were in the beginning. When they come, I just wait them out. Once I do it a few times, I realize it's possible, and that makes it easier to do it again. That's what I have learned: Change isn't easy, but it is *possible*.

In one of our daily phone calls, I tell Mom about the eight-week class and how much I like the people and how much I think it's helping me. "It's a lot cheaper than therapy and it addresses the real issues," I say.

"What do you mean?"

"I mean my big problem is my behavior today. Anne keeps wanting to focus on things that happened to me in my childhood. I'm not opposed to exploring my past to figure out why I'm behaving like I am today, but I think the more immediate problem is dealing with the behavior first and then worry about the rest of it. In fact, I'm getting so frustrated with Anne that I'm thinking about not seeing her anymore. I just don't think our philosophies sync up. I mean nothing really bad ever happened to me as a kid. So my dad was emotionally distant and had high, unrealistic expectations for me. Boo-hoo, poor me. This therapy thing just seems so self-indulgent."

"No Eva, getting help for your problems isn't self-indulgent. Using drugs is."

I freeze. This hurts because it's true and she's absolutely right.

"Look Eva, you may not have been molested or abused as a child, but somewhere along the way you learned to believe that you weren't worth loving. But even if you can't remember that you're worth loving, you have to think about how much I love you and how much your sister loves you and how much Will loves you. We can't bear to see you hurt."

The thing is, as much as I struggle to believe in my own inherent self-worth, she's right. I know without a doubt how very much these people love me and how much I love them.

Chapter 39

Increasingly, the idea of marrying Will doesn't fill me with joy but with fear. I'm not having full-blown anxiety attacks, but I feel edgy about the prospect of getting married. And I feel guilty for feeling this way. I feel guilty for feeling doubt. I feel guilty about having stopped planning the wedding, when Will has no idea I'm thinking any of this. One of the things I'm learning in therapy is how to communicate better, and I think that in some ways, I'm improving. Like take last night, for example: Way back when I started planning the wedding, I asked Will to write up a guest list so I could know how many people to invite. His list included forty-one "definites," thirteen "maybes," and sixteen "maybe, but probably nots." Putting my list of fifty definites with his list, I start working with the number seventy-five, since I know not everyone will be able to make it. At the time, I didn't even look at his list, I just wanted the number for planning purposes. I told him to get everyone's name and address to me electronically so I could mail them an invitation, but that there was no rush, because I wouldn't be mailing the invites out until two months before the wedding. Just the other day, out of nowhere, Will said he'd gotten everyone's name and address together on a disk, and he handed me a hard copy of all the names. On his "definite" list, ninth from the top, was his ex-wife. When I saw her name, my heart began thrashing around in my chest. I thanked him, put the list down on the table, and went into the bathroom and took several deep breaths. All the nights of sleep I'd lost over this woman, and he wanted to invite her to our wedding. A woman who was well-known for being a party animal, whose drunken antics were legend, and he wanted to invite her to our wedding. A woman who he once vowed to spend his life with, and he wanted to invite her to our wedding.

As I breathed in and out, trying to keep my anxiety in check, I wondered if I was being unreasonable. After all, he and X were still friends. They rarely see each other, but they speak on the phone and email every now and then. *That* doesn't bother me, because I have that exact same friendship with my ex, Rick. But to invite her to the wedding . . .

I took one last deep breath, exited the bathroom, and walked into the living room, where Will was sitting on the couch, watching TV.

I took the remote and hit MUTE. Will looked at me. "What's up?" he said.

"Will, can I ask you something?"

"Sure."

"Why did you put your ex-wife on our guest list?"

"Because I know that if she had a wedding, she would invite me. We're friends."

He didn't have to say that she had been a huge part of his adult life. He met her when he was twenty-four, married her at twenty-eight, and stayed friends with her even after divorcing her when he was thirty-two. I know she's been a huge part of his life, and that's exactly what rips my heart out. "Will, I feel very strongly that I don't want her at our wedding."

"Okay."

"Okay?" That was it? No argument? No protests? No, "you're being an idiot"?

"It's your wedding."

"It's our wedding."

"She'll understand not getting invited. I don't want you to worry about her being there. I don't want you to worry about anything. I just want to marry you."

"Thanks, Will."

And that was it. It doesn't sound like much, but I had a strong emotion, I expressed it to Will after only a mild, low-grade anxiety attack, and voila, problem solved, concern addressed. Look how great this communication stuff is!

But how am I supposed to tell Will I'm having doubts about getting married? I'm hoping it's just a run-of-the-mill case of cold feet, but whatever it is doesn't change the fact that we're not going to have a wedding to go to if I don't get my ass in gear and finish planning the thing.

I talk to my therapist, Anne, about my fears.

"It's very common to be anxious before a wedding. Marriage is a huge deal," Anne says.

"I know. Of course I know that. I just—I'm feeling very unsure. I'm not sure I want to marry Will. I want to be with him forever, it's not him I don't want, it's marriage. It's so scary. I've heard so many people say how love can die. What if that happens to Will and me?"

"There are no guarantees, Eva."

"At first I was dying to get married to him, but now I feel too scared. Will was married once before, did I tell you that?"

"You mentioned that he had an ex-wife."

"I can't stand that he was married before. I've never been a jealous person before, but when I think of his ex-wife, oh, it just kills me. She was a former stripper and a total party animal. I worry that because I'm not like that, I'm somehow a disappointment to Will."

"Your jealousy is an expression of your insecurity."

"I know."

"As we work together to improve your self-esteem you'll

stop worrying about how you measure up to other people. You'll start thinking about how lucky Will is to have you instead of how you're not perfect. Why don't you tell me why Will is lucky to have you?"

I think about how I've been considering calling off the wedding. It will break Will's heart. So is Will lucky to have me, a woman who is incapable of making major life decisions without being thrown into a crippling panic? I don't think so.

"I make a good living," I say. "I'm good at my job. I'm well read and well educated. I can be funny. I'm pretty smart."

"I'd say Will is a lucky man indeed. You just keep reminding yourself until thinking well of yourself becomes second nature."

The guilt about the wedding is going to do me in. Ridiculously, I try to get myself to think of the wedding as a test I have to study for like the SAT. I was always a good test-taker. I just need to buckle down and study, or, in this case, plan.

As a little girl, I remember distinctly having paper dolls with wedding dresses I could dress them in. I loved those paper dolls and I played with them until their clothes were ripped and crinkled into oblivion. I was a flower girl in three weddings, and I always thought there was something so wonderful about the flowers and pretty dresses and cakes and elaborate meals. Why can't I resurrect some of the wonder about weddings that I had as a little girl? Certainly the meaning of the event is heavy with import, but somehow, when I look through the wedding magazines and books, I don't get a sense of wonder or a feeling of magic. Instead I feel tired and more than a little annoyed with forking over so much cash for an event that's only going to last a few hours. Maybe it would have been easier if I'd gotten married at twenty-two and just stuck Dad with the bill after all. I can't stop thinking of other ways Will and I could spend this money. Maybe we could go on a three-week trip to Hawaii instead of the nine days we were planning on or maybe we could go on a trip through Greece or the British Isles or an extended cruise through the Caribbean. Should I be worried that I'm more excited about the honeymoon than the actual wedding itself?

Every day I sit down with the stacks of books and magazines I bought and will myself to forge ahead with making phone calls and ironing out details, but just thinking about it makes my heart tight with worry and my thinking fuzzy.

Maybe the problem is that I've never been good at "girly" stuff. I couldn't sew a curtain to save my life. I can barely toss a throw pillow.

That night, I have a dream that I'm walking down the aisle, and I step on the back of my bridal gown and the entire back end of my dress comes off. I'm not wearing any underwear or even nylons, and my fat ass is on display for all to see, except somehow I don't know this. I say my vows all teary-eyed and emotional, while the audience snickers in hilarity behind me. I wake up breathless. I look around. Will is sleeping. A glance at the red lights on the digital clock reveals it's 3:34 in the morning. It was just a dream. Just a dream. Okay.

After a couple minutes, my breathing returns to normal. I close my eyes and drift in and out of sleep. I have another dream. In this one, Will and I are in a big house at a party with a bunch of people I don't know. We're at the party for quite awhile. It's a large house, and we endlessly go from one room to the next as people talk and mingle all around us. When the end of the night comes, Will tells me he has to go back to Michigan where he really lives. He cares for me, but he has to leave me. I wake up again, anxious and upset, and again, it takes me a minute to register that it's just a dream. I actually have to sit there and think for a moment about whether Will is really from Michigan. Of course he's not. He's never been to Michigan in his life. He grew up right here in Colorado. He's not leaving me. This hasn't all been a giant fling. I close my eyes and my body and mind linger in a nebulous netherworld that's not quite sleep. I have a third dream. In it, I learn that Will is a serial murderer. The cops have been searching for months for the person who committed a series of brutal murders, and I stumble upon the clues that lead me closer and closer to the truth. Just when I learn the murderer is my fiancé, he attacks me. Again I wake up, my heart pounding, my breath jagged. It's 5:52 in the morning, and I've had a terrible night of sleep. My eyes sting from the lack of rest.

I can't do this. I can't get married. It's going to be the end of me.

My thrashing and out-of-control breathing has woken Will. "What's up?" he says groggily, his eyes only half open and straining to focus.

"I haven't been able to sleep all night. I've been having bad dreams."

"I'm sorry, hon."

"I think we have to talk."

"What about?"

"Will, I love you, but I'm not sure I have what it takes to be married. I thought marriage was what I wanted, but now I don't think it is."

"Eva, you just had a bad dream."

"No. It's more than that. I haven't done anything with the wedding. Not since that night I spent in the hospital."

"You've just been under too much stress. Let's just elope."

"It's not the wedding I don't want. I just don't want to be married. I've thought about this a lot."

Tears well up in his eyes. I've never seen him cry before. You're going to think I'm awful, but I'm actually touched—happy even—by the sight. I think, *this man really loves me*. I think I knew that before, but in a logical, cerebral way. His tears make me understand his commitment to me in a more real, emotional way, some place deep in the core of my soul.

"Will, I think I've stopped planning the wedding because deep down I have too many conflicted feelings about being married. I think the truth is that I don't want to be married. I mean, if I wanted kids, I would definitely want to be married for legal reasons, but I don't want kids, so I don't see the point."

"I'll tell you what the point is," Will says. "The point is that I want to make a commitment to you and I want you to make a commitment to me and I want to do it in front of everyone we love and care about. I want to let the world know that there is no one in the world I would rather be with. No one."

"But you thought that when you married . . . Elizabeth," I get her name out, her real name out, stumbling over it only a little. "You know better than anyone how you can enter a marriage believing it will last forever only to end up divorced a few years later."

"I got married when I was twenty-eight years old. I was young. I know much better now what marriage means, and what you need to do to make a marriage succeed. You and I have both been in love before, but what we have together you and I, it isn't the young, naïve love we've had with other people. We're older and wiser and we know what marriage and commitment really mean. I don't think things will always be easy in our lives, but I believe that if we're together, we could be happy most of the time. And when we do go through hard times, I want to get through them together."

"I'm sorry, Will," I say, slipping the beautiful antique platinum engagement ring off my finger. "I want to be with you, but I don't want to be married to you."

Chapter 40

The first few days after I break things off with Will are horrible, absolutely horrible. He's devastated and walking around like a zombie. I thought I would feel relief when I called the wedding off, but I still feel anxious and unsure. Worse, I feel awful for making Will so sad.

I make dinner for us and we eat in tense silence. After dinner I say that I rented a movie, and he nods. We go into the living room and I pop *Dead Men Don't Wear Plaid* into the DVD player. We sit next to each other and watch it, but instead of being entwined around each other, which is how we normally watch TV—with his arm draped behind my shoulder, his other hand on my leg, and me curled up into his chest, my arm around his stomach—we sit several inches apart like polite strangers.

"Have you told anyone?" I ask him. "About how the wedding is off?"

"No."

"Why not?"

"I'm hoping you'll change your mind. I'm going to keep the ring."

"We have to tell people who are out of town so they don't buy plane tickets. We'll have to tell people eventually. They'll wonder when they don't get an invitation."

He just shrugs.

"I still love you. Very much," I say.

"I know," he says quietly.

I begin kissing him. He kisses back stiffly and without passion. I reach my hand down to his pants and he stops me—this is the first time he's ever turned me down.

"I'm not rejecting you," I say. "I'm rejecting marriage."

"I know," he says. "I'm just not in the mood."

But you're never not in the mood, I think.

I call Sienna and my mother and Gabrielle and Rachel and tell them about how the wedding is off, about how I love Will and want to be with him, but I can't take the pressure of marriage. Sienna and Gabrielle and to an extent Rachel all understand my fears. Sienna and Gabrielle have conflicted feelings about marriage, so they respect my desire not to get married. Rachel believes in marriage, but knows it's not for everyone. My mother, though, is absolutely devastated. She cries on the phone, saying she's so disappointed not to be able to see her daughter get married. She starts lamenting about where she went wrong as a mother and how she blames herself and my father for this, because it was their terrible marriage that soured me on the idea of it. I tell her I don't blame their divorce for me not wanting to get married. I feel so awful when I get off the phone with her I wish like hell Will and I had never gotten engaged in the first place.

I feel a powerful, overwhelming feeling to call Sandy, but I know that if Will finds out that I've used again, he will leave me. That is not what I want. I couldn't bear that. I love him, without question and without conditions. I manage not to call her. It's not fun, but I manage.

One of the biggest snowstorms in sixty-two years hits Denver. Will, inexplicably, still has to go into work. He emails me when he finally gets there saying it took him two hours to get to work when it normally takes half an hour and that he thinks the staff at his office will be allowed to go home shortly. I am supposed to meet with the WP execs today, but I feel certain that they'll cancel the meeting. I call just to confirm that. Kyle tells me the meeting is still on.

"Can I just conference call in on the meeting?" I ask.

"You have the handouts on the figures to give out and the PowerPoint presentation to present."

"I know, but . . ." I walk over to the window and look out. It's a whiteout out there.

"We're counting on you," he says gruffly.

"Okay. I'll be there."

If the weather were nice, I would have no trouble getting to the WP office with time to spare, but with the weather the way it is, I have to haul ass. I'm snowed in because, since Will left for work, the street plows have dumped a ton of snow at the end of the cul-de-sac where I live, blocking in my driveway. Shit! I don't own a shovel. I think quickly of what I could use instead of a shovel. A plastic bowl? A dustpan? A salad spinner? Then I see my neighbor across the way shoveling his driveway. He's finished and going back to his garage to put it away, and he's no doubt about to take off for work. I have no time to spare! I go rocketing out of my house wearing nothing but sweats and slippers.

It's impossible trying to race through snowdrifts that are as tall as me. (Can you hear the theme music to *Chariots of Fire* blaring behind me as I plunge forward in my heroic quest?) But eventually, breathless, I beg my neighbor for his shovel and he gives it to me. I run back home where I put on boots, gloves, and a jacket. Thus attired I begin the process of clearing the snowdrift so I can leave my home. After just a very few minutes, I realize that this shoveling is not easy, particularly when you're an out-of-shape weakling like myself. After twenty minutes of this, I'm sweating and the muscles in my arms and back are screaming, and I've barely gotten anywhere.

By the time I clear the driveway, there is no way I can make it to WP on time. I race through a shower and grab all my things and hit the road. The highways are treacherous. The high winds keep threatening to hurl my car into the median, and a thick blanket of snowflakes drifting leisurely from the sky makes it impossible to see. Several times the wind jars my car so badly my heart races with the thunderous fear I felt when I got into a car accident in high school. (I didn't get hurt, but the experience was terrifying nevertheless.) I'm sitting on edge, my hands holding the steering wheel in a crocodile-death-grip, and I curse stupid Kyle Woodruff for not being leader enough to postpone our meeting to a day that doesn't coincide with one of the biggest snowstorms in history. The thought flickers briefly through my mind: What if I died today? Wouldn't he be sorry? Then I realize, no, of course, he wouldn't be sorry. He doesn't care about anyone except himself. He wouldn't even feel responsible for forcing me to drive through this weather.

I get through the meeting despite wanting to strangle Kyle with my bare hands. I have another terrifying and LONG drive back—it takes me three times as long as usual to get home. But once I'm safely in my house, I open the window and look out onto the snow, which is glistening in the moonlight. Now that I'm not in that snow driving a two thousand-pound vehicle, I can appreciate how beautiful the snow is. I get a craving to go sledding, which is something I haven't done since I was a kid. I could take a day of hooky tomorrow and just go have fun playing in the snow. The one problem is that I don't know of any hills within walking distance, and I don't want to drive a car through this mess again, so unless I can be teleported somewhere, I guess it won't be happening.

I tell Anne about calling the wedding off. I'm not sure if I'm imagining it, but I sense disapproval from her.

"You don't think I made the right choice?" I ask.

"If you feel you needed to break things off, then it was the right choice." The room falls silent for a moment, then Anne says, "So, do you feel relieved?"

"I feel sad. Sad about hurting Will. And I feel confused. I thought marriage was what I wanted. Ever since our second date I thought it was what I wanted. My feelings for Will were overwhelming. Are overwhelming."

"Why did you fall for Will in the first place?"

"The usual stuff. We were attracted to each other, we had fun together, and when I was with him, I felt like I could be myself."

"That's interesting because you said once you started dating that you started doubting yourself."

"But that wasn't because of him. It was just my own . . ." My own what? Insanity? Craziness? Lack of self-esteem? "It was just my own thing. I've had other boyfriends in the past who have made me feel insecure. Like I dated this guy named Chris once. Chris was a big fitness buff. He ran a jillion miles a day and was always Rollerblading and racing in marathons. He had a great body, really muscular but not in that weight lifter scary way, you know? But he kept telling me that I should lose ten pounds and work out more. I always felt like he tolerated my body but never liked it. I knew it was his own issue. I'm not going to spend my life worrying about being ten pounds skinnier than I am. I want to be healthy, but I have better things to do than worry about every calorie I consume. But the thing was, sometimes when we'd be having sex, when he'd close his eyes, I'd think about if he was closing his eyes because he couldn't bear the sight of me naked, and that . . . well, it didn't make me feel good, that's for sure. And this other guy, I only went on a couple dates with him. On our second date we were trying to figure out what to do with ourselves, and he suggested that we go bowling. I said I was a terrible bowler. Then he suggested that we play pool. I told him I don't play pool. He asked what I did for fun, and I said I'd been busy launching my own business and I'd never really had time for hobbies. So he said, 'Do you cook?' 'No.' 'Garden?' 'No.' 'Golf?' 'No.' 'Ski?' 'No.' Then he says, 'How do you expect to find a husband?' I think he was kidding. I think he was one of those guys with a dry sense of humor that can say something they think is funny and you never know if they are joking. But at the time, I was in one of those moods you get into after you go on one bad date after another and you start thinking that maybe the problem really is you, that there's something wrong with you that you can't find a guy you're compatible with. I know it's ridiculous, to start worrying that I'll never find love because I can't bowl well, but that's how I felt at the time. Will . . . he's never made me feel bad about myself. Sometimes he says he wishes I had more time for him, but I wish I had more time for him, too. Anyway, the point is, Will accepts me for who I am, which is why I love him. Somehow I decided that I loved him so much I wanted to be a better person than I was. I wanted to plan a perfect wedding and learn how to cook. Instead I got addicted to an illegal drug . . ."

Anne studies me for a moment. "Why don't you like bowling?"

Huh? We're talking about how I've broken off my engagement and am battling an addiction and she wants to talk about bowling?

"Uh . . . well, I've never been a big fan of sticking my feet into hot smelly shoes a million other people have worn. I don't even like used clothes that have been washed, let alone sticking my feet into what can best be described as a potential fungus farm. And, I don't know, it's a silly game. What have you accomplished after you've gone bowling?"

"Why do you feel the need to accomplish something?"

I realize I completely set myself up for that. At first, I don't want to broach the topic of how I have such a hard time relaxing, but then I realize the whole point of therapy is to deal with issues I'd rather not deal with. I give her my theory about how my father taught my sister and me to feel we constantly need to be productive.

"Tell me about your father. What sort of work did he do?"

"Sales. He hated his job. He also made furniture and sold it on the side, but he never made much from that."

"Was he successful at his job?"

"Do you mean did he make a lot of money?"

"Is that how you define success?"

"When it comes to work, I think being a success means having a job you like or, if you can't manage that, then, yes, to make money at whatever it is you do. Either way, my father wasn't a success. He hated his job and he made enough to get by, but he never made a ton. He never got promoted, things like that."

"Is that why you think he was so hard on you? Because he wanted you to achieve the success that he never had?"

I'd never thought of it that way, but it seems plausible. I nod. "Maybe. He really struggled to keep us in a good neighborhood so we could go to good schools. Money was always an issue. It's one of the big reasons my parents got divorced. He probably wanted to make sure I didn't have to struggle like he did. His father died when he was young, so he started working at a young age to bring in money. He and my mom got married when he was just twenty and she was only eighteen because she was pregnant with me."

"Do you feel guilty about that? About being the reason your parents got married?"

I shake my head. "No. I think my parents would have ended up married to each other even if it weren't for me. They really just always seemed like they belonged together. There has always been this fire between them. I think that if money hadn't been such an issue and if they'd had better communication skills, they could have had a good marriage to each other. I do feel bad that my father and mother had had so much responsibility heaped on them at such a young age, but I know that's not my fault."

I think about how my mother married zany fun Frank be-cause she was ready to have some fun or how Dad has mellowed out now that he's done raising kids and has Annabella in his life. He pressed Sienna and me to succeed because that was the only way he knew how to be a father. He was just trying to do his best to raise Sienna and me in a world where men aren't given the skills they need to communicate their emotions. He didn't do everything right, but my issues aren't his fault. And it's about time I start learning how to relax, so my relationship with Will doesn't combust like my parents' relationship did.

"Are you still having cravings?"

I study Anne's office floor. She has chocolate brown carpeting that has to be at least twenty years old it's so worn.

Finally, with a sigh, I admit to her, to myself, "Yes. Usually it's just a quick flash. A thought that comes into my mind that leaves as quickly as it comes. One time I had a craving that was really awful. I was so cranky I felt like I could tear Will's head off. The next day I got lunch with Rachel and she said that Sandy's boyfriend is in jail. Sandy is sober again and she promises to stay away from her ex. I felt sort of stupid, you know, that I spent all these hours fantasizing about something I couldn't have gotten anyway."

"You probably could have found a way. Sandy's ex-boyfriend isn't the only drug dealer in Colorado."

"But a bigger part of me doesn't want to use. A much bigger part of me."

"How is the group you're going to?"

I shrug. "It's good. The people in the group with me all used for a much longer period of time than I did. The stuff they did . . . well, they did things I never want to do. And I know that if I use, I will go down that road. I do not want to go down that road. I have far too much going for me."

Chapter 41

Woodruff Pharmaceuticals officially buys Ridan Technologies in early February. Kyle Woodruff fires Michael Evans shortly after the purchase, saying he doesn't want anyone who's "not on board with a forward-thinking agenda" which is CEO-speak for "I only want to be surrounded by people who'll do my bidding and kiss my ass."

As I suspected, Kyle asks me to sign another contract for the rollout of their new product. I tell him my fears regarding timelines. He's not amenable to me bringing in another consultant, and though he says we can work out timelines we both agree on, I don't believe him. I tell him I'll think about it.

Before I have to get back to him with my response, I check my email, and in it there is a Request for a Proposal (RFP) from a woman who owns her own business in Montreal. She found me through my website after doing a search online. I so rarely use my website I forgot I even had one. My site has my bio and highlights some of my successes as a consultant on it. The woman, whose name is Maggie, tells me that she started her own jewelry-making business a year ago, and ever since some of her work was featured in *Vogue*, she hasn't been able to keep up with demand for her designs. She wants help figuring out how she can grow her business. She has questions about hiring additional staff and how she would work the finances to pay their salaries and health insurance and so on. She has questions about the whole gamut of small-business ownership, and this kind of thing is right up my alley.

One thing about being a consultant is that you're always having to sell yourself to get the next project. It's like endlessly having to go on job interviews. It's hard for someone like me to brag about all of my accomplishments when my natural tendency is to focus on all of my faults, but I'm intrigued by Maggie's business and am interested in securing the project. So I write up my proposal, including examples of how I've helped small businesses like hers in the past.

SUCCESSES:

Company: An importer/manufacturer of furniture was suffering from poor budget controls and weak sales.

Major Initiatives:
- Installed budget controls
- Arranged several refinancings of eight-figure debt
- Brought in venture capital investors

Outcome:
Sales rose from $5M to $70M during this period.

Company: $8M, seventy+ person designer, manufacturer, and wholesaler of women's shoes, with sales sagging and an inability to ship orders on schedule.

Major Initiatives:
- Introduced lean manufacturing, Six Sigma, and total quality management concepts, techniques, and tools
- Advised the owner on financial and strategic options and communicated plan to key internal and external stakeholders and investors

Outcome:
Increased sales by 36 percent, gross margins by 5 percent and net income by 110 percent within seven months

Company: A national film production firm was running at a loss due to several bad investments, causing a severe cash shortage that negatively impacted operations creating vendor dissatisfaction. Shipments were late and quality was poor. The sales department was fragmented.

Major Initiatives:
- Consolidated the sales organization
- Hired a VP of Sales and Marketing
- Consolidated and renegotiated raw material purchases
- Developed operating budget with corrective action programs

Outcome:
The company increased sales by 25 percent in four months. Costs of materials were reduced by 20 percent.

As I review my successes, I remember what it is I like about my job. Thinking back to when I helped the furniture company, I remember what a great high it was when, within a few months of implementing my management changes, sales and profits turned around dramatically. The owner of the company actually cried, he was so thankful for my help. I smile at the memory and email Maggie a PDF of my proposal.

Moments after I get the proposal off, I get a phone call from Kyle Woodruff.

"Kyle, hi, what's up?" I say. I look at my ring finger of my left hand. It looks strange without the ring there. Without

that ring, no one knows my story. I could be single or in a serious relationship, strangers would have no way of knowing. I
can't decide if I like my personal life to be secret or not. When
weird-looking guys hit on you, engagement rings can come
in pretty handy.

"Eva, I need you to get started on the first phase of the
branding project right away. I want focus groups. I want
logos. I want taglines. I want . . ."

"Whoa, whoa, whoa, Kyle, I haven't agreed to go forward
on the next stage of this project. In fact, I think it might be
better if we parted ways."

"What? But you agreed to do this."

"No, I never agreed. I said I'd think about it. I've thought
about it, and my answer is no."

"But why?"

"Kyle, I spoke to you earlier about your expectations regarding deadlines. They are simply too—" I pause for a
minute, straining to think of an appropriate euphemism—
"ambitious."

"I knew I shouldn't have hired a woman. Women always
lose their edge. They always end up on the Mommy Track."

"The Mommy Track?"

"You lose your career ambition and focus all your time
and energy on your kids."

"But I don't even have kids."

"But you will."

"I'm not planning to, but even if I did . . ." I don't even
know what to say. I'm so mad right now, it's a damn good
thing that Kyle is twenty miles away and not in the same
room as me, because if he was standing in front of me, I
would do my best to gouge his eyeballs out. *I never should
have hired a woman. Mommy Track. Lose their edge.* On behalf
of myself and women everywhere, I want to cause Kyle
Woodruff grievous bodily harm. Whether I had children or
not, I hate that Kyle assumes that if work isn't the entire
focus on my existence, that means I'm not a good employee.

"Kyle, what you just said to me is so offensive, I don't even know where to start. Maybe I could start by telling you that that kind of statement is the kind of sexist crap that could get a lawsuit slapped on you so hard and so fast your head would spin. Or maybe I could start by telling you that what we need in this country is not a Mommy Track, but a Personal Life Track, where whether you are a parent or not, your boss respects that you have a life outside of work. You, Kyle, do not respect that I have a life outside of making Woodruff Pharmaceuticals a success, and that's why I'm turning down additional projects with WP. I wish you the very best of luck running this company, Kyle. Good-bye."

I hang up the phone. My entire body is shaking. I will never be a fan of confrontation even if I go to therapy for the rest of my life, so that is part of the reason I'm upset by what just happened. But I'm also shaking because I don't have another job lined up. How could I turn down work no matter how awful, without another job to go to?

Even as I tremble with the panicky feeling of *Oh God! What have I done?* I smile, thinking about how I didn't run away from conflict. I told Kyle his comment was inappropriate. I stood up for myself and my needs. It's a baby step, certainly, but I'm damn proud of myself anyway.

That night when I tell Will what happened, he congratulates me for turning Kyle down and telling Kyle off.

"But I don't have any other work lined up. What am I going to do for money?" I say.

"Eva, I make enough money that I can take care of the household expenses until you get more work."

"Will, I know we aren't about to go to the poorhouse, but money is power. I've been making my own money for a long time now. I don't want to rely on you for money."

"I don't see what other choice you have."

He's right, and the idea terrifies me. But this is what partnership is, right? If Will lost his job, I'd take care of him. That's love. I can do this . . .

For the next few days I start trolling for leads on projects in case this Montreal thing doesn't go through. I keep busy, but not crazily so. It's strange to realize that if I want to make the time to go to a yoga class, I can. So I do. And I absolutely love it. It's so relaxing to breathe and stretch and get my atrophied muscles moving. My arm and leg muscles are sore after the first several workouts. Somehow I never realized yoga was a real, actual workout.

Gabrielle wants to talk to Will and his friends about online gaming for her dissertation, so on Friday night, Will and I pick up Gabrielle and we drive down to Mickie's Pub together. I introduce her to Richard, Abby, and Jerry who are already there with beers in hand.

"This is Gabrielle Leveska. She's working on her dissertation in sociology. I met her when we were in grad school together," I say.

"What's your dissertation on?" Richard asks.

"It's about representation of self and social interaction via online gaming."

"Are you much of a gamer?" he asks.

She nods. "I was an Everquest junkie for awhile."

"Me, too!"

And they're off, talking about the games they like and the weird world of Internet gaming: Sharing their stories about people who got so addicted that they lost their jobs and their families and were unable to relate to humans anymore; and of other people for whom gaming broadened their circle of friends, because they took the people they met online and extended that relationship into the real world.

Gabrielle and Richard talk so feverishly, nobody else can get a word in. Abby, Jerry, Will, and I start a conversation of our own. Our conversation goes from everything from religion, to politics, to healthcare, to reality TV shows, and upcoming movies. When we talk about politics or religion, I can slip in historical trivia, and I feel, in those moments, that my degree in history was good for something. This is the knowledge I bring to our little group. As for the guys, they are all capable of quoting lines from "The Simpsons" episodes and a wide array of B-movies that I've never heard of, and no matter how many times they repeat these lines, they never stop busting a gut with laughter. I don't know if this is common to all men or just all men who work with computers for a living. Is there a secret geek test all these guys have to pass before they're allowed to create Web applications and software programs? I don't know, but I suspect there might be.

When I've finished my second beer, I excuse myself to use the bathroom.

I go to the bathroom and choose the stall that doesn't have the *You are not the first . . .* graffiti. It has graffiti of its own, however. It reads, *For a good time, fuck patriarchy.*

A smile spreads across my entire face.

Chapter 42

On Valentine's Day, Will takes me to a fancy restaurant. As we share a plate of exotic cheeses and sip our rich Merlot, I tell him about how I landed a new consulting project. "I'll need to go to Montreal to meet with her. She's bilingual, obviously, since I don't speak a word of French. Anyway, I thought maybe you could take a few days off of work and we could make a long weekend of it."

"Sure. That sounds fun."

"Great. I'll get the plane tickets and let you know what days you should tell your boss you need off."

I notice a man at the table next to us getting up from his table and getting down on one knee. Will notices too, and after the woman accepts the ring and marriage proposal, the restaurant erupts into cheers and applause.

The rest of the evening is awkward for Will and me. We go home and we don't make love.

Things are still awkward between Will and me the next morning. We kiss each other good-bye and tell each other to have a good day at work, but it feels like we're not ourselves, like we're auditioning for parts in play or something.

I work for a little while and then I call Gabrielle and ask her what she thought of Richard.

"He's a total babe. I can't believe he's still single. What does he think of me?"

"I don't know. I didn't ask. But I can shoot him an email and we can see if he'd be up for going on a double date. Are you free tomorrow night?"

"For him, absolutely."

As soon as I get off the phone with Gabrielle, I email Richard and ask him what he thought of Gabrielle.

To: Richard@magellansoftware.com
From: eva@lockhartconsulting.com

Hey, Rich, what did you think of Gabrielle?

A few minutes later, I hear back from him.

To: eva@lockhartconsulting.com
From: Richard@magellansoftware.com

She's very cute. And so bright. There's nothing sexier than a smart woman. She's not single, is she?

To: Richard@magellansoftware.com
From: eva@lockhartconsulting.com

She is. She thinks you're really cute, too. Would you be up for a double date tomorrow night? I thought we could get some dinner and then see a show at The Bovine Metropolis Theater.

To: eva@lockhartconsulting.com
From: Richard@magellansoftware.com

I'd definitely be up for that.

I feel gleeful as I write him back that I'll buy the tickets and set everything up. When I call Gabrielle, she makes me repeat four times what he said about her being cute and bright. She practically squeals with delight.

When Will gets home, I tell him about my triumphant scheming to get Richard and Gabrielle together.

"That's great, hon. I hope it works out for them."

I've tried matchmaking a few other times and the results have always been disastrous. Even so, I'm delirious with excitement over the potential for Gabrielle and Richard. Despite everything, I will always believe in love.

Chapter 43

The double date starts off well. At first, the four of us sit down together at the upscale restaurant and look over our menus in silence. Once we order, we all spend a few moments looking at each other and smiling stupidly.

"Um, so, Gabrielle did her undergraduate degree in film," I say as a not-so-subtle icebreaker to Richard.

"Really?"

Gabrielle nods.

It appears for a moment as if the conversational thread has died. I try valiantly to resurrect it. "So have either of you seen any good movies lately?"

"I just rented *Leprechaun 6: Back 2 tha Hood*," Richard says.

"I haven't seen that one yet!" Gabrielle says.

"I'm sorry, but what the hell are you talking about?" I say.

"The Leprechaun series. Number five was called *Leprechaun: In the Hood*. Number six is *Back 2 tha Hood*," Richard explains carefully.

"Leprechaun? You're watching movies about leprechauns?" I ask.

"He's a murderous leprechaun in search of his gold," Gabrielle explains. "Didn't you love it when, God, which one was it, *Leprechaun in Space* maybe—"

"Wait, wait, wait," I say. "Why are you watching movies about murderous leprechauns in space?"

"Because it's hilarious!" they say in unison.

"And there were six of these movies made?" I ask, incredulous.

They try to explain the entertainment value to me, talking about their favorite moments in murderous leprechaun history. Here they are, a woman who is earning a doctorate and a man with a master's degree in computer science, talking about the merits of a leprechaun on a rampage. Just when you think you know someone, it turns out you know nothing.

After dinner, we go to a show at the Bovine Metropolis Theater. Rattlebrain does sketch comedy shows and is Denver's answer to Second City. As always, the show is hilarious, and all of us have a great time. When we leave into the cold winter air, Gabrielle says, "I'm having so much fun! Let's go get drinks somewhere."

I take a quick look at my watch. It's after eleven. Way, way past my bedtime. But I want Richard and Gabrielle to get together, so, in the name of love, I agree.

We go to Mickie's and, as usual for a Saturday night, a band is playing. Gabrielle and Richard go off to get us drinks, and it's not until they've left that I realize they didn't ask what we want. When they return, they have Irish Car Bombs for everyone.

"Car Bombs?" I say. "This could be dangerous."

As it turns out, they are dangerous. Gabrielle and Richard order another round of Irish Car Bombs about ten minutes after we've had our first, and by the time Richard suggests yet another round, I'm so buzzed this seems like a very reasonable and in fact good idea.

We're standing at the edge of the dance floor, not really dancing but sort of bopping to the music. The band is good but the beat is really too slow to dance to. An older woman wearing a very slutty outfit that she's falling out of chooses to stand right in front of us. She has a good body, but she looks like a sixties groupie, aged beyond her years from decades of too much drinking and drugging and tanning her skin into a leathery crisp. Still, when there is someone standing in front of you who is half naked, it's hard not to watch out of morbid curiosity if nothing else. She desperately wants to dance, but it's just not dancing music. She's all hussied up with no place to go.

The strap on her cropped tank top (excuse me, but it's the middle of winter—I mean really) keeps falling off her shoulder and she looks drunk enough that I don't think she'd noticed if it came off completely.

"She's wearing so few clothes you'd think she could at least keep the clothes she has on," I say to Will.

Richard may or may not have gotten us another round of drinks. By this point, facts are blurred, details are trivial.

The groupie chick decides she needs to get to the bar to get another drink and she stumbles, and she really does almost come out of her blouse completely.

"She's wearing so few clothes you'd think she could at least keep the clothes she has on," I say.

"You just said that," Will says.

"I did?" I wave my hand dismissively. "But that's the great thing about drinking. You can have the same conversations over and over again and it's like new every time."

I don't know how many beers later it is when we leave, but when I wake up, I realize I'm asleep on Richard's living room floor desperately hung over and being assaulted by the putrid stench of Richard's dog Bear sniffing at my face. I don't recommend mixing acrid dog breath with a hangover if at all possible. Just a little tip from me to you.

I lift my head. The side of my face is covered with carpet lint. Through mostly closed eyes I see Will asleep on the couch. I get up and go over to him.

"Hmm?" he says, waking.

"Hi. What happened last night? Why was I sleeping on Richard's floor?"

"We decided to come to his place because we were all too drunk to drive and he was the only one with a place within walking distance. You volunteered to sleep on the floor."

"I did? Why would I do such a thing?"

"You just kind of flopped down and were asleep in about eight seconds. You don't mind that I took the couch, do you?"

"No."

I get up and go to Richard's bathroom. I suck down three Advil and a vitamin and return to the living room. I return to my spot on the living room floor and get another hour or two of sleep before Richard and Gabrielle wake up.

We go to a diner and order huge breakfasts. In my opinion, there is nothing like heavily salted home fries to assist in getting over a hangover. I watch as more than once Richard lightly touches Gabrielle's back or she briefly lays her fingers on his arm. Things are looking good.

After breakfast, I say I need to use the bathroom. "Gabrielle, do you want to join me?"

"No. I don't need to go."

I glare at her.

"I mean, sure," she says.

In the bathroom, I attack. "So? Did anything happen?"

"We kissed. That was all."

"Was it good? Do you like him?"

She smiles. "It was great. I like him a lot."

"He seems to like you. Do you think the height thing is going to be an issue?"

"He did have to do a deep plié to kiss me, but it's not an issue for me. He's got my number and he already asked me out for dinner for tomorrow night."

"Awesome!"

Chapter 44

Gabrielle and Richard see each other several more times over the next couple of weeks. Gabrielle and I email back and forth and she tells me all the details of how well they are getting along. She also emails me ideas for how we can celebrate her thirty-fifth birthday. Together we work out all the details.

She ends up throwing a party in Nederland, which is a small town north of Boulder. Will and I have a heck of a time negotiating the winding mountain roads to get there. The party is in a tiny bar that was once a house and is now just a big room—the walls have been torn down and you can see the seams in the ceiling where they once were. There is only enough room for a smattering of wood tables and two couches with the stuffing popping out of them. Gabrielle has gotten an astrologer/psychic to do tarot readings at the party, and when it's my turn, I approach the astrologer with trepidation. The astrologer is a woman in her early fifties with white hair that falls to her shoulders. I've never believed in psychics or astrology, but the moment she starts reading my cards, I start crying. She says that I have several fire cards, which she reads to mean that I have a tremendous drive and desire to succeed. She says that I'm so focused on money and success that I have a tough time living in the present, and I need to learn to slow down and get in touch with my spiritual side. This is stuff I already know. These are the same issues I've been talking to

my therapist about twice a week for the last several weeks, so
I have no idea why it is that her telling me this makes me cry
so much, but I cry for most of the reading, nodding my head
vigorously and saying again and again, "That is so true.
That's exactly right!" After Gabrielle and Rachel have their
readings done, we all compare notes. All of us cried through
the readings, and we start crying again when we recount the
highlights to each other. Both Rachel's and Gabrielle's readings are lessons that apply to me as well—and I suspect they
apply to all women. Lessons about the communication issues
with our mothers, lessons about how we tend to take on the
problems of everyone around us and not focus on our needs,
lessons about facing change. Will and Richard watch the
three of us sobbing women curiously.

When I break apart from Rachel and Gabrielle, Will says,
"I thought you don't believe in psychics or tarot cards."

"I don't believe in it. But getting your cards read is like
going to a therapist. She can say something general and you
can instantly apply it to your life. At least for me, I usually
know what my problems are. It's doing anything about them
that's the challenge. Getting your reading done or your chart
read is just another opportunity to reflect on how to improve
yourself, how you want to lead your life."

Will still looks incredulous. Guys just don't get it.

At some point, a local band gets on the small stage and
starts playing. I watch Richard and Gabrielle dance. Their
height difference is kind of funny, but they have a blast dancing together, and it makes my heart happy.

Will and I sit on one of the torn-up couches across from
two girls that Gabrielle used to go to school with. Almost all
of Gabrielle's friends are unique and different and highly political. The two women and Will dig into the bowl of Goldfish crackers that is on the coffee table in front of us.

"These things are addictive," one of the girls says. She's
wearing her hair in short ponytails and is wearing clothes

that are seventies-era inspired and so tattered looking they appear to actually have been worn every day since 1972.

"My dog loves Goldfish," the other girl says. "I use them to train him."

"You could train *me* with them," Will says, taking another handful.

The three of us chuckle, and then I look at Will with a gleam in my eye, wondering what I'd want to train him to do exactly.

When the band takes a break, I pull Gabrielle aside and ask her how things are going with Richard.

"Things are wonderful."

"Awesome. How's the rest of your life going?"

"Good. My research is going well, and one of my old professors has asked me to help her do some research, so I think I'll be able to quit my job and just work part-time on that and the rest of the time on my research."

"That's amazing!"

"I know. Isn't it exciting?"

"What is the professor you're going to work for doing research on?"

"She's studying the discrimination women face in the police force and how this leads to poor police work. I'm actually trying to get into the police academy so I can do my research incognito. I went to the academy the other day and I realized that for me to pass there, I'm going to need to take all my angry political bumper stickers off my car. I just don't fit in there at all, but it'll be interesting."

"That is so cool. Good for you."

"I know. For the last two years my life felt like it was falling apart. I was worried that things would never come together for me again."

"But you got through it, and now look how things are."

"I know. Right now I'm actually happy Dan divorced me. We were so young when we got together that I really didn't know any other way to be in a relationship, but I feel so much more freedom to be myself with Richard than I ever was with Dan."

I start crying again, thinking about how, sometimes, things really are better the second time around. I hug Gabrielle, and we hold each other for a long time.

Chapter 45

I've scheduled our trip to Montreal so that I meet Maggie first thing and then Will and I have the rest of the long weekend in Montreal to have fun.

I meet Maggie a couple hours after our plane arrives. Maggie is an eighty year old who launched her own business a year ago. After the jewelry she creates got featured in Vogue, demand for her products has skyrocketed, and she can't keep up. She wants help figuring out how to expand her business, which is called "Beauté Cachée," which is French for "hidden beauty."

Will and I catch the subway to the Mont Royal side of town where Maggie lives (she works out of her home).

I leave Will at a café where he can hang out until my meeting is over and walk down the street to Maggie's place on my own.

I knock on her door. A full minute passes, but then the door creaks open and Maggie greets me with a trembling voice like she's talking directly in front of a whirling fan.

"Come in, come in," she says.

I follow her inside. Maggie is very slender. Her hair is thin and sparse.

As soon as we enter the living room, it becomes obvious that Maggie has lived through far too many Christmases.

Her coffee table, two end tables, entertainment center, and dozens of shelves are burdened with ornate knickknacks. There are garish china dolls in leering reds and oranges and plates with pictures of Scarlett O'Hara, playful puppies, and angels praying. It's a kitsch nightmare in here.

Maggie exits the room saying something about getting tea.

As she makes the tea, I study her house. I count eleven candy dishes and four ashtrays between her two end tables. Eleven candy dishes! All of them empty. There isn't even room to set a drink down.

I have to say I'm a little surprised that an artist has a home that's decorated with such clashing decorations. I stand and walk over to one of the shelves on the wall and study the bric-a-brac. There is no apparent theme. The only commonality is that the objects are cheap and ugly.

Maybe she's purposely trying to be kitschy? Maybe it's one of those modern art things like all-blue paintings that I'm just not cool enough to get?

"Tea?" she asks.

"Please. That would be nice, thank you. So Maggie, all these decorations, were they gifts from grandkids? Were they things you found when you were looking for material for your art?"

She nods. "A little of both, garage sales, things like that."

I nod.

"It's an eclectic mix, I know. I grew up during the Great Depression in upstate New York." Maggie speaks slowly and with a quavering voice, but her words are articulate and clear. "Even when it was over, we were poor for many, many years. It makes me feel safe, somehow, having these things around me. Some of them may not be considered very pretty by some people, I know, but somehow I like them anyway. There's something about them . . ."

As soon as she says it, I feel guilty. She lived through the

Depression. She feels safe being surrounded by things. There is nothing wrong with that, and I hate myself for being judgmental.

"Have you always collected things?" I ask.

"Always."

"When did you start making jewelry out of things you found?"

"About a year and a half ago, I found a tiny chess piece when I was at a café. My granddaughter, Emilyn, loves chess. Christmas was coming and I always have a hard time deciding what to get her. She's a college student and it's hard for me to keep up with what kids her age like. I brought the chess piece home and set it on my sewing table, which is really just a junk table. Well, I suppose you could say every table I have is a junk table." Maggie laughs. She has a wonderful laugh. "On that same table I had a penny that had been flattened on a train track. I liked the way the black chess piece contrasted with the copper penny. On a whim I glued them together along with a tiny sepia-toned picture of my mother, making it into a pin. I was happy with the results, and when I gave it to Emilyn as a present, she went on and on about how much she loved it. She told me I should start making more jewelry, so I did. I had nearly all day to work on making things, so soon I had made more pieces than my grandchildren could wear. Emilyn suggested that we put up a website and try to sell some of the things I made. She said we could get a site up at almost no cost because she would work on it with friends. It would be something for their portfolio. All I had to pay for was the domain name, which hardly cost a dime, so I thought, why not?"

I love, love, love that this frail woman with a trembly voice knows what the hell a domain name is. I know that if you're open to change you can learn and grow all your life, but I know so many people over the age of fifty who get so set in their ways, resisting change of any kind that it's refreshing to hear this little old lady throwing Internet terms out there with ease.

"Not long after that, Emilyn was in New York, and that's where the editor from Vogue saw her wearing some of my designs and asked her where she got her jewelry. She told the woman and gave her the web address. A small article about the jewelry appeared a couple months later, and since then, I haven't been able to make stuff fast enough to keep up with the orders we're getting."

"Wow. That's a great story. Is running a business new for you or did you ever run another business before?"

"I've never had a job outside being a mother. I raised four kids, four great kids. In my day, women with kids didn't work outside the home."

"Sure, sure. It must have been a big adjustment for you."

"It was a little scary at first. My husband bought me a few books on running a small business. He was a professor before he retired, so he didn't know the first thing about running a business, but he's been real supportive."

"That's wonderful, Maggie." Maggie and I sit down on the couch and she pours us each a cup of tea. Her fine bone china teacups don't match. Mine has a periwinkle blue pattern with gold trim. Hers has delicate pink flowers with pale green leaves.

I move on to collecting information on the financial health of her business and where she'd like to see it go, that sort of thing. I leave our meeting that afternoon feeling the kind of physical exhaustion I often get after several hours of intense work. I don't plan on starting on my report with my recommendations to Maggie until Will and I get back to Denver, which leaves Will and me free to enjoy the city.

Will and I go for a leisurely lunch, then we take an unhurried stroll through Parc Mont-Royal, a large park designed by the same architect of New York's Central Park. We walk for about an hour when we come upon musicians banging away on bongos in the middle of the park. We sit down in the grass to rest our feet and enjoy the music.

I smile, enjoying myself thoroughly. It's a chilly but beautifully sunny day out. As much as I'm having fun, I realize that I'm starving. I go to report this to Will. Instead of saying, "I'm ravenous," which is what I meant to say, I loudly pronounce, "I'm ravishing!"

"You are ravishing. And quite full of yourself."

It takes a minute for the synapses going from my brain to my tongue to figure out where I went wrong. "I meant to say ravenous, not ravishing, ravenous. I'm hungry, that's all I was trying to say."

"Oh, sure. You're gloriously beautiful and you know it."

"Shut up!" I give him a light slap on the arm and laugh. "You know that's not what I meant."

"My ravishing girlfriend!"

"Stop it! Shut up!" I tickle him and he tickles me back. We lie back on the grass tickling and giggling with each other. I squeal with laughter. I try to stop his tickling hands, but he's about a million times stronger than I am and he's got my wrists held tight. I can't tickle him back. I struggle to free myself from his grip, and we wrestle around on the ground. I realize how much fun I'm having. I realize that I'm actually allowing myself to be silly and have fun.

It is a simple but wonderful feeling.

Eventually we get up and continue exploring the park. We walk and walk and walk and barely manage to see a tenth of what the map tells us there is to see, but we're too tired to continue on. The park offers a tremendous view of the city. You can see McGill University and the Biosphere and everything. It's a gorgeous view, with the sun reflecting off the cars parked on the street, twinkling like stars.

That night we have a wonderful dinner at one of the zillion or so restaurants there are to choose from. It's a romantic meal and I think about how much I love traveling. I almost ask Will what he would like our next trip together to be, and then I realize our next trip is going to be our non-honeymoon. Our vacation to Hawaii that was supposed to celebrate our marriage to each other, but will now be nine days of rubbing in the fact that we didn't get married.

I opt to keep my mouth shut.

The next day we go for a walk through Parc-des-Iles, which is where the Grand Prix is held every year. There are several lush parks, an amusement park, a casino, and the famous Biosphere from the 1967 World Expo. The Biosphere is a steel skeleton of a sphere. Inside the 3-D dome is an architecturally intriguing building that serves as a museum dedicated to educating people about environmental issues.

We walk for hours and get a delicious lunch at a Thai restaurant, then Will and I go back to the bed-and-breakfast we're staying at to take a nap. The B&B is a charming place with one brick wall, wood floors, and high ceilings. It's quaint and homey and old-fashioned. The bed is so high off the ground it's like climbing up onto a cloud.

We're both wiped out from all the walking, but as soon as we lie down to nap, instead of sleeping we begin kissing and groping. We make slow, passionate love.

Afterward, we lie in each other's arms. I smile as I bury my face into Will's chest. Things are starting to feel normal again. I feel like we're starting to heal the rift between us.

On our last day in Montreal, Will and I go to the modern art museum (the Musée d'Art Contemporain). As we stroll through the museum, there is a group of schoolchildren with their teacher. The teacher asks them a question in French, and the children answer "yes," which in French is "oui." It sounds like they are on a museum ride saying "wheeee!" in unison. It is utterly heartwarming. I squeeze Will's hand and he smiles at me. I look into Will's beautiful hazel eyes and I wonder for a moment about what a child of ours would look like. Adorable is my guess.

Chapter 46

When we return from Montreal, I begin working on my report on my recommendations on how Maggie can expand her business. Working on this project reminds me what I love about my job. It makes me feel wonderful to feel passionate about my work again. This project could take me as little as a week, but I decide that I am going to give myself two weeks to write it up. I'm going to develop a new pattern. I will work out for half an hour on the treadmill at the gym, then I will spend an hour generating new business leads, then I'll spend seven hours working on whatever project I'm currently working on.

I won't let myself work longer than that. I will curb my workaholic tendencies, whatever it takes.

Going to the gym turns out to be more relaxing than I would have thought. It feels good to sweat and work hard. This is going to sound strange, but it's actually something of a relief to see the naked women in the locker room because they remind me what real women look like. The last time I saw a porno film I was in college and I dated a guy who lived in a dorm. Going into a male dorm is like walking into a sex shop—it's all porn all the time. Even though it has been a decade since I've seen porn, the fact is that the only women I ever see naked are the women dancing nude in the background of movies and HBO series for no good reason except for the fact that directors like to have naked woman dancing in the background whenever possible. Those women, of course, have all been surgically altered so their breasts are essentially connected to their collarbone. When I go into the locker room and see what real women's bodies look like, even women who are fit and in great shape, it is so unbelievably different from the plastic women I see on the movie screens. It's a relief to remember that my body looks fine, as long as I don't compare it to women who bought their figures from plastic surgeons.

Oh and about the porno in college, here's how it went down: I was sitting with my boyfriend on his bed and we were talking. In the dorms in college, everyone kept their doors propped open all the time so people could come in and out. Aaron's roommate was the only guy on the hall to have a VCR, and so while Aaron and I were talking, some random guy came in and popped a porno in. One moan from the woman on the screen was all it took. It was like a cattle call beckoning the herd home. Suddenly you could hear the stomping footsteps of guys coming running from every direction. In about ten seconds flat, Aaron's floor was covered with guys sitting Indian-style, staring zombielike at the screen, mouths agape and drooling. I was the only woman in the room, and considering what was going on on the screen, I felt supremely uncomfortable. I had to tiptoe through the pack of men, because there wasn't enough room on the floor for me to walk any other way to get out of there. It was then that I came to this epiphany: Men are simple, simple creatures.

Chapter 47

It's a snowy, cold, gray February day when Rachel calls me crying and frantic.

"Rachel, what is it?"

"It's Julia. Car accident. She's been in a car accident." It's hard to make out what she's saying between her sobs, but I understand the gist of it. Rachel says something about Julia being with Sandy, and something about Ed, Sandy's ex, but that's all I can make out. I tell her I'll get to the hospital as soon as I can.

I race to the hospital, ask at the front desk where I can find Rachel and Julia, and then I run in the direction that the receptionist tells me to go. Outside the room is Rachel, tears streaming down her red and blotchy face, her hand covering her mouth as she peers in through the window into the room where doctors and nurses are working on Julia. Julia looks so small, just a tiny wisp of a thing.

I hug Rachel. "How is she?"

"She's not good. There's internal bleeding. She may have punctured her spleen. The doctors are going to have to operate."

"Oh. Oh." I start crying, too, and then sniff away the tears. I need to be strong for my friend right now. "I am so sorry. What happened?"

"Ed was high," Rachel says, crying and sniffling. "He came after Sandy screaming that he was going to kill her."

"I thought Ed was in jail."

"His lawyer got him out. Sandy was babysitting Julia, and Sandy ran to the car with Julia to get away, and he went after them, crashing into Sandy's car with his."

"Is Sandy all right?"

Rachel nods. "She's fine. A couple bruises. Ed hit her car on the right side, the side Julia was on, not Sandy's."

"Rachel!" I turn and see Jon barreling toward us. Jon takes Rachel in his arms. "How is she? How is she?"

Rachel tells him the same thing she told me. They hug and cry. After several minutes Rachel pulls away from Jon's embrace and asks him where their son, Isaac, is.

"I left him with Beth. I wasn't sure if he should be here."

The three of us stand in mute shock until Julia is taken into surgery. We spend the next several hours tense with fear. I think what scares me more than anything is watching Rachel. She looks so awful it terrifies me. Her face is blotchy from her crying. Her makeup is blurred around her puffy eyes. Rachel and Jon never sit down. They just stand and hold each other.

I watch how Rachel never takes her hand from where it's nestled in Jon's hand. They never let go of one another. Sometimes he wraps her in his arms. She leans into him, letting him support her.

At some point, Rachel begins sobbing so hard she can no longer stand upright. She begins to sway and Jon eases her down into one of the chairs. He holds her as she cries.

I feel so powerless to do anything about my friend's pain. And I think about how an adorable little girl's life is in jeopardy because of Sandy's loser ex-boyfriend.

I find myself tearing at the skin around my fingernails. I don't even notice I'm doing it until I've peeled so deep I start bleeding and need a Band-Aid.

"I'll be right back," I say to Rachel and Jon. Rachel's too out of it to notice me, but Jon nods. I go to a nurse at the front desk who gives me a Band-Aid, then I go to the bathroom, ostensibly to wash up, but as soon as I'm in there I lock myself in a stall and weep in great heaving sobs. I'm scared. I'm terrified for Julia and Rachel and Jon. I hate the fact that this little human being's life is in the balance, and there's not a damn thing any of us can do about it but wait and hope and pray. Love is such a precious, fragile thing. It can be lost quickly after an accident or slowly over one too many fights over garage shelves. But it's too damn important to give up without a fight.

I return to the waiting room with Rachel and Jon. We sit tensely as the minutes pass with agonizing slowness until at last a doctor comes to speak with Rachel and Jon. My heart stops in anticipation of his words. When he tells us she came through the surgery with flying colors and all signs indicate that she will be just fine, the tears come again, but this time they are tears of relief. Through eyes blurred with tears I watch Rachel and Jon take each other in their arms.

As I watch Rachel and Jon, I understand for the first time what marriage really is. It's bungee-jumping off a cliff without a rope—you have no idea what you're getting into. It's scary and terrifying flying off into the great unknown, but as you do it, you're doing it with the person you love most in the world, hand-in-hand.

I realize, suddenly, that I want to be with Will forever, weathering the tough times with him at my side. I want to marry him. I was afraid to be wrapped up in something that would be hard to get away from—because my entire life I've run away when the going got tough. But I want to learn how to get through challenges, not by running away but by facing them dead on. I want to be entangled enough that when difficulties come up, I don't just flee as I've done with so many things in my life. I want to face the hard times with Will at my side.

* * *

I call Will on my cell phone and ask him if he can meet me at
The Falling Rock. It's a casual bar with good food and a wide
selection of beers—and it happens to be the place where we
met for our first date.

I get to the place before Will does and slide into one of the
long booths. I order a beer and as I wait for Will, I watch a little blond-haired boy. I'd guess he was around eighteen
months old. He squirms out of his father's lap, wanting to be
put down. There is music playing overhead, and the little boy
dances to it. He has two main dance steps. With the first, he
keeps his feet glued to the floor and rocks his upper body
back and forth from side to side like a dashboard hula dancer.
His other dance step is marching in place. He is the cutest,
most precious little thing, and I smile and stare shamelessly
at him. The boy smiles, too. He is filled with complete and
utter joy, the absolute happiness of hearing music and letting
his body express his delight with it. I want to run up to him,
take him in my arms, and hug him and snuggle my nose into
his soft baby skin. I don't think his parents would appreciate
that, however.

It occurs to me that the little boy hasn't actually done anything to win my affection so completely. He hasn't jumped
through any intellectual hoops. He isn't a successful entrepreneur who has saved businesses from the brink of bank-
ruptcy. He doesn't have to worry about whether he's cute
enough or thin enough or funny enough or smart enough.
He is just *being*. And that is more than enough.

After a time, Will appears at the door, all bundled up in
his wet, snowy coat, hat, and gloves. Even though we've been
together for a year, I still smile and feel a flutter of excitement when I see him.

He takes off his coat, hat, and gloves. He shoves the gloves
and hat into his coat and hangs the coat on the hook on the

outside of the booth. He sits next to me and leans in to give me a quick kiss. "How's Julia?"

"Julia's going to be okay. She should be able to go to home in a few days."

"Thank God."

"I know. It was really scary for awhile there."

I give him more details on the accident and Julia's condition. I've pretty much gotten him up to speed when the waiter swings by and takes Will's drink order. After the waiter leaves, I just stare into my beer, taking a moment to summon my courage.

"Will, I asked you to meet me here for a reason."

"Yeah? What's up?"

"Do you remember where we had our first date?"

"Of course I do. We met right here. You were sitting at the bar and I saw you and I remember thinking, *that can't possibly be her. She's much too pretty.*"

I smile. "Right, we met here, and that's why I thought this would be a good place for me to ask you to marry me."

"What?"

"I do want to marry you. I've wanted to all along. I have my fears, but I want to work through them instead of running away from them."

"How . . . when . . . what changed your mind?"

"Today, when I watched Jon and Rachel together, I don't know, the way they were there for each other, it was so amazing. I mean what they have together isn't perfect, but it's really incredible, and I want that with you. I want to share my life with you."

Will smiles, gets up from the booth, and fumbles through his coat, unzipping one of the inner pockets. In it is my ring box. He sits down, opens the box, takes the ring out, and slips it back on my finger.

"You've been carrying that around with you all this time?"

"I was hoping you'd change your mind. I had a pretty good idea that you would."

"Really? How?"

"Because we were meant for each other, Eva."

I eye the glittering ring on my finger. The ring is absolutely perfect for my hand and my taste in jewelry. It's perfect, and it's about the only thing in our relationship that is. We're two flawed people with messy pasts who still have enough optimism and hope to dream that our relationship can do what so many others don't—make it.

"I was thinking that we won't do the whole big wedding deal," I continue. "I don't want to get stressed out. I thought we could go to the justice of the peace and then go to Mickie's with our closest friends for a few beers or something."

"Great. That sounds great."

"We'll lose our deposit money on the DJ and the reception hall."

"Fine. No big deal. We'll still save a lot of money over all. When do you want to do it?"

"Well, I want to give Mom, Dad, and Sienna enough time to buy their plane tickets. I think we should have it on the same Saturday in May we planned to have it originally."

"Sounds good."

"You're a tough guy to make happy, you know," I tease.

"I just want to marry you."

"I still want us to dress up a little for the pictures, but I think if you get a nice suit and I buy a new dress, that should cover us."

"I'll start shopping for a suit tomorrow."

"You don't have any?"

"I work with computers. I don't think I've ever had to wear a suit in my life. I'll wear a tie for job interviews, but that's about as far as I need to go."

"So it's decided then. We're getting hitched. I believe this deserves a toast." We raise our beer glasses and clink them together. "To love," I say.

"To love, forever."

We sip our beers and then kiss. I feel, for the first time in months, the serenity that comes with certainty.

In the days that follow, I feel calm and happy. I feel certain I'm making the right choice, with none of the doubts that plagued me before. I've decided to resume my habit of stopping by Rachel's shop every now and then for no other reason than to shoot the shit. Today when I go to her shop, I have to wait for a few minutes while she rings up a customer.

When the customer takes her bag and leaves, I come around behind the counter and sit on my stool.

"Hey, you," I say. "How's Julia?" Julia had gotten home from the hospital three days earlier.

"She's going to be just fine. Her spirits are really good. Last night Jon was reading her a story and she was all animated and happy. It was such a beautiful thing to see I just started crying. What's up with you?"

"Well, the wedding is back on."

Rachel whoops and claps her hands together. "I knew it. I knew you two would get married ultimately. Congratulations."

"I've decided just to have a few friends watch Will and me sign the marriage certificate and then go get a few drinks after, someplace casual. I don't want to kill myself trying to plan a wedding."

"That makes sense."

"I still want to get a pretty dress though. Not a wedding dress, just something pretty that makes me feel special."

Rachel gets wide-eyed and points her finger at me. "I've got the outfit for you. You said you wanted a nontraditional dress. This is nontraditional." Rachel goes to the back of her store where she keeps new items before putting them out on the shelves.

"Is it used?" I ask.

"Think of it as preowned. It's going to look perfect on you."

"You know I don't like used stuff."

"Honey, please, for me. I saw it and it just screamed Eva to me."

She dangles the dress in front of me. It's red satin, very sumptuous. It does look sort of pretty.

"Okay," I say.

We go back to the dressing rooms and I try the dress on to placate her. After Rachel zips me up, I spin around and look into the mirror, and I gasp. I am a goddess. The dress is breathtaking, and in it, so am I. It has a sweetheart neckline and short off-the-shoulder sleeves. It's tight in the bust and sucks in my stomach, playing up my hourglass figure. The skirt is loose and flowing, making it comfortable to move in. The fabric is sexy and sensual.

"Oh, my God, Rachel, it's beautiful."

"It looks perfect on you."

"But it's used," I protest again, with less feeling this time.

"Maybe. But this dress was made for you. Some things just fit."

She's right. I keep turning and twisting in the mirror, trying to find anything that's wrong with the dress, but I can't find anything.

"How much is it?"

"It's my wedding present to you."

"It's so beautiful. It looks pretty pricey."

"The fabric is exquisite. I'm sure the woman who owned it before paid a mint for it."

"Did she tell you the story about why she was selling it?"

"She didn't really sell it, she basically gave it away. She brought me a whole bunch of clothes. She didn't even want to haggle with me. She actually said she didn't need any money. She was just trying to downsize so she could move to Paris."

"Why?"

"She said to pursue her true love. I got the feeling she wasn't talking about a guy, but about another kind of passion. Singing maybe. She had a sultry lounge singer sort of look to her. She was curvy like you. She gave me a whole bunch of clothes and only took fifty bucks in payment. The clothes were worth several times that."

"Still, you shouldn't give it away if you could make some really money selling it."

"People who come to used clothing stores are on a budget. They couldn't pay what this is worth anyway."

That gets me to thinking that maybe even though this dress is gorgeous, maybe it's just a well-done knockoff of the real thing. Cubic zirconium masquerading as diamond.

"The cloth is pricey, but how do you know that it won't fall apart while I'm wearing it?"

"This is a well-made dress. Look at how carefully it was put together." She runs her fingers along the top edges of the dress and along the sides. "If you have quality material and take the time to put it together right, the results can be spectacular."

I don't know why I can't just accept that the perfect dress has fallen from heaven into my lap, but I just keep worrying about what could go wrong. "What if I spill something on it? What if I catch it on something and it tears?"

"Then you'll have a gorgeous dress that fits you like a glove with a stain or tear in it. I can't sprinkle fairy dust on it and guarantee that nothing will happen to it, but I can say that as an amateur fashion maven, this dress was made for you."

"You're right. Thank you so much, Rachel. Thank you so much." I hug her tightly. She smiles. I feel immensely relieved to have something to wear for my wedding at last. I change and we return to the storefront and sit on our stools behind the counter.

"Hey, so has anything ever happened with your email flirtation with Shane?" I ask.

"I finally told him I had to stop. I deleted every last email. I learned my lesson when Julia landed in the hospital. My family is the most important thing in the world to me. I'm not going to do anything to mess that up."

"Are you going to tell Jon about it?"

"I don't think so. I don't want to hurt him if I don't have to."

"How did Shane react?"

"I think he was disappointed, but not surprised. He knew I didn't want to leave my husband."

"I have to say I'm relieved. I think you're making the right decision."

"I know."

When I get home from Rachel's store, I call Sienna. "Guess what? Will and I are going to get married after all."

"That's wonderful! What changed your mind?"

"He knocked me up. No, I'm just kidding." I tell her about Julia's accident and how watching Jon and Rachel get through it together made me realize that marriage is what I want after all. "I'm thinking we'll still have it on the original day we planned, but I kind of just want to do it without thinking about it anymore. It's not very romantic to say this, but I just want to get it over with. I'm sorry if you have to cancel any performances . . ."

"No, don't worry about it. I'll be there. I can't wait to see you. Are you going to have a party afterward?"

"I thought maybe we'd grab some food and some beers some place. Something casual. It'll just be Will and my closest friends, you and Mark, Will's Mom, and Mom and Dad and their significant others."

"Mom and Dad are coming out?"

"They are. Mom and Dad in the same room—that hasn't happened since you graduated from college six years ago."

"And boy was that fun."

"Wasn't it though? I think I'm more afraid of the two of them together than pledging to spend my life with Will."

"Well, I can't wait. Congratulations again. I'm really happy for you."

The Saturday afternoon that Will and I vow to spend our lives together is a warm, sunny, beautiful day. We head down to the county clerk's office accompanied by Gabrielle and Richard, Rachel and Jon, Sienna and Mark, Mom and Frank, Abby and Jerry, Dad and Annabella, and Will's mom. We all troop to the justice of the peace office to sign the marriage license. Sienna is taking pictures like mad. She is a cheap, but perfectly adequate photographer.

It's nearly two when we've finished the paperwork rigmarole and have posed for about seven million pictures.

"So, I was thinking we could head over to this bar called Mickie's . . ." I say to everyone. "It's located at, um, it's right on, where is it again?" I ask Will. Luckily, unlike me, Will is able to think straight, despite just signing his life away to a psychopath such as myself, and gives everybody directions.

"We'll all meet over there, okay?" I say.

After getting about a thousand more hugs and congratulations, Will and I pile into his car.

"I want to stop at home for just a second," he says.

"Okay." I'm too nervous to argue. I clutch his free hand as if my life depended on it and don't say a word the entire way home. I just keeping thinking the words, *I'm married, I'm married, I'm married, I'm married!*

I feel nervous, but I actually think I'm doing pretty well considering the enormity of what we've just done. In fact, I feel pretty good, happy even. I look over at Will and smile, he smiles back and gives my hand a squeeze.

He pulls into the driveway. "I'll wait for you here," I say.

"No, why don't you come in."

"Why?"

"Ah . . . I sort of got you a present."

"Oh." I'm beaming like an idiot.

Instead of going inside, he opens the fence gate and I follow him around the side of the house to the backyard. My jaw falls open.

"Surprise!"

About fifty people—friends, acquaintances, aunts, uncles, grandparents, and various coworkers are milling about in a backyard decorated with flowers and ribbons and bows. A long table overflowing with food lines one side of the yard.

"A surprise wedding reception?" I say.

"I didn't want you to be stressed out by the wedding plans," Will says, "but what did you think, I was going to marry the girl of my dreams and not loudly let the whole world know?"

"How the hell did you get everybody here on such short notice?"

"Never underestimate the superhuman powers of a man in love. Do you like the flowers?" he asks. "I was worried about choosing the wrong ones."

"You could have decorated the place with swamp algae and I would have loved it. The flowers are perfect. Everything is perfect. And it's quite a spread you got there," I say, nodding in the direction of the buffet. "I bet there isn't a single nut on the menu."

"Not a one."

Tears pool in my eyes as I look across the lawn at the people I love most in the world. In all of their dazzling imperfection are my mother, my father, Sienna, Gabrielle, Rachel, Richard, Jerry, Abby, all of my extended family and friends, and, of course, the love of my life, Will.

And I feel profoundly blessed.

Sometimes in this life, it's hard to remember to love yourself. Sometimes, it's easier to hate yourself, to focus on your faults, on the ten pounds you still haven't lost, the scars, the cellulite, the creeping signs of age. And because you don't always remember, it's imperative to surround yourself with people who love you, even when you can't manage it yourself.

In this world, having someone there to look out for you, to love you, to catch you when you fall, to remind you that you're pretty damn special, not despite of, but because of the flaws and imperfections that make you you—that is no small thing.

That is everything.

Please turn the page for an exciting sneak
peek of Theresa Alan's next novel
SPA VACATION
coming in 2008!

Chapter 1

The Tuesday before the trip

Amy Harrington had never been the kind of woman who was consumed by lust. Desire was a messy and fickle thing. Amy didn't act recklessly or hastily. She wasn't a big fan of spontaneity. She liked making rational decisions based on the best information available. She was a sensible girl, always had been.

That was why what was happening to her now was throwing her world into a frenzied, baffling orbit. She had never experienced such an immediate carnal reaction to anyone before, and the feelings were making her thinking blurry and confused.

Amy couldn't focus on what he was saying. She watched his lips moving as he sat behind the desk in his tastefully decorated office, but she couldn't seem to actually put together what the words coming our of his mouth *meant*.

He was good-looking, certainly, but that wasn't enough to explain what was causing this reaction in her. She'd encountered hundreds of sexy, handsome men in her life and none of them had turned her insides into quivering mush like Brent Meyer did.

Amy's friend Caitlyn, the poet, would be able to find a

turn of phrase that could explain exactly what it was about his smile that was so captivating. She would have the words to describe the precise bright green shade of his eyes. Stoplight green maybe? No, that conjured traffic and headaches, not beautiful, brilliant Oz-emerald eyes. Amy didn't have Caitlyn's gift with words, that was obvious.

Amy's friend Leah, the scientist, would be able to explain the exact chemical and physical reactions that were happening in Amy's body. It involved an increase in adrenaline, probably, and maybe something about pheromones, but Amy didn't know about that sort of thing. She knew about financial planning and making budgets and ensuring that all the numbers at the bottom of the spreadsheet added up. Love? Attraction? Lust? These simply weren't her areas of expertise.

Amy imagined that their meeting would run long and he would ask her to dinner. The meal would go on for several hours and many drinks. She'd have a little too much alcohol, and he would offer to drive her home. She would say that was very generous of him. She would get in his car and relax in the comfortable leather seats. He would say he needed to stop by the office for just a moment. She would accompany him in. In the empty office building of the software company he'd founded, they would sit beside each other on the comfortable gray couch in the reception area. He would put his hand on her leg. She'd pretend to protest, but only for a moment. He would slide his hand up her leg, beneath her skirt . . .

Amy realized suddenly that he'd asked her for something, and she had no idea what, since she'd been too busy fantasizing about an illicit tryst with him. "I'm sorry, what did you say?" she asked.

"I asked when you're getting married."

He gestured to her left hand. She followed his gaze and saw that she'd been spinning her engagement ring around and around her thumb.

"Two months."

"Still getting used to the ring, huh?"

"Yeah, I suppose so." *And still getting used to the idea of being married, apparently.*

Amy suspected that it wasn't a good sign to be daydreaming about having sex with other men when she wasn't even married yet.

It's just a fantasy, Amy assured herself. She could *think* about anything she wanted. She just couldn't *act* on those feelings. And she didn't *want* to act on the feelings anyway because she loved Eric. He was the love of her life.

Right?

Amy and Brent continued discussing budgets and economic forecasts for another hour or so, with Amy struggling to focus on doing her job and trying to keep her lust toward a man she'd only met a couple hours ago in check.

When the meeting with Brent was over at last, Amy put on her winter coat and her leather gloves. She picked up her briefcase, gave Brent a big, confident smile good-bye, and exited the Meyer Technologies building into the cold March air of the Colorado Rocky Mountains.

She got into her car, turned on the ignition, and sat for a few minutes as the car warmed up, staring blankly at her dashboard in a daze of confusion.

What was wrong with her? She *never* fantasized about hurling a strange man across his desk and doing X-rated things to him.

Amy just didn't do things like that.

Maybe that was her problem. Maybe that's why things had fallen into such a rut at home. Sex between Eric and her was always so . . . *polite*. It had always been like that. When they first dated, she thought of Eric as clitoral heroin. They use to have sex for hours; there had been a time when they couldn't get enough of each other.

That time was long gone.

It wasn't that she was having problems with her husband-to-be. Not exactly. On the surface, everything was perfect. They'd moved in together eight months ago and they rarely fought. They were comfortable financially and lived within their means. Neither of them gambled or drank to excess. In other words, their lives were unbelievably boring. And Amy had no idea what to do about it.

Lately, Amy's life felt hallow, empty. A husk. A shell. Something barren of substance. Her life was a memory. An aftertaste. Something that could be imagined, but was not actually there.

She knew this was not how a bride-to-be was supposed to feel. The truth was that even amid all the hubbub of planning her wedding, her days were gauzy.

As she pulled out of the parking lot and into traffic, she thought for the millionth time of how much she was looking forward to her trip and getting away from the prewedding insanity.

Amy had arranged to meet her college girlfriends Caitlyn and Leah at a spa in Mexico for two weeks. She wanted some sort of aerobic dominatrix to force her to get in shape for her wedding pictures. This way, she could get in shape while catching up with her two best friends. Caitlyn and Leah were going to be her bridesmaids, but she knew they wouldn't have any time to talk at the wedding. Things would be much too crazy for that. They'd been drifting apart ever since graduation—when Leah took a job as a biologist in Portland; Caitlyn had returned to Chicago where she'd grown up; and Amy accepted a position as a financial consultant in Denver. Amy supposed that there was no way to help the fact that they weren't as close as they'd been in school, but that didn't mean she liked it. On this trip they'd be able to relax and catch up and become skinny, sexy vixens while they were at it. It would be great.

Sun. Exercise. Friends. She would be feeling like herself again in no time.

When she got back to her office, Amy dropped off her coat and briefcase and went to the kitchen to heat up a low-calorie, taste-free frozen meal. She brought it back to her office in time to hear her extension ringing. She figured it was her wedding planner calling yet again to ask her about yet another detail. Amy had done the financing on major corporate mergers that were less stressful and time-consuming than planning a wedding. It was just one more reason she couldn't wait to get away.

"Hello?" She sat in her chair, setting her lunch on the desk in front of her.

"Hey, babe." Eric's voice sent a jolt of guilt through her.

"Hi. What's up?" She attempted to sound casual; she wondered if she was pulling it off.

"Christine and Adam want to know if we want to go to dinner Thursday night before you leave for your trip."

"Oh," Amy said, disappointed. It wasn't that she didn't like Christine and Adam, she did, it was just that every time she and Eric got together with them, they talked about how they'd spent their weekend sky-diving or hang-gliding or deep-sea diving or engaged in some other life-threatening activity. Amy never had any desire to do any of the potentially deadly or injurious things they did, but it made her feel dull by comparison. All Amy could add to the conversation was, *Well, this weekend Eric and I ordered in pizza and watched a NetFlix movie so we didn't have to leave the house even once. It's not quite as thrilling as parasailing or hiking up Kilimanjaro, but we live a full life anyway as you can plainly see.* "Sure, that would be fun."

"Great. I'll let them know. How's your day?"

"My day? Oh, you know, the usual. And you?"

"It's going well. Do you want me to cook tonight?"

"Cook? Yeah, that'd be great."

"Okay. I'll think of something good. I love you."

"I love you, too."

"See you tonight, hon."

"Tonight," she repeated dumbly before returning the phone to its cradle. She stared at the phone for a moment as her heart thumped painfully, as if Eric could somehow psychically know all the traitorous thoughts she'd been having.

Exhaling, she turned to her computer and opened an Excel file. Listlessly, she took bites of her chicken and vegetables, luckily not tasting any of it. When she dropped a sliver of a carrot into her keyboard, she turned the keyboard over and banged on the back of it as if she were attempting to make a baby burp, watching the food go flying out from her technological Heimlich maneuvers.

She tossed the rest of her lunch into the garbage and swiveled in her chair, her eyes taking on the glazed look of someone drooling at the asylum.

That glazed look was replaced with bright, alert eyes when her email pinged to let her know she had new mail and she saw the name on the FROM line. As she read the email, her heart raced.

To: amyharrington@attbi.com
From: meyer@meyertechnologies.com

I really enjoyed meeting you this morning. You're an incredibly beautiful woman. And smart, too! Can I take you out for a drink after our meeting on Friday? Strictly for pleasure, no business.

She blinked, then tentatively she hit REPLY.
To: meyer@meyertechnologies.com
From: amyharrington@attbi.com

Thanks for the offer, but I don't think my fiancé would appreciate me going out for drinks with a handsome entrepreneur.

Before hitting SEND, she stared at the word "handsome." She knew she was being deliberately flirty and provocative. She was never flirty and provocative. But just now, she didn't want to be herself. She wanted to be daring. She wanted to be a risk-taker. As adrenaline surged through her veins, she hit SEND.

She stared at her computer screen for a full minute. Oh God. Had she stepped over the line? Had she . . .

Her email pinged again.

To: amy harrington@attbi.com
From: meyer@meyertechnologies.com

Your fiancé doesn't have to know.

Amy swallowed and tried to get her breathing to return to normal. She clearly wasn't cut out for a life of crime or high adventure if sending a few emails nearly gave her a heart attack.

To: meyer@meyertechnologies.com
From: amyharrington@attbi.com

It's tempting, but I'm leaving for Mexico on Saturday and I need to pack.

She was already packed; the truth was that she didn't trust herself alone with Brent and alcohol.

The ringing phone made her jump. She'd been so focused on watching her computer screen for a reply from Brent, that the shrill sound of the phone made her feel like a burglar who'd been caught, and the alarm was signaling the police. It was the reaction, she knew, of a guilty person. She wondered for a moment if it might be Brent calling her.

"Hello?"

"Amy, hi." It was Gretchen, her wedding planner. "Listen, have you made any progress on the dress?"

Amy exhaled. "I told you, I'll make my decision just as soon as I get back from the spa. I want to lose a few pounds before I make my final choice."

"Amy, you know how important the dress is. The seamstress can always take it in when you lose a few pounds. I just don't get you. You searched for three weeks straight so you could find the perfect periwinkle blue shade of tablecloths, but when it comes to something as vital as the dress, you leave it to the last second. I've never had a client with more exacting taste than you. I like it, I'm a perfectionist myself, so I appreciate a woman who knows what she wants, I'm just saying . . ."

"Gretchen, I appreciate your concern, I really do. I've narrowed it down to two dresses. I promise I'll pick one just as soon as I get back." One of the dresses was simple and conservative. It fit Amy perfectly, she felt comfortable in it, and it suited her personality completely. The other dress wasn't Amy at all—it had elaborate beadwork and looked like something Cinderella would wear to the ball. It showed off Amy's cleavage and Amy never showed her cleavage, even when she was home alone. But she'd fallen in love with the dress when she'd tried it on. Maybe it was that when she tried the dress on, she felt like the woman she wanted to be instead of the woman she was. "Look Gretchen, I really . . ."

"Wait, wait, I need to ask you about . . ."

Amy's email pinged. "Sorry, I need to go. I'll talk to you before I leave for Mexico, I promise."

To: amyharrington@attbi.com
From: meyer@meyertechnologies.com

A rain check, then?

Amy hung up the phone and, before she could think, she wrote back.

To: meyer@meyertechnologies.com
From: amyharrington@attbi.com

We'll talk on Friday . . .